Serenity

Of

Passion

F. Y. Dawn

Dawn2Dawn Publishing
8810c Jamacha Blvd #136
Spring Valley, CA 91977

Published by Dawn2Dawn Publishing 02/2014

ISBN-13: 978-0991400027(sc)
ISBN-13: 978-0991400034(e)

Library of Congress Control Number: 2010903247

1

"Dearly beloved, we are gathered here today to join Paul Matthews and Sheena Walker in holy matrimony." Jaleel sat in the sanctuary of Zion Pentecostal Church listening to Pastor Hawkins as the exchanging of vows commenced, wondering how he'd let his life get this far out of control. The woman he loved was marrying someone else. Even though Jaleel was married, he always found comfort in the fact that Sheena wasn't. He always assumed if his marriage didn't work out, Sheena would be waiting patiently to take his hand in marriage.

He gazed around the church which was elegantly decorated, each pew covered with sheets of white satin and fresh white roses resting on the ends. Rose petals were scattered down the center aisle by a flower girl who was now standing at the altar twirling her flower basket. The bridesmaids and groomsmen were all standing tall with smiles on their faces, some with tears in their eyes. Everyone in attendance seemed to be so elated. Their faces were plastered with smiles, full of joy and excitement for the new couple. Tears had begun to well up in Jaleel's eyes as he silently wished the ceremony to be over, for his torture to end, and for someone to stand up and object. He knew, however, he was the only one who wanted to object; yet He was married to the bride's cousin.

His wife, Delisa, saw his tears and silently prayed they were tears of joy. She put her hand on his knee and leaned over to whisper in his ear. "Isn't this beautiful?" He looked at her with hurt, pain, and disgust, but was glad she was so caught up in the ceremony that she couldn't see the torment through his eyes.

Jaleel looked toward Sheena at the altar and nodded. "Yes, this is beautiful," he said, referring to the bride, not the ceremony. She was petite, slender, five-foot-five with a creamy, caramel complexion and had mesmerizing brown eyes. She had nice, trim legs, slightly curvy hips, and a flat stomach. Her silky black hair normally flowed down her back and draped across her shoulders, but not today. Today it was pinned up, exposing her long, slender neck that had a beauty mark on the left side, which Jaleel often dreamed of kissing.

It was strange how he was in love with Sheena, but when they first met, it was Delisa who'd caught his eye. He was eighteen years old, a freshman in college, full of arrogance, confidence, and determination. He walked into his composition class five minutes late. Delisa was the first person he'd seen right before the professor reminded him that he was no longer in high school and tardiness would not be tolerated. Jaleel tried to explain that he had gotten lost, but the professor told him to plan better in the future and dismissed him from class with a smug grin on his face. As he left, he heard Delisa trying to muffle her laugh.

Although he was really embarrassed about being kicked out of class, he waited outside, telling himself that he needed to get the notes from someone, but he actually stayed to talk to Delisa. As she walked out of class, he grabbed her by the arm and pulled her to the side.

He slid close to her so he could whisper in her ear. "I couldn't leave without knowing your name." He looked deep into her eyes as a slow, sexy grin spread across his face. He was used to playing this game, used to playing and winning, and was not quite ready for Delisa's response.

"I don't know you like that so back up, and didn't your mother ever tell you not to talk to strangers?" Delisa said with disgust. She didn't like brothers stepping into her personal space trying to run game. She walked away, leaving Jaleel and Sheena standing with their mouths hanging open in shock.

Sheena was brought up in a Christian home and was taught that being rude or unfriendly to people would turn people away from God. So, with all sincerity, Sheena looked at Jaleel and tried to correct her cousin's actions. "Hi, I'm Sheena. Please forgive my cousin." Sheena noticed that since she moved to San Diego from San Antonio she seemed to be apologizing a lot for her cousin. "She's just a little cranky from sitting in that boring class."

"You don't have to apologize for her. I like a challenge. So are you going to tell me her name?"

"Look, I gotta go. If you want her name, you gotta get it from her." Sheena walked away confused, wondering how her cousin could be so rude and still get a guy's attention. They were the same age, and Sheena had never had a real boyfriend.

Over the next few months, Jaleel tried to get with Delisa whenever he saw her, but she responded with the same rude attitude. Sheena was always there with a smile and apology. The last time he approached her, it seemed as though she was going to give in, but some of her girls walked up and Delisa's attitude quickly returned. Jaleel saw what game she was playing and decided she wasn't worth anymore of his time. He didn't even like her that much and was only pursuing her because his ego was wounded. He was always the aggressor and hadn't come across a woman, until now, that could resist him.

He turned to leave while Delisa and her girls giggled behind him. He ran smack into Sheena who was walking with her head stuck in some book. As he bumped into her, the book fell to the ground. They both bent down to pick it up and their heads collided, which caused both to fall backward. Delisa and her girls were bent over in a riotous laughter, causing everyone around to look and see what was so funny. Jaleel was so embarrassed that he jumped up and grabbed the book and Sheena, pulling her by her arm out of everyone's eyesight.

"Agghh!" Jaleel yelled in frustration. "Sheena, what is wrong with your cousin? She is the rudest person I know. You know, she never told me her name. One of her little followers accidentally told me."

"Jaleel, calm down."

"Calm down? How can you be calm after she just embarrassed us in front of all those people?"

"Do you know what your problem is?"

"No I don't, but I'm sure you're going to tell me."

"If a man thinks himself to be something when he is nothing, then he deceives himself."

"What?"

"Galatians 6:3." Sheena saw Jaleel roll his eyes. She had been waiting for the opportunity to witness to him and was not going to let his frustration deter her. "You're so concerned about yourself and your image that you don't realize arrogance is a turn off to some women. You're used to being the man, and you can't take it when someone disagrees. I want you to write down my cell number. I want you to go to church with me. I haven't found one that I want to join, but I visit quite a few. So, will you go to church with me?"

"I don't need you to preach at me. I get enough of that from my father. And you may be able to overlook the craziness of your cousin, but I can't. Tell her I'm done. She doesn't have to worry about me trying to get at her anymore, because I am done." Jaleel walked away overwhelmed with anger and embarrassed, because he knew Sheena was right. His father had told him the same thing several times. He always thought his dad was just being soft as usual, so he never listened.

The following Saturday night, Jaleel sat on his bed in the dorm. It had been a few days since he had last spoken to Sheena and he was still unable to shake what she said. Although he saw her in class, he refused to speak to her or Delisa. He was no longer angry, but felt more like an idiot than anything. He picked up Sheena's number and decided to call and apologize. As he waited for her to answer the phone, he couldn't believe how nervous he was. He had never apologized to a girl before. If they got mad at him he would just shake them loose and move on to the next one. When Sheena finally answered the phone he stuttered, trying to figure out what to say.

"This isn't Sheena, and don't tell me you are going start bugging my cousin now. Your game is played I doubt it will even—"

Sheena snatched the phone from Delisa before she could finish her sentence. "Jaleel, I'm sorry. I asked her to answer because I didn't recognize the number."

"Like I told you, you don't have to apologize for her. I was actually calling to apologize for how I acted the other day. You were trying to help and I was being an idiot. If the offer still stands I would like to go to church with you tomorrow."

"You know it does. Service starts at eleven so meet me at the bus stop at nine and don't be late—"

Jaleel interrupted before she could finish. "Did you forget that I have a car? So, meet me at the bus stop at ten thirty and I will drive us there. I also want to take you to this church I know if you don't mind. I think you might like it."

"Okay, I'll see you at ten thirty." Sheena hung up the phone, shocked that he had called, and even more shocked that he wanted to go to church.

Over the next few weeks, Jaleel and Sheena went to church together every Sunday and to lunch afterward. She liked the church he took her to and eventually joined. He was already a member, but hadn't attended in a while. He continued going to church with Sheena so she would not have to ride the bus. Before long, he was excited about going to church. He felt different and Sheena often told him he seemed different.

Before long, it was winter break. Sheena flew home to see her parents. Jaleel continued to attend church. Her absence made him realize how much he enjoyed being around her. Not only at church, but they studied together and sometimes met for lunch in between classes. He realized how much he cared for her and wanted to be more than her friend. He decided to let her know as soon as she returned.

Sheena didn't call Jaleel the whole two weeks she was on break, so he was really anxious to see her. He went to their usual meeting place to pick her up, but she wasn't there. He waited half an hour then decided to go to church, thinking maybe she rode the bus. He arrived at church late. Sheena was there, but because he was so late there were no seats next to her. He sat impatiently through the whole service and nearly ran to Sheena after the benediction.

"Hey, how was your trip?" He asked, trying not to sound like a nervous wreck.

"My trip was great. Look Jaleel, we need to talk. Do you want to go out to eat?"

The look on her face made his heart drop into his stomach. Here he was getting ready to profess his feelings for a girl whose facial expression said she could not stand the sight of him. Once seated in the restaurant, Sheena began talking immediately.

"Jaleel, you are a really good friend and I don't want to lose your friendship. I also don't want to be another notch on your belt. I know you have changed over the last few weeks and I am proud of you. But, I am not interested in anything more than friendship. I kind of sensed that you were looking for something more and I cannot give it to you."

Jaleel couldn't help but wonder where all this was coming from. How could she have possibly known he had feelings for her? If by some chance she'd read his mind, she was right about his feelings, but totally missed the mark about his intentions. He tried not to let his disappointment and hurt show.

As he spoke, he chose his words carefully. "I enjoy being around you and if friendship is what you're offering, I'll take it."

Clapping and cheering brought Jaleel's mind back to the present. He had missed majority of the ceremony caught up in his memories, but it was for the best. He didn't know how much more his heart could take. He stood and joined the other attendees as they applauded Mr. and Mrs. Paul Matthews.

During the reception, Jaleel forced himself to have a good time, grabbing his wife and pulling her to the dance floor, holding her close, trying to wrap himself in the comfort and security of her love for him. He needed to be loved and Delisa loved him. While Luther Vandross sang softly in the background, Delisa leaned into him placing a trail of kisses down his neck and whispering in his ear.

"Baby, take me home. Take me home and love me." It had been awhile since they'd been intimate and she wanted him desperately.

Pulling back to look at his wife, he saw eyes glossy with tears. Without saying a word, he took Delisa's hand, retrieved their things, and drove her home.

Neither of them spoke during their ride home. Jaleel looked over at Delisa and she had a look of anguish on her face and he knew he was the cause.

2

Delisa sat in the car thinking about her husband's reaction to Sheena's wedding. The tears threatening to fall from his eyes, his rigid body, and the look on his face during the ceremony spoke volumes. She knew he used to be in love with Sheena and sometimes felt that he settled for her since he couldn't have Sheena, but she always pushed those thoughts out of her mind. He was her husband. She was determined to make him forget about Sheena, and thought she had succeeded, but now she wasn't so sure.

They pulled up to their four-bedroom home located off of Campo Road in Rancho San Diego. Delisa's pulse began to race, remembering why they left the reception and how Jaleel held her while they were dancing. Despite her suspicions, Delisa wanted this man, loved this man, and didn't want to live without him. She watched as he got out of the car and came around to get her out. Jaleel's gray, pin-striped Sean John suit fit his body perfectly. His dark-chocolate face, light brown eyes, and perfectly trimmed goatee made him look like walking art.

He opened the door and stepped close to her, helping her to her feet. He stepped so close that she couldn't help bumping into him as she stood up and she instantly felt his arousal slide down her arm as she stood. Knowing he desired her sent Delisa over the edge and she held on to the car door to steady herself. He leaned over to pry her hands from the door and placed his lips upon hers, exploring her mouth as if he had never kissed her before.

Delisa melted into his arms. Her knees became weak. It had been months since he'd touched her and she had been craving his affection. It seemed like as the days ticked by and Sheena's wedding approached, the more withdrawn he became. Delisa wasn't sure what had caused the change today, but she welcomed it. She forced herself to forget about the why and just enjoy the now. Jaleel forcibly tore his lips from her and bent over, swooping Delisa up into his arms and carrying her inside the house.

Once inside, passion exploded as Delisa used her hands and mouth to ravage his body. She took him down to the ground right there in the entrance of their house. Her kisses across his chest caused Jaleel to groan with pleasure. He wanted to make love to her, to take her to a point of ecstasy where all of her pain would disappear. The look on her face in the car had pricked his heart, and he wanted desperately to soothe her anguish. He carried her to the bed, giving her everything she desperately needed.

Delisa laid there relaxing in the cradle of Jaleel's arms, reminiscing about how their relationship began. She'd lied to Sheena. Jaleel's focus had switched from her to Sheena and the ugly green-eyed monster of jealousy reared its head. One little lie about Jaleel only wanting her for sex was enough to push her overly religious cousin into action.

Even though Delisa was successful in making Sheena back away from Jaleel, it was still a couple of years before they hooked up. The guilt she felt for interfering consumed her. Sheena was family and a good girl who didn't deserve what Delisa did, so Delisa stayed away from Jaleel on a romantic level.

During their senior year, Sheena had already graduated, completing in three years what took most students four years, Jaleel came down with a severe case of pneumonia and Delisa was there with him every step of the way. She visited him every day in the hospital, coming right after her last class and staying until visiting hours were over. Delisa also talked to all of his professors and got him extensions on his assignments.

Once Jaleel was released from the hospital, Delisa came by his house every day, helping him get caught up on his assignments, making sure he got a decent meal, and she even cleaned his apartment. Most nights she stayed so late trying to complete her own assignments that she was usually too tired to drive home. So, she crashed on his couch and left early to shower and change before her first class.

One night, shortly after falling asleep, Delisa heard Jaleel stirring around in the kitchen. "Jaleel, are you okay?" She whispered through her sleep-laden voice.

"Yeah, I'm all right. I just have a lot on mind and was hoping some butter pecan ice cream would help take my mind off of things. You want some?"

"Yeah, I'll take some, but you sit down and rest. I'll get that," she said as she stood up, raising her arms in the air to stretch her body.

"Delisa, you don't have to do that. You've already done so much. You really saved me these past few weeks. If it wasn't for you, I would have ruined my GPA and probably would have to do another semester before I graduate."

"Jaleel, we're friends. I would like to think you'd do the same thing for me." She watched him as he scooped ice cream into the bowls. She could tell there was something on his mind and had to know what was making him so restless. She stepped closer to him and reached out to touch his shoulder. He shuddered as her fingers brushed across his bare skin. Shocked by his reaction, Delisa ran back to the couch and began packing up her things.

"Delisa, what's wrong? You don't have to leave."

"Jaleel, I realize that I was a horrible person when we first met. I just didn't realize that my touch would disgust you. I've changed if you haven't noticed."

"Is that really what you think?" He grabbed her by the arm and turned her around before she could make it to the door. "I noticed the change, noticed the woman you've matured into, and these past few weeks with you under my roof so close to my bed have been torture. Every night I wake up, come out here, and watch you sleep, wanting so badly to..." He pulled her close, gently kissing her mouth. "...to do that. If you don't mind, I would like to spend more time with you outside of this apartment and away from school."

Delisa placed her things on the floor by the couch and went back into the kitchen to finish scooping ice cream into the bowls. Jaleel crept up behind her, pressed his body against hers, and whispered in her ear. "You can't ignore me. I know you want me as much as I want you. No matter what you say, you do not take care of someone who's just a friend the way you took care of me." He ran his fingers through her hair and planted small kisses on the back of her neck.

Turning to look him in the eyes, Delisa asked, "Is sex the only thing you want from me? Because Jaleel, I want your heart. I have tried to fill the void in my life with other guys. No one compares to you, but I won't settle for anything less than your heart. If you can handle that, take me to your bed and hold me tonight."

Without saying a word, he picked her up and carried her to his bed, pulled her close, and pressed her head against his chest. He held her all night and never tried anything sexual. Delisa woke up the next morning feeling more rested than she had in a long time. Jaleel was still asleep and she leaned over and kissed him awake. Seductively, she whispered against his neck, "Make love to me."

"Are you sure? I can wait until you're ready, until you know that it is more than sex for me."

"I'm sure. I have wanted us to be together for almost three years, and now that I am finally in your bed, I have never been more certain." He made love to her that morning; they both gave more to each other than they had ever given to a lover.

Remembering the history they had together reassured Delisa that her husband loved her. They had been so in love and happy at one point. She was determined to get that happiness back. Although things happened so fast and an unplanned pregnancy prompted them to get married right after graduation, their life was good and everything seemed to fall into place.

Delisa had a degree in Early Childhood Education and was the director of the church's preschool. Jaleel had a BS in Computer Science. He was a system administrator for Grossmont Hospital in San Diego. They

13

had a beautiful home and a gorgeous daughter. Jaleel was a deacon at the church, and they both loved the Lord. Surely, they would make it past this rough spot in their marriage.

3

The music was blasting from the DJ's speakers and just about everyone at the reception was on the dance floor, including Sheena, who he could now call his wife. Sitting at the table in awe of her beauty, he watched her dance with person after person. When single men who weren't relatives put their hands on her waist to dance, Paul's anger was apparent and he had to close his eyes and breathe deeply to keep from losing it. A couple of those men were lawyers who worked at Paul's law firm. Anger said, *fire them as soon as you return from your honeymoon.* Good thing he never let his anger lead him.

Paul knew that dancing with the bride at the reception was tradition. That was the only reason he agreed to it, but now he'd had enough. He made his way to the dance floor. The closer he got to his wife, emotion overwhelmed him and tears filled his eyes and flowed down his cheeks. He tapped the man she was dancing with on the shoulder and before the man could move Paul grabbed Sheena and pulled her close.

"Paul, what's wrong? Why are you…"

Paul covered her mouth with his finger before she could finish her sentence. He lifted Sheena off the ground for better access to her mouth. As they kissed, everyone seemed to disappear, the thumping of the music faded, and they became lost in each other's kiss. They didn't realize how long they were kissing, but when they finally parted, all eyes were on them. The room erupted in a thunderous roar of applause, whistling, and howling.

Placing Sheena back on the ground, Paul whispered in her ear. "How much longer do we have to stay here?"

"Paul, you know we have to cut the cake and throw the garter and the bouquet."

"I have a surprise for you. I have been working really hard to make sure it was ready by today and now I'm anxious to give it to you." Paul leaned in and kissed her again, trying to persuade her to leave that very instant.

"Well, I have a little gift of my own that I have been waiting to give to you. So if you can give me one more hour, we can leave and begin our life together."

Paul kissed her again desperately, hungrily, insistently, and as if sensing their anguish, a voice came over the speakers calling all single women to catch the bouquet. Sheena tossed the bouquet into a crowd of single women. Some there for the fun of it; others filled with anticipation of a wedding myth. Moments later, Paul tossed the garter, forcing his hormones into subjection after having slid the garter down Sheena's leg. It took the power of God to keep him from dragging her out of the reception hall. He had given his life to Christ shortly after he met Sheena and was determined to abstain from sex until he married her. Now that the day was here, Paul was overwhelmed with anticipation. With bouquet tossed, garter thrown, cake cut, and goodbyes said with flinging rice, they were on their way.

Leaning up against her husband, Sheena looked at him with mischievous eyes. "Where's my surprise Mr. Matthews?"

"In due time, Mrs. Matthews, in due time." Pausing for a second, Paul thought about what he said. "I can't believe you are finally my wife, not my friend, not my girlfriend, not my fiancé, but my wife. Mrs. Matthews." Pulling her closer, Paul explored her body with his mouth and hands. He was inching his hand up her wedding gown when the limo slowed to a stop.

"Paul, where are we? I thought we were going straight to the hotel from the reception?"

"Yeah, but I have to stop here to get your surprise. Come inside with me. It won't take long, but I don't want to leave you by yourself."

16

Seeing the look of frustration on Sheena's face, Paul hurried to help her get out before she could protest.

Walking toward this massive gray and white stucco two-story house with a finely tailored lawn and boxwood shrubs, Paul couldn't believe how well everything was falling into place. "Go ahead and make yourself comfortable. This will only take me a couple of minutes." Paul knew Sheena well and knew she would be walking around admiring the house, which is exactly what he wanted. Sheena loved looking at houses, and they had looked at quite a few before he convinced her to move into his condo downtown after the honeymoon, which was his first step in setting his plan in motion.

Just as he suspected, Sheena was walking around checking the house out when he returned. "Paul, this house is beautiful. Whose house is this?"

"Would you like to see the rest of it?" He jumped in, sensing her question and not wanting to respond. He led the way, showing her four spacious bedrooms with adjoining bathrooms, a home office, a beautifully decorated kitchen with a breakfast nook, formal living and dining areas, along with a family room and fireplace. Then, stopping in front of double doors on the second floor, Paul turned to Sheena. "Are you ready for your surprise?"

"Paul Matthews, what are you up to?"

Ignoring her question, he opened the doors and led her inside a room filled with lit candles, vases of red roses with a few petals scattered across the king size bed, and Luther Vandross' *If This World Were Mine* playing softly in the background.

If this world were mine, I would place at your feet
All that I own, you've been so good to me
If this world were mine
I'd give the flowers the birds and the bees
And it'd be your love beside me
That would be all I need
If this world were mine, I'd give anything

"This is our room. All of this is ours."

"Ours? What do you mean ours? Are we staying here tonight instead of the hotel?"

"Sheena, baby, this is our house. This is your surprise. I signed the closing documents a few days—" Paul was interrupted by Sheena's loud, ear-piercing scream. He stepped back and watched her as she jumped up and down letting out excited shrills, spinning around in awe, trying to take in everything.

"Honey, you bought me a house?"

"Yes, I did. I've set it up for our things to be moved in. When we return from our honeymoon, this will be our home. The place where we build our lives together, raise our children, and this…" he said, pulling her toward the bed, "…is the bed where I will make love to you and cause you to scream over and over again with excitement and satisfaction, starting tonight." He planted tender kisses on her shoulder. She shuddered when his lips brushed her bare skin. Those kisses trailed up her neck, to her ear, and rested on her mouth. As his lips consumed her mouth, his hands were undressing her. His strong hands gripped the delicate fabric of her wedding gown and eased the zipper down. The dress brushed across her skin as it fell to the floor.

He heard Sheena gasp and felt her body tighten as she pulled herself from his embrace. He watched as she stepped out of her gown, laid it on the chaise, and then stood in front of him with her head held down. He waited for her to speak, sensing that there was something heavy on her mind. When she finally lifted her head, her eyes were filled with tears and she opened her mouth several times to speak, but couldn't seem to find the words to say.

"Sheena, you know you can tell me anything. I love you and it hurts me to think that something I did or said has upset you on our wedding day. I wanted this day to be perfect."

"Honey, I'm not upset. This day couldn't have been more perfect. I'm crying because you make me so happy. I have never had a man love me the way you do, and I have never loved anyone as much as I love you.

I am ecstatic to be your wife…I told you I have a gift for you, too."

Paul sat on the bed and pulled her onto his lap. "Baby, you didn't have to get me a gift. You being my wife is more than enough."

"I know and that is one of the reasons I love you so much. You have given me so much and the only thing you have ever asked me for is my love, which I have gladly given. Tonight I want to give you something else." Sheena paused to kiss Paul, making his curiosity and desire for her increase. "I probably should have told you this a few months ago, but Paul, I have never been with a man before and my gift to you tonight is my body, pure and untouched. You will be my first, my last, my only."

Paul's heart raced with passion as the words came out of Sheena's mouth. They had talked about past relationships, but never mentioned sex. He just assumed she had been with a man before, because she'd been in serious, long-term relationships. Paul wasn't saved at the time and just figured that if a man and a woman dated for more than three months, it was safe to assume they had sex.

"You are an awesome woman. The stand you take and the life you live for the Lord amazes me. The gift you are giving me is priceless and I will treasure this night for the rest of my life." Paul felt his body trembling and laid his head on Sheena's chest in an attempt to calm his emotions, but was unsuccessful. With a voice shaken with unfathomable love, he said, "I am going to take my time loving you and enjoy every inch of the gift you have given me. If I do anything you don't like or it hurts, let me know and we can stop."

Slipping the remainder of Sheena's clothes off, Paul carried her to the bathroom and prepared her a bath. He washed her gently and thoroughly, making sure his hands touched every inch of her then placed her on the bed. He continued the exploration of his gift, finding and ravishing all of her passion zones. He felt her body squirm with need and he knew she was ready for him. Sheena's body stiffened as they connected and he wanted to stop, but she felt his hesitation and begged him to continue. He kissed her deeply, taking her mind off the pain and allowing her body to relax. Pleasure rolled through them as they consummated their union, clinging to each other as if they would die if separated.

Paul wanted to pull her close and hold her tight while they slept, but he knew they had to shower and change the sheets. He placed her in the shower, rushed to change the bedding, and then joined her in the shower.

"Baby, are you okay? Did I hurt you?"

"I am a little sore, but that is to be expected, right?"

"Right."

"Then don't worry, I'm fine. What I want to know is how soon can we make love again?"

Paul smiled as he looked down at his wife's naked body for the first time. When he washed her and made love to her he was not able to take in the fullness of her body. She sensed what he was doing and tried to turn away from him, but he grabbed her by the arm. "Don't hide from me. You're beautiful. Let me look at you."

"Paul, I have never stood naked in front of a man before."

"Well you are going to have to get used to it because your body belongs to me, and with a body like that I am going to be looking every chance I get, and I see you trying not to look at me." Paul could no longer contain his laughter. He couldn't believe they were having this conversation. He had to get her to loosen up. He grabbed her by the hand and led her into the bedroom.

"Sheena, look at me, I don't want you to be embarrassed to look at me. I want you to enjoy looking at me."

Paul backed away from her so she could see all of him and slowly, he turned around. He watched as her eyes scanned his whole body and they stood in silence for a few seconds, admiring each other. "You are more gorgeous than I ever could have imagined, and if we don't put some clothes on, I will not be able to control what I do to you."

"That sounds pretty tempting, but you do need time to recuperate, so let's sleep minus the clothes, and in the morning we can talk about what you are going to do to me."

4

Sheena sat aimlessly at her desk, silently reliving the past two weeks. Her wedding, beautiful new house, honeymoon, and gorgeous husband consumed her thoughts. Focusing on work was next to impossible, so she decided to call the source of her frustration. "Good afternoon, Counselor Matthews." The smile could be heard in her voice and it split across her face, making her glow with overwhelming happiness.

"Good afternoon, Principal Matthews, how's your first day back at work?"

"Very unproductive. I can't seem to get my mind off of you and onto running this school. Do you have any suggestions to keep me focused?"

"It sounds to me like your mind is in the right place."

They both laughed so loud their secretaries came rushing in to see what was going on, and in unison they said, "Please shut my door." They laughed again.

Everything had fallen right into place after their wedding night. There was no longer any awkwardness. They learned each other's sleep patterns. Both liked the same side of the bed, but Sheena realized that as long as her head was on Paul's chest she could sleep on either side. Paul used to stay up late in the home office preparing for court cases, but every night he'd hear Sheena running bath water and couldn't resist joining her. Sheena, who used to sleep wrapped in the covers, soon found that the heat from Paul's body was all she needed. They fell into step with each other and the single lives they once led faded into the background.

"Do you think you will be home on time today?" she asked.

"Probably not. Tomorrow is my first day back in court since our honeymoon and I have a couple of last minute things to take care of."

"Can you work at home? I can help. I just want to be in your presence. It doesn't matter what we're doing." Sheena smiled. She could hear his soft groans and knew he had a hard time telling her no.

"I'll tell you what, let me get back to work and I promise I will be home on time, and Sheena, don't think I don't know what you just did."

Doing her best southern belle impersonation, Sheena asked, "Why Paul, whatever are you talking about?"

The playful lilt to her voice made him smile and shake his head. This woman turned him inside out in a short time and he loved every minute of it.

With whispered *I-love-yous*, they ended the call. As soon as Sheena hung up the phone, she hit the intercom button and told her secretary that she was leaving for the rest of the day and if there were any emergencies she could be reached on her cell phone. Sheena had a reason for wanting Paul home early, and if she left work now she would have just enough time to plan something nice.

In the two weeks of their marriage, they had not spent one relaxing, quiet night at home. They were either eating out or she was slaving over a hot stove trying to be the best wife she could by preparing huge meals. Tonight she wanted to relax, she wanted him to relax, and fall into a normal, more realistic routine. With their demanding careers, eating out was more realistic, but she didn't want to be that type of wife. She wanted quiet evenings at home, not at a restaurant. With school starting soon, she'd need those quiet evenings more than ever. With all errands complete and everything she needed in hand, Sheena made her way home to set up.

The minutes ticked by as Sheena waited for Paul to come home. Her anxiousness turned to anxiety as she paced back and forth across the kitchen floor. She kept checking the pots on the stove, ensuring the small meal she'd prepared wasn't drying out. It was soon seven and she abandoned her attempt to salvage dinner to give him a call. The call went

22

straight to voicemail. Thoughts of her husband stranded, wounded, and alone racked her brain. She called his office, no one answered and she wanted to kick herself for not taking the number to his direct line.

He'd tried to give it to her so she could reach him even when his secretary was screening his calls, but trying to be a good, understanding wife, she had told him, "If you are that busy, I don't want to interrupt." She hadn't thought about having to reach him after hours.

By nine, Paul still wasn't home. Sheena had long since tossed out the dried out chicken and overcooked potatoes and attempted to watch a movie to stay calm. Five minutes into the movie and she was right back to her earlier behavior, relentlessly calling Paul's office. Her neck was tense and chest tight with worry; she'd paced so much her legs felt like she'd run a marathon.

In such a short time, Paul had become her world. What would she do if something happened to him? After nearly driving herself crazy, she decided to do the one thing that would calm her nerves: pray. *"Dear Heavenly Father, I am worried about my husband and I don't know what to do. I know that you know all and see all..."* Sheena heard the door open and ran into the kitchen.

"Paul!" She didn't know whether to kiss him and cry, or slap him and scream. She chose screaming and crying. "Where have you been? I have been worried sick, and here you come walking in like everything is okay!" Tears streamed down her cheeks and she nearly collapsed from the force of her relief and anger colliding.

"Sheena, calm down!"

She could not believe he raised his voice at her. "Calm down? I was about to lose my mind worrying about you! Why didn't you call me?" Her voice rose to match her rising ire, and she had no choice but to walk away before things got out of control.

"I'm sorry." He reached to grab her arm, but she snatched away and ran up the stairs.

By the time she reached the top step she was an emotional mess, a bath and bed was exactly what she needed. Like always, the hot bath calmed her and helped evaluate a long day. She felt foolish. Without question, she'd overreacted. She cut her bath short and went in search of her husband. He still hadn't come upstairs, so she searched the dark house, hoping he hadn't left. Back on the first floor, a light peering from under the family room door revealed his location. She crept inside and the sight of Paul on his knees praying sent more conviction than she'd ever experienced; without hesitation she dropped to her knees and joined him in prayer.

"Paul, I am so sorry." She pleaded for his forgiveness as soon as he acknowledged her presence. "I allowed my fear to consume me and when you came home I was angry at myself for not having the number to your direct line and angry at you for not calling. Please forgive me for not handling my anger properly." She was so ashamed of her behavior she couldn't look him in the eye.

In the year that they dated, Paul had never raised his voice at her. "I'm sorry for raising my voice. I think we are both tired and didn't handle the situation properly." He pulled her onto his lap. "I should have called. I had more stuff to do than what I had originally anticipated and time just got away from me. My cell phone always dies at the end of the day because I use it so much, and Ellen, my secretary, leaves at six. That's why you weren't able to reach me."

"Paul, you are married now and some of the things you did when you were single won't work. I married you knowing you were a lawyer and would have to work long hours, but don't promise me that you will be home on time then stand me up without calling."

"You're right, but you have to realize that I am not an employee. I am the boss and I have extra responsibilities. I may not always be able to drop what I am doing and pick up the phone. That's why I need you to have the number to my direct line to keep you from worrying."

Not wanting to keep going back and forth, they both decided to let it go for now knowing that they'd both need to compromise for this not to become a major issue. They went to bed, but sleep did not come easy for either of them.

Sheena lay in bed, frustrated for being mad at Paul. It was that same hardworking, determined, going the extra mile work ethic that had initially attracted her to Paul.

She had returned to her office after taking a short lunch and Marcy, her secretary, informed her that there was a man waiting who wouldn't talk to anyone other than the principal. There were only two months left in the school year and the visits from angry parents regarding their children's grades were mounting. "Where is he?" she asked, trying to stave off her irritation.

"Vice Principal Adams' office; he wants to talk about Latrell Jones."

"Send him in and bring me Latrell's discipline file." Discipline issues were usually handled by the vice principal, but Sheena was well aware of the Latrell problem. He had been written up numerous times, suspended twice, and was in danger of having to repeat the ninth grade. They tried several times to set up parent conferences, but were unsuccessful. When Latrell was caught vandalizing cars in the staff parking lot, they had no choice but to involve the police. Now here, two days after Latrell's arrest, his father decides to show up. Why wait until it's too late before you get involved?

There was a knock on her door. "Come in." Sheena looked up and in walked the most gorgeous man she'd ever seen. His smooth, brown, muscular physique and dimpled cheeks took her breath away. He walked up to her and she cleared her throat in an unsuccessful attempt to hide her attraction. "I'm Principal Walker." The heat from his palm resonated through her body as they shook hands.

"Paul Matthews. How's your day been thus far?"

"Just fine, Mr. Matthews. Please have a seat and tell me how I can help you."

"Well I'm not going to beat around the bush. I want you to

drop the charges against Latrell."

"Mr. Matthews, what is your relationship with Latrell?"

"Call me Paul, and I'm his mentor."

"Since you're not a parent I cannot discuss—"

He interrupted, "Mrs. Walker..."

"It's Miss Walker."

A smile spread across his face and made Sheena melt. "Forgive me, Miss Walker, Latrell's mother is in the hospital dying of breast cancer, his father has never been in the picture, and he has been staying with his elderly grandmother. I understand your privacy policy, but Latrell needs help and right now I am the only one capable of giving it to him."

"Your wanting to help is commendable, but my hands are tied. The only way I can discuss this with you is if you get a notarized letter from the mother authorizing you to handle his education."

"Okay, have dinner with me tonight. I can have the letter by then. We can discuss alternative disciplinary action, and it may be inappropriate to say, but I can't help myself. I would really like to get to know you better."

Sheena couldn't believe she agreed to have dinner with a man she had just met. His sexy smile and charm made her come unglued. He had her eating out of the palm of his hand during dinner; agreeing to drop the charges in exchange for community service around campus, and developing a plan to get him caught up on his school work so he wouldn't have to repeat the ninth grade. Before the night was over, Paul had managed to get her personal cell phone number, her home phone number, and an agreement to meet him for coffee the next morning.

They saw each other at least twice during the week and every weekend. She kept trying to break things off because he was not a Christian. She had been taught that believers shouldn't date unbelievers, but she couldn't resist his charm.

26

After a few months of dating, she accepted the fact that she loved him and did not want their relationship to end, so she invited him to church. Everyone at church was shocked that she had a boyfriend, especially Delisa and Jaleel. Paul gave his life to Christ that day, being baptized in Jesus' name, and filled with the Holy Spirit. He never looked back.

Now here she was, his wife, becoming irate at the same qualities he used to pursue and win her heart. Having fully beaten herself up over her temper tantrum, she decided to follow through with her previous plan of seduction. She slipped out of bed and put on the lingerie she'd purchased. It would be her first time wearing something so seductive. She lit the candles around the room quietly and grabbed the bottle of massage oil.

It was four in the morning. Paul had been asleep for about five hours and she hadn't slept at all. She straddled him and began placing small kisses across his chest until she felt his hands caressing her thighs. She looked up and saw him watching her. She'd never initiated their love making and hoped she didn't screw it up. Drizzling the massage oil on his chest she began to massage it in, deeply caressing his finely cut torso.

"Roll over so I can do your back."

"Get up, so I can look at you. When did you get this? Is this what I missed out on by coming home late?"

Feeling really bold, she stood, still straddling him on the bed. "Something like that, but let's not dwell on it. Do you like it?" She could see excitement in his eyes and knew she'd made the right choice.

"I love it." He sat up to grab her, but she put her foot on his chest and pushed him back down.

"Where do you think you're going?"

"I'm going to make love to you. You standing over me dressed like that is driving me crazy. Now come lay down."

"Sorry, I'm making love to you, so you are going to have to be patient." She assaulted his body with brutally arousing foreplay and when she'd fully conquered him, they parted, both panting heavily, laying in a

27

silence only broken when the alarm clock went off to wake them for work.

5

Paul and Sheena arrived almost an hour late to Jaleel and Delisa's house because Paul couldn't keep his hands to himself. Even as they stood there waiting for someone to open the door, his lips were on hers while his hands wandered up her shirt.

Delisa looked through the peephole then cleared her throat as she swung open the door. "Sheena, you have not been on time for anything since you got married. Paul, maybe you could keep your hands off my cousin long enough for her to wish me a happy birthday."

They laughed, greeting one another with hugs and kisses. They walked inside and greeted the other guests who were already caught up in a 'husbands vs. wives' game of Pictionary. Jaleel's cousin, Marlon, was up at the board drawing what looked like rows and rows of bushy eyebrows. Marlon was a good guy, but Sheena never quite understood his and Alicia's marriage. She hoped with all her heart that Paul would never be as withdrawn from her as Marlon seemed to be from his wife. Paul, with his competitive nature, immediately joined in the game. Sheena followed Delisa into the kitchen to help bring out more snacks.

Jaleel's heart dropped into his stomach when he saw Sheena walk into the room carrying a platter of hot wings. He watched her as she passed out plates and offered wings to everyone. He hadn't realized he was holding his breath until she disappeared into the kitchen. Since she got married he had not seen her as often as he used to, and even though he was trying to get her out of his mind, it seemed like every time she came around he was right back at square one. He knew it wasn't fair to Delisa; she deserved better. He didn't want to lose her, but he couldn't help it.

Every time Sheena came into the room, her presence made everything else fade into the background. Jaleel became caught up in the sway of her hips, the softness of her voice, and the sparkle in her smile. Her knee accidentally brushed against his leg while she was passing out drinks; instantly, he hardened. He forced himself to pay attention to the game which had now switched to Taboo without him noticing.

Paul had enough. He could no longer sit there and allow Jaleel to seemingly undress Sheena with his eyes like no one was in the room. He always assumed Jaleel had a thing for Sheena, but told himself that Jaleel was married to a beautiful woman. He had an adorable little girl and too much to lose if he made a pass at Sheena. Tonight he was going to say something. "Jaleel, can I see you in the kitchen for a second?" He waited until Sheena and Delisa had finally taken a seat.

Jaleel leaned up against the kitchen sink, staring at Paul, waiting for him to speak, but curiosity got the best of him. "What's up, Paul? Is everything all right?"

"I should be asking you that question. From what I can see, you're having a problem with your eyes wandering around, lingering in places they shouldn't." Paul stepped close to Jaleel and looked him straight in the eye. "I just thought I'd warn you that the next time I catch you checking out my wife I'm going to hurt you." He tried to remain calm, keep his hood side at bay, and let his diplomacy prevail, but Jaleel's smug little grin was making that impossible.

"Man, I don't know what you're talking about, but I do know if you don't get out my face we're going to have a problem." He stared Paul down and matched the fury in his eyes. He was not about to be the punk in his house.

Paul chuckled. "Jaleel, don't let the suit and the law degree fool you. I grew up in the 'hood the same way you did. If I catch you eyeing my wife again you'll get beat down."

Sheena walked in to see Paul and Jaleel standing toe to toe, face to face, nostrils flared, brows furrowed with contention. She tried to step between them, but neither would budge. "Baby, go back and play Taboo,

I'll be done in a minute." Paul tried to dismiss her, but she was not having it.

"I am not going anywhere until you tell me what's going on."

Keeping eye contact with Jaleel he grabbed her hand and backed up. "Nothing's going on. I just had to put your boy in his place."

"Keep running your mouth, pretty boy. I promise you don't want none of this."

Paul stepped back into Jaleel's face, both of their six-foot frames heaving with anger. "None of what? A pathetic, lovesick little punk who walks around embarrassing himself and his wife over a woman he can never have?"

Delisa heard yelling coming from the kitchen and ran inside just in time to see Paul and Jaleel square off and go to blows.

Sheena screamed. "Paul, baby, please stop. Don't do this. This is stupid!"

His rage had taken over and he couldn't hear her plea. Paul repeatedly rammed his fist into Jaleel's face. He stammered and had to regain his balance when Jaleel swung at him, making contact with his mouth. Paul tried to slam him on the ground, but wasn't able to overpower him. Both men tried to gain the upper hand and spun each other around the kitchen, knocking dishes and food on to the floor.

Delisa couldn't believe what she was seeing and ran to get Marlon and some of the other brothers to break up the fight. They rushed in, grabbing both men and tearing them apart.

Marlon drug Jaleel off where they could have some privacy. "Jaleel, what's up with you tonight? The way you've been trippin' since she arrived, I'm surprised it took Paul this long to knock you upside the head." Jaleel's eyes widened with shock and denial was on his lips, but Marlon wasn't having it. Jaleel was more like a brother than a cousin and they always kept it real with each other. "I saw you, Paul saw you, and everyone else probably did too. Care to tell me what's up?"

Jaleel's shoulders slumped in resignation and in exasperation he rubbed a bloody knuckled hand down his face. "I'm trippin... I'll get it together." It was neither the time nor the place to discuss the things running through his mind and he hoped Marlon understood, but wasn't going to wait around to find out. He pushed off the wall and left his cousin alone in the hallway.

Once things had settled down, Delisa looked around the kitchen. There were broken dishes on the floor along with her trampled birthday cake. She looked at Paul; blood was running from his mouth. Jaleel stepped back into the kitchen with blood oozing from his nose. Then she looked at all her guests who were now crowded in the kitchen. Silence crept over everyone and was broken by the eerie calm in Delisa's voice. "Everyone, please go home." Tears flowed down her cheeks as she stared at her husband.

Without a word, everyone grabbed their coats and purses and left Paul, Sheena, Jaleel, and Delisa standing in the kitchen. Sheena grabbed a broom. "Let me help you clean up this mess. It's the least I can do since my husband was the cause."

"No, don't worry about it. Jaleel and I need to talk. Take Paul home and I'll talk to you later." They embraced and Delisa promised to call as soon as she got to the bottom of things.

Hearing the front door close, Delisa turned to her husband who had finally gotten his nose to stop bleeding. "Why would you ruin my birthday like this?"

"Baby, it wasn't my fault. Paul got up in my face accusing me of some nonsense."

"From what I saw tonight, I'm surprised he didn't kill you. Your eyes were all over his wife. I should have checked you on your feelings for her a long time ago."

"What is wrong with you guys? I am not in love with Sheena!" Jaleel couldn't believe he was actually having this conversation with his wife.

"Yes, you are." She paused to check her emotions. "I have seen you look at her and tonight you were watching her as if Paul and I weren't even there."

"Delisa I love you and—"

She cut him off. It was time she took control of the situation and didn't want to be sweet talked into settling to be his second choice. "I believe you do love me, but you have never looked at me the way you look at her. Your eyes light up and your desire for her radiates from within you. I saw the look on your face at their wedding and it cut me so deep I may never heal. I am done being your second choice. I'm leaving. Don't bother to call until you are ready to love me and only me."

Delisa packed her and their daughter Jalisa's bag while Jaleel followed behind her, begging her not to leave. With each plea her heart shattered a little more, but she kept a stone face. She loved this man and couldn't imagine a life with anyone else, but she loved herself too and deserved better. With a shattered heart and frayed nerves she went to the car, put Jalisa in the car seat, and looked at Jaleel as he pleaded one last time.

"Baby, please don't leave me."

Then, she got in and drove off, not once responding to his pleas.

Paul and Sheena's ride home was quiet. Paul watched her as she drove. He had never seen her so angry. Her jaws were clenched so tight, seemingly taking all her strength to keep from lashing out at him. "Sheena…" He mustered up enough courage to speak. "Did you expect me to do nothing while he had his eyes glued to your body all night?"

Sheena pulled into the garage, lowered the door, and went into the house. Paul sat in the car trying to figure out how to calm her down. Deciding it would be best to give her the space she needed, he went into the house to clean his mouth. He started toward the stairs and heard the shower running and realized that tonight would be the second time since their wedding that he would shower alone. He was headed up stairs to prepare for a long night of the silent treatment when the doorbell rang.

Seeing that it was Delisa, Paul opened the door apologizing. "I am sorry for ruining your birthday. Please forgive me."

Paul grabbed her bags and a sleeping Jalisa. "I forgive you, and I thank you. Tonight you did what I should have done years ago. I have always known how he felt about her, and I never had enough courage to say anything. I just settled for whatever he gave me. I'm done settling. I left him... I can't believe I left him." Delisa broke down, tears rolled down her face, her chest tightened, and with every breath her sobs spiraled more and more out of control.

Paul hurried to lay Jalisa in one of the guest rooms and when he got back to Delisa she collapsed against him. He held her and silently prayed for God to give her strength to make it through this trial. Paul was still standing in the doorway when Sheena came to the top of the stairs.

"Paul, what is going on? What is all that noise?"

Paul turned so she could see Delisa. "She left Jaleel and needs to stay here for a while," he explained.

Sheena ran down the stairs and embraced Delisa.

"Don't tell me you left your husband because of the foolishness Paul was talking about."

"It is not foolishness and everyone can see it except you. Sheena, Jaleel has been in love with you since our freshman year in college. While you were away at grad school, I kept him company and took care of him while he was sick. It took his mind off of you for a while, but as soon as you came back, he only had eyes for you, but we were already married. Don't be mad at Paul. He only said what I should have said a long time ago."

"Let's say that he is in love with me. The Bible tells us that if we see our brother overtaken in a fall, we who are spiritual are to restore him with meekness. We don't beat him up and we don't abandon him when he is at his lowest state. Leaving your husband is the easy way out. You have to stay and fight for what is yours."

"I am tired. Since the day we got married I have fought for our marriage."

"Being tired is something we all experience. We just have to make sure we don't give up."

"I hear you, Sheena. I just really need some sleep. I will talk to you tomorrow." Delisa joined her daughter in bed. Tossing and turning, she cried herself to sleep.

Sheena and Paul stood facing each other, trying to read each other's thoughts through their eyes. She didn't want to argue with him, but felt she needed to explain her frustration. Her eyes scanned his face, landing on his lip, swollen and encrusted with blood. She ran her hand across his face, stopping to inspect his puffy right eye. Grabbing his hand, she led him into the kitchen where she grabbed paper towels and a bag of ice to tend to her husband's injuries.

"Paul," slowly and softly she spoke, "Do you plan on beating up every man that looks at me?" She didn't wait for a response. "I am your wife. You're in covenant with me. I'm the only wandering eye you should be concerned about, and I only have eyes for you."

When she finished cleaning his wounds, she placed the ice pack on his eye and led him to the bedroom to continue their conversation. "We have to keep ourselves connected to God, so that when we find ourselves in situations like this we don't get angry with the person, but we recognize the spirit that is influencing them and attack the spirit not the person."

"Baby, I am not perfect. I've only been saved for a little over a year."

"Neither am I. We learn and grow from our mistakes."

Paul grabbed Sheena's hand. "Will you pray with me? I feel like an idiot for getting out of control." Getting on his knees, Paul repented for his actions. He prayed for strength and wisdom, for Jaleel to find peace, and for him and Delisa to reconcile. For the first time, he laid hands on his wife, praying for her with fervor, taking authority over the adversary, he proclaimed her victory at work and asked for wisdom while she governed the school. The power of God engulfed them as they cried and prayed in the spirit.

Jaleel walked around the kitchen looking at the mess he and Paul made. He stepped over broken dishes and birthday cake. He could not believe his behavior. He tried to make himself stop looking at Sheena, but every time she came into the room he couldn't think straight. She was a beautiful woman, but it was more than her beauty that captivated him. She was very considerate and caring, always putting others before herself. She was a good listener. You could talk for hours and still have her undivided attention, but what he loved most was her innocence. Even though she was married and had given that gift to Paul, Jaleel was still attracted to the fact that Sheena had not been with a lot of men.

Jaleel silently cleaned the kitchen, ashamed of the mess he'd made in the house and everyone's life. He knew his actions were way out of line and had to do something before he lost everything. He was done pretending to be over Sheena. He needed to really get over her. Getting closer to the Lord was the only way to do it. He made up his mind to pray, fast, and consecrate unto the Lord for a spiritual renewal.

6

"A day late; a dollar short." Delisa's eyes returned to whatever she was working on when he arrived.

Without a word, Jaleel placed the bouquet on her desk and backed out of her office. Her rejection hurt more than he ever thought it would. She was angry. She had every right to be, but he wasn't done wooing her. He wouldn't be satisfied until they were all back under one roof, living the happy life they once had.

Jaleel headed over to the preschool class. The beautiful smile on his little girl's face and her excitement to see him instantly lifted his spirits.

"Daddy!" Jalisa screamed, ran across the class, and jumped into his outstretched arms.

He had to chastise her for disrupting the class, but the big hug and kiss he gave her more than made up for it. They exited the classroom and he tickled her ribs and blew raspberries on her cheeks all the way to the car. Her tiny body wiggled in his arms as her feet flailed from the torture. Her shrills of enjoyment pierced his ear. Jaleel loved every minute of it.

Jaleel regretfully tied her into her seatbelt. As he climbed into the driver seat, his cell phone rang. He checked the screen and tapped accept.

"Hey Sheena, what's up?

"I was wondering if you had few minutes to talk this evening when you drop Jalisa off."

"Is everything okay?

"I hope so. We really need to talk to know for sure."

Jaleel's head dropped to the steering wheel and he rested it there for a moment before he replied. He knew this moment was coming. The day his feelings became public knowledge, he knew he'd have to look Sheena, his friend, in the eye and own up to everything. It was time to face the music. "Sure, I've got plenty of time."

Sheena ended the call, feeling good about her decision to get involved. She was becoming more and more concerned for her cousin. She had to do something to help them reconcile, but first she had to talk to Jaleel and discuss his feelings for her. She buckled down on the work load sitting before her. Within two hours, her work was complete and she headed out for the day.

Pulling up in front of her house, Sheena saw Paul and Jaleel outside talking. Having flashbacks of their last encounter, Sheena rushed up to them.

"Is everything okay?" She asked, feeling a bit relieved seeing the lighthearted look on their faces.

"Everything is fine. Jaleel called and told me you wanted to meet with him. He wanted to make sure it was all right with me, and I needed to talk with him too, so I took off from work a little early."

"I hope you don't mind," Jaleel tried to explain. "I just didn't want to make things worse if Paul came home and saw us talking. While I have both of you here, I just want to say, I know I was way out of line and I should have put my feelings in check a long time ago. Please forgive me." Feeling the heaviness and the tension of the burden being lifted, he hugged both of them.

Paul was still a little skeptical about this sudden change in Jaleel, but decided to give him the benefit of the doubt and wait to see if he had really gotten over Sheena. "Sheena, give me and Jaleel a few more minutes, then he is all yours."

"That is not necessary. He has already answered all my questions. I wanted to make sure he was dealing with the issue and I wanted to invite him to Thanksgiving dinner. I already talked to Delisa and she wants you to come, so I won't take no for an answer." Not waiting for his response, Sheena walked away, leaving them to finish their conversation.

Sheena walked in the house to find Delisa standing in the foyer waiting for her. "Why is Jaleel still here?"

"Were you watching from the window?" Sheena laughed at her cousin's jumpy nerves.

"Yes, I was watching. I miss him so much. I wanted to ask him to stay, but..."

Sheena interrupted, "No, buts. If you love him and miss him, why play this game? Go home and be with your husband."

"I am not playing games. I cannot go back until I am sure he has you out of his system."

"I believe God is working on him. He apologized for not checking his feelings a long—"

Delisa cut her off with a deep gasp. "You mean he finally admitted that he has feelings for you?" Her eyes swelled with tears and the pain of betrayal tinged her heart.

"Assuming he had feelings for you was one thing. I could convince myself that I was trippin' to help myself sleep at night, but having those assumptions confirmed hurts more than I ever imagined." Delisa sank to the floor and rested her back against the front door.

Sitting next to her, Sheena wrapped her arms around Delisa. "Hey, what happened to the bold, sassy woman he fell in love with? Maybe you should take this time to get in touch with her. Under all the pain and frustration, I know she's still in there somewhere. She wouldn't just rollover and take this. She'd stand up and make her man take notice of what he was missing out on. I know it hurts, but don't give up on him. He loves you."

"I am not giving up, but I see how Paul loves you, how your presence brightens up his face. Your touch takes his breath away, and his eyes never stray. I want that kind of love; I deserve that kind of love. That's the way I love him. Why doesn't he love me that way? What if he can never love me that way?" Delisa cried uncontrollably at the thought of Jaleel not being able or willing to reciprocate her love.

All of the feelings Delisa had been keeping bottled up were finally released. Sheena was glad Delisa was finally talking. She had been keeping all her emotions contained and would change the subject whenever Sheena tried to talk about Jaleel. Deciding not to slap Delisa with scripture after scripture, Sheena became a friend, a shoulder to cry on, an ear to listen, and when asked, a voice of advice.

"You know he cried at your wedding," Delisa spoke through her sobs. "He was sitting right next to me, his wife, and his heart was breaking for another woman. We left the reception early and he made love to more passionately than he had in a long time, but I couldn't help wondering if he imagined he was making love to you."

"Delisa, I am so sorry. You have to know that I didn't do anything to lead him on."

Delisa chuckled amid her tears. "That never crossed my mind. You have always been clueless when it came to men. I was shocked when you showed up with Paul. I couldn't believe you noticed a man was interested in you and had taken the time out of your busy schedule to date him."

"Well, Paul was never subtle. He was aggressive and weaseled his way into my time by using his lawyer skills to persuade me to see him. I remember wondering how he got me to agree to everything he wanted. Then I found out he was an attorney who manipulated people for a living. I was good and ready to tell him off, but he kissed me, our first real kiss. His kiss heated my body, and I knew I had not been manipulated. It was my body's reaction to him that allowed him to get anything he wanted from me. Even though I tried, the one thing I could not ignore was how his presence affected me." They laughed. Sheena's light hearted confession lifted the haze that had settled on them.

The next morning, Sheena was awakened by Paul's cell phone ringing. He checked the caller ID, answered the phone, and then left the room.

Sheena stared at the clock. *It's only five. Who is calling this early in the morning, and why can't he talk in the room?* Sheena's thoughts were spinning out of control. If it were a family emergency, he would have talked in the room. Maybe it was work. He would definitely leave the room if it was work, but would they call this early? She searched for anything that would ease her mind and erase the fear that was looming in the back of her mind.

Thirty minutes later, Paul came back into the room. Sheena sat up, waiting for him to explain. She watched his every move, tried to make eye contact, but he was getting dressed and wouldn't look her way. She watched him put on jeans and a sweatshirt. Her heart raced with fear. "Are you wearing jeans to work?" She asked, hoping he had planned some sort of casual day at his office.

"No, it's Friday, I'm not going in to the office today, remember?"

"Then, where are you going so early in the morning?"

"Baby, you feeling all right? We talked about this all week." He sat next to her on the bed and felt her forehead to see if she was warm. He looked into her eyes and didn't understand what he saw. "My brother's flight comes in this morning. Remember he's coming in for Thanksgiving and will be staying with us for a while?"

Sheena breathed a sigh of relief. "So, that was your brother that just called?"

"I'm not going to lie to you and I don't want a whole bunch of questions. That wasn't my brother."

"Then who was it?" Sheena asked, trying to contain her anger and fear.

"I can't tell you who it was. Just trust me." He kissed her long and hard trying to soothe the fear and worry his actions left lingering in her mind.

She pulled away and looked in his eyes. "I trust you," she said. He had never given her a reason to distrust him, and she knew he would never purposely hurt her. That thought was enough to get Sheena through the day.

Sheena left work a little early. She wanted to make a special dinner

41

for her brother-in-law and had to stop by the store. She was going to prepare Paul's favorite meal: smoked salmon, salad with spinach greens and strawberries topped with red wine vinaigrette, roasted red potatoes with scallions and peppers, and for dessert, strawberry cake with cream cheese icing.

Pulling her car into the garage, Sheena grabbed all of her grocery bags and shuffled her way into the kitchen only to find her husband, brother-in-law, and Jaleel sitting at the table having a heated discussion about the San Diego Chargers with two empty pizza boxes in the middle. They were talking so loud no one heard her come in.

"Tim, you cannot deny that the Chargers are cold this year," Paul said to his brother. "I know you are a diehard Steelers fan, but you have to give the Chargers their props."

"What? Big brother you've been in San Diego too long. If my memory is correct you also used to be a diehard Steelers fan."

"I think I had something to do with his conversion." Sheena stepped further into the kitchen.

"Hey, you're home early." Paul grabbed her bags, placed them on the counter then pulled her close. He had been craving her kiss all day and was not going to allow Jaleel or Tim to stand in his way. His kiss was slow and deliberate. He wanted to taste every inch of her mouth. He caressed her cheek as he deepened his kiss and was getting ready to slip his hand under her shirt when he heard someone clear their throat.

"We're still sitting here." Tim couldn't believe how Sheena had changed his brother. He had never seen Paul get lost in a woman the way he did with Sheena. "And if you don't mind I would like to give my big sister a hug."

"Uh-oh," Paul stepped away from Sheena and out of the line of fire. "Sorry little brother, I can't help you with this one."

"What? What happened?"

Sheena smiled and stepped closer to him. "Don't you mean your little sister?"

"What? Oh, that's right!" Tim laughed. Looking at Paul, he placed his arm around Sheena's shoulders. "I forgot Paul was robbing the cradle." Tim and Jaleel's laughter roared through the house.

Sheena playfully punched Tim in his side then greeted Jaleel. "Keep laughing and I'm going to put you out." She slapped his shoulder. "What are you doing here anyway? I thought you were taking Jalisa for the weekend."

"I am, but Delisa said it would be easier for me to pick her up here instead of daycare since I had to get her clothes. I say it would have been easier if she had packed a bag and brought it with her, but she wanted me to meet her here, so here I am."

"Delisa is your wife, Sheena's cousin, right? And lives here?"

"Right, it is a long story." Jaleel answered, anticipating his next question they heard the front door open, little feet pattering on the floor, and Jalisa screaming, "Daddy, Daddy, Daddy!" She ran straight into his arms and Jaleel smothered her with kisses.

Jaleel's eyes widened when Delisa walked into the room. He put Jalisa down and she ran off to her room. Jaleel held his breath as he scanned his wife's body. His pulse accelerated and his mouth watered. "Baby, you look beautiful."

Delisa walked up to him. It had taken her all night and all day to build up the courage to do what she was getting ready to do. She walked passed Sheena and winked. Placing her hand behind Jaleel's head she pulled him down and covered his lips with hers. Her tongue roamed his mouth, becoming reacquainted with the taste and feel. Jaleel's knees buckled and Delisa stepped back to look in his eyes.

Jaleel's heart was racing; he couldn't believe she was in his arms. He stood there with his forehead resting on hers looking down into her eyes. Neither of them spoke, only lived in the moment, forgetting about the eyes that were on them and their estrangement.

Tim's voice broke the silence. "Sheena, if this is the affect all the women in your family have on men, please do not introduce me to anyone. I love being single and I'm not ready to be hemmed up like Jaleel and my brother." Tim looked at Paul then back to Jaleel. "I can't believe you guys.

These women walk in the room and you lose consciousness. Don't get me wrong. They are gorgeous women, but I will never let a woman control my senses like that."

Delisa was mortified. She hadn't noticed Tim at all. "I'm sorry. I didn't know we had company. You must be Tim. I recognize you from the wedding." She stepped toward him and extended her hand. "I'm Delisa. It's nice to finally meet you."

"There is no need to apologize. From what I can see, love makes people do things they wouldn't normally do. If you lovebirds would excuse me, I am going to lay down for awhile and give you guys some privacy."

Sheena waited until Tim left the kitchen. "So does this mean you guys are getting back together?" They all looked at Delisa.

She didn't want to lead Jaleel on. "What this means is I'm in love with my husband and I've missed him." She stepped back into his arms, relishing in the heat of his embrace. "Jaleel, you mean a lot to me, but I will no longer settle for part of your heart. We both need to strengthen our relationship with God before I will come home."

Jaleel felt his heart breaking all over again. He knew she was right. He had already started taking steps to get closer to God, but their kiss made him hopeful. Still holding her in his arms, he resolved to accept what she was giving him at the moment, and strive to do all he could to get her back. He offered her another kiss. Willingly, she accepted, and promised he wouldn't let her down.

7

It was noon and some of Sheena and Paul's dinner guests had started arriving. It was a Walker family tradition that Thanksgiving dinner be served by two, and everyone always arrived early to sit around laughing and talking, catching up, or reminiscing about old times. Sheena and Delisa loved to hear stories about their fathers' childhood. Delisa's father was a year older, but the two looked and acted like twins; they were very close and raised their daughters to be the same.

Sheena and Delisa always went to the same schools and spent all of their free time together. Then, right after eighth grade, Delisa's father's job transferred him to San Diego. Their decision to move affected the whole family, but was hardest on Sheena. Delisa had a sister, three years younger, who she could spend time with to keep from being lonely. Sheena's sister was seven years younger and on a completely different path. Delisa was more outgoing and made friends easily while Sheena was a little shy and the only friends she had were really Delisa's friends. So, after Delisa moved away, Sheena lost herself into church and school where she earned the nickname 'Bible Nerd' because she tutored some of her classmates and started each session with prayer and scripture.

Sheena had done so well in high school that she could have gone to any college she wanted, but the thought of college overwhelmed her. High school was socially difficult for her even though she had gone to school with most of her classmates since elementary school. The thought of moving to a new state and having to meet new people scared her. When she heard that Delisa had been accepted to San Diego State University, her decision was easy. But once she was there, Sheena realized she didn't need Delisa as much as she'd thought.

It was a quarter to two and all of their guests had arrived except for Delisa's sister, Camilla, who never was on time to anything. Sheena's parents, James and Linda, had flown in the night before with her sister, April. Jaleel showed up at noon with his dad, Mr. Wright, and Delisa's parents, Johnny and Felicia, arrived around one.

The table had been set and dinner was in full swing before Camilla arrived with her five-month-old daughter, Adrianna. She walked into the dining room and made the same comment she always made. "I can't believe you guys started without me." The table erupted in laughter.

"Cammie." Delisa got up and grabbed Adrianna. "If we waited for you we'd starve to death."

Camilla looked around the table at everyone laughing at her and smiled. She loved the holidays. Even though she was usually the butt of everyone's joke or the one being fussed at, she still enjoyed being with her family. "Uncle James, you haven't seen me in a year, at least you could have waited for me." She leaned over to kiss his cheek.

"Please," Johnny chuckled. "My brother isn't going to let food sit in front of him for too long." They laughed loud and hard. James grew up with the reputation for being a big eater and used to be called 'Munch' when he was a child. Camilla hugged and kissed everyone at the table and stopped when she got to Tim.

"I don't think we've met before. I'm Camilla."

"I'm Tim, Paul's brother; pleasure to meet you." He stood and slightly bowed in greeting.

"The pleasure is all mines." Her eyelashes fanned down to her cheekbones and her shy smile did nothing to hide the sudden color highlighting her cheeks. Camilla moved away from the intriguing stranger, finally took her seat, and piled her plate with turkey, candied yams, mashed potatoes, collard greens, macaroni and cheese, stuffing, and green beans. For a moment, no one talked and all you could hear was smacking, slurping, and forks clanking against the plates.

"Baby, you put your foot in these greens," Paul said with a mouth full of food.

"You ain't lying," others at the table joined in.

Finishing up his second plate of food, Paul settled back in his chair and watched his extended family. They were a very close family and he was honored to be a part of it. He loved how they never treated him like an in-law and never even referred to him as such. He was always introduced as son, nephew, or cousin. His mother died when he was young, his dad worked long hours, and his grandparents weren't in the picture because both his parents grew up in foster care, so Paul never really had much of a family life. He was grateful for the family God had blessed him with.

Paul noticed that Tim had suddenly gotten quiet like his mind was preoccupied. Paul had to ask him several times to pass the mashed potatoes before he responded. When he finally passed them, he knocked over a glass of water then fumbled nervously to clean it up. Paul scooted closer so no one could hear. "What's wrong? You don't seem like yourself."

"What? Umm...I guess just a little jet lag. The time difference is finally catching up with me."

Paul knew it had to be more than jet lag. He had been in San Diego for a week and that was plenty of time to get adjusted. He wanted to press the issue, but his cell phone rang. Paul excused himself from the table to take the call. Sheena watched him as he walked away. All she could think about were the early morning phone calls that he received every day.

No matter how much she wanted to trust him, she couldn't help but think he was having an affair. She tried to convince herself that he was a good Christian man and would never do such a thing, but all of the secrecy got the best of her. She was afraid her marriage was over before it began. Sheena could not shake the gloomy feeling that had come over her. Once dinner was over, all the men gathered in the family room to watch the game while the women sat around in the kitchen. Sheena's mind was still on Paul and all his secret phone calls.

Noticing the change in Sheena's mood, Delisa pulled her to the side. "What's up with you? And don't tell me nothing. I've been watching you for the past hour and something is on your mind. Spit it out."

Tears welled in Sheena's eyes as she turned to Delisa. "I am probably overreacting, but I just can't shake this feeling. For the past week, Paul has been getting these secret phone calls early in the morning before we wake up."

"Did you ask him what's going on?"

"Of course I did. He told me to trust him and wouldn't tell me who was calling."

"Sheena, you have to talk to him again. You can't let stuff like this slide. Look where it's gotten me."

"But I want to trust him. There has to be a logical explanation, and I know he'll tell me eventually. Besides, I want him to know that I trust him."

"Well, pray about it. God knows and sees all. There is no need stressing over something that God already has the answer to."

Sheena looked at Delisa. She couldn't believe how different her cousin was. Delisa had never been the level headed one offering advice. "Wow Delisa, look at you. Sounds like you really have been getting closer to the Lord."

"I have, and I know I have a long ways to go, but I feel closer to Him than I ever have. I pray at least twice a day. I've even fasted a couple times. Even though Jaleel and I are separated, I have this peace that is beyond words."

"Do you think you're ready to go home?"

"I don't know, but I will say this. Tonight, I purposely sat on the opposite side of the table than Jaleel so I could watch him. Every time I looked up, I caught him staring at me. We made eye contact, and he gave me a smile that made my heart skip a beat. The best thing is that he never looked your way. It is obvious some change has taken place, I just don't want to mess it up by going home too soon."

"Going home? Who's going home?" Camilla came barging into the dining room with Paul, Jaleel, April, and Tim. She saw the tears in Sheena and Delisa's eyes and instantly her voice softened. "What's going

48

on? Is everything okay?"

Paul pulled Sheena into his arms and whispered into her ear. "Baby, why are you crying?"

"I was just a little overwhelmed. Talking to Delisa really helped." She stepped out of his embrace before he could press the issue, but that never worked with Paul. He grabbed her and molded her body to his.

Paul whispered against her lips. "It's okay if you don't want to talk to me about it, but don't push me away." He parted her lips, deepening his kiss to soothe her mind and help her relax.

"All right, all right, cut all that out. I thought we were going to play Taboo, Scrabble, or something, not sit around watching these two. You guys are sickening. I think I'm going to lose my dinner." Tim placed his hand over his mouth, pretending like he was going to throw up.

Camilla laughed and grabbed Tim's hand. "You are crazy. You can be my partner. Finally, someone who thinks these lovebirds are sickening."

"Camilla, please," Delisa chuckled. "You and Tim will never be able to beat the connection between a husband and wife. You were never any good at Taboo, anyway."

"Well, big sister, that sounds like a challenge."

Seeing that she was the seventh wheel, April quietly excused herself. She was used to being by herself at family functions, and she did not like the competitive sides of Delisa and Camilla. They were always trying to outdo each other and the games usually ended in an argument.

The game was underway and the trash talking in full swing. The first round went to Paul and Sheena with four points. The others tied with three points. The next round, Camilla and Tim took the lead by scoring five points. They were jumping up and down high-fiving each other. Camilla got in Delisa's face, screaming, "Now, what was that about the connection between husband and wife?"

"Oh please, the game just got started—"

Sheena interrupted, "Yes, the game just got started and I do not want the night to end early because of your sibling rivalry. Don't get started. We're only playing for fun."

Camilla and Delisa both ignored Sheena's warning. Neither liked to lose, and losing to the other was the ultimate defeat. In Taboo, you were only as good as your partner. Jaleel kept missing the mark. Delisa gave great clues, but Jaleel simply wasn't catching them. The clues he gave were so far-fetched that no one knew what he was talking about. He tried and tried, but couldn't get into the game. The final outcome of the game left Tim and Camilla as the clear winners. Camilla was gloating and enjoying her win too much. It was making Delisa furious.

"Cammie, do you have to be such a poor winner?" Delisa asked.

"Delisa, stop whining. You beat me all the time and act the same way. Now that I'm enjoying my win you want to act like a big baby."

Sheena was just about to intervene when Delisa conceded. "You're right, I am a poor winner."

Jaleel, Sheena, and Camilla looked at Delisa with wide eyes, their mouths hanging open. "Okay... What have you done with my sister?" Camilla couldn't believe Delisa was trying to take the high road. "She would never take losing to me so calmly."

"Trust me, it is not easy, but I'm trying to change. If this had been about two weeks ago, I'd probably have my fist half-way down your throat by now."

Jaleel laughed, remembering how many fires he had to put out when Camilla came to visit. Delisa and Camilla were loving, caring sisters until they played cards, went to the gym, watched Jeopardy, or anything else that allowed for someone to come out on top. He watched Delisa trying to be the better person, but he could tell she was still heated.

"Well, I'm going to get a drink to celebrate finally beating you at something. Since this house is full of Christians, I know there is nothing here with a little kick to it. I'm going to run to the store. Does anyone want anything?"

"That sounds like a plan. Do you mind if I ride with you?" Camilla nodded, and Tim stood to escort her out.

Walking to the car, Camilla looked up at the sky. The sun had moved west across the sky, preparing to set. She loved watching sunsets and it had been a while since she'd a chance. There was a place called Sunset Cliffs where she would go to watch the sunset. She hadn't been able to since giving birth to Adrianna.

"I know we don't really know each other, but there is this place I like to go to watch the sun set. I was thinking since I have free babysitters maybe we could go, if you don't mind. I won't stay long, and then we can stop and get a drink on the way back."

"That's cool, but we should grab our jackets. It's a little cold out here." They grabbed their coats, and then were on their way down the highway.

8

Tim and Camilla arrived at the cliffs, bundled up in their jackets, and sat on the hood of the car. The call of the seagulls and sound of the waves crashing against the rocks were hypnotic. They sat in silence, enjoying the peace of the ocean and the beauty of the fiery orange sky. A bone-chilling breeze blew through them and Camilla shivered. It was the end of November and although San Diego didn't have much of a winter, the temperature could drop quite a bit in the evening. With the breeze coming off the ocean, it felt like a true winter.

Tim watched Camilla's hair blow in the wind and her nose turn red from the chill. The orange hue in the sky brought out the amber flecks in her eyes. She was the most beautiful woman he'd ever seen. Besides looks, her fire and energy added to her beauty. He could sense her confidence, but it was not overbearing. She knew who she was and loved herself. He watched as she enjoyed the sunset, her body shivering occasionally from the cold.

He sat behind her and pulled her between his legs, wrapping himself around her to shield her from the cold. Under normal circumstances, Camilla would have protested a man she barely knew putting his hands on her, but she was freezing and there was something about him that seemed so familiar.

Tim took a deep breath. He had to pull himself together. Her presence had him unglued from the moment she had walked into the dining room. After several deep breaths, Tim forced his mind back on the sunset. "I can see why you like coming here. This is breathtaking."

"I know, I used to come here all the time to clear my head.

While all of my friends were cramming at the last minute during midterms or finals, I'd be out here. I came here the day I found out I was pregnant. I left the clinic and came straight here. The nurse had given me information about abortion, adoption, and a list of obstetricians in my area. I sat on my car reading all the information and crying. I couldn't believe one night of stupidity was changing the rest of my life. Some friends and I decided to go out for one last hoorah before senior year and our entrance into adulthood. Long story short, I met a man, had my very first one night stand with a total stranger, and never got his name or number. So, I sat here on my car trying to make a decision that would affect my life until the day I die."

"Wow, that couldn't have been easy. Especially since your family is full of Christians."

"Well, I'm a Christian too. I have just always marched to the beat of my own drum, which made telling my parents a little easier. It seemed like they were waiting for me to screw up, so they didn't really get upset. I guess they were just happy I went to college and was about to graduate."

"What do you have your degree in?"

"Well, two months before my due date I had some pregnancy issues and was placed on bed rest. I had a few inconsiderate professors who gave me incompletes and the rest is history. But, I will be graduating in December...Business Administration."

"Really, I have a B.S. in Business Administration with a Masters in Accounting."

"I'm going into accounting. I already have a couple of job offers. I'm having a hard time deciding which to choose."

"Who knows? My brother has been pressuring me to move out here and open my own firm. Maybe I'll hire you."

"I just might take you up on that." Camilla searched his face for a sign of deception. He seemed too good to be true. He actually seemed interested in what she had to say.

"Okay." He marveled at how he was getting so caught in this woman. "That explains why we didn't meet at Paul and Sheena's wedding. You must have just had the baby."

"Yes, I had her a few days before. So, I have given you my life's story. What's yours?"

"There isn't much of a story. I never met my mom, and my dad worked two jobs trying to make ends meet. By the time I started school, Paul stepped in as dad, making sure I ate, got to school on time, did my homework. We barely speak to our father now, but Paul and I couldn't be closer."

"If you don't mind me asking, how is it that you've never met your mother?"

"She died while giving birth to me. Paul was only five. I used to think he blamed me for taking her away. When I was seven, I caught him crying while looking at a picture of her. It shocked me because I'd never seen him cry, not even when our dad would come home drunk and beat us for not having food in the house, or some other nonsense."

Camilla wished she could take away the pain from his past. Her heart was bursting with compassion and sympathy for this man she hardly knew. She caressed his cheek with her finger tips and turned his head to look in his eyes, but before she could speak he did. "Your hands are freezing. Maybe we should head back to the house."

They had talked for so long the sun had set and nightfall rested upon them. She stared into his eyes and felt familiarity and such comfort that she'd have sworn she knew him all her life. Gradually, she stepped back and made her way to the driver side of the car.

Camilla turned the heater on in the car to take the chill out of the air. "Do you still want to get that drink?" She asked as she headed back toward the highway. Before he could answer, she noticed seven missed calls on her cell phone. "On second thought, maybe we should head on back. I have quite a few missed calls from Sheena and Delisa."

Camilla checked her voicemail and her heart sank when she heard Sheena's voice. "Camilla, I hate to leave this kind of message, but we've been trying to reach you. It's Jalisa. She fell and hurt herself. Please get to Zion Hospital."

Tim saw her face and knew something terrible had happened. "Baby, what's wrong?" He couldn't believe the endearment that came out of his mouth. He really had to get himself together before it was too late.

"They had to rush my niece to the hospital." Foreboding of tragedy rose over Camilla. She tried to brush it off, but it surrounded her like the heat blowing out of the car vents. Her foot leaned heavy on the accelerator. She drove without regard to the speed limit.

They arrived at the hospital and were greeted by Paul and Sheena. Paul eyed his brother, wondering where he had been for the past few hours and why he hadn't answered his cell phone. Now was not the time to question him, but Paul was determined to get some answers.

Camilla located her parents sitting next to her aunt and uncle in the ER waiting room. "Mom, what's going on? How is Jalisa?"

"Cammie, where have you been? We have been trying to reach you for hours."

"I wanted to watch the sunset, so I took Tim to Sunset Cliffs. We were sitting outside and I left my cell phone inside the car. I didn't hear it ringing," Camilla explained.

Johnny and Felicia knew how much their daughter loved going to the cliffs, and how she always lost track of time while she was out there. Felicia embraced her daughter. "Calm down, Camilla; it's okay. I know you would've been here sooner if you could. Delisa wanted you to go back as soon as you got here. So get back there and help your sister. Make sure she knows we are all out here praying for Jalisa."

Camilla hadn't realized she was still holding Tim's hand until she turned to walk away. Even though she barely knew him, his masculine strength was exactly what she needed and when the nurse asked if they were immediate family, Camilla told her they were Jalisa's aunt and uncle. She still didn't know what was going on and needed someone to lean on if the news was bad. Tim didn't protest. He wanted to be there for her and felt honored that she needed him.

Camilla walked into Jalisa's hospital room. Jaleel and Delisa were sitting side by side, her head resting on his shoulder. Camilla walked up and placed her hand on Delisa shoulder. "Hey, how is she doing?"

Delisa jumped up and wrapped her arms around her sister. "She fell down the stairs. I don't even know why she was up there. Before I noticed, she was tumbling down. I tried to get to her before she hit the bottom, but I wasn't fast enough. She landed at the bottom and the back of her head smacked on the floor. She just laid there and wouldn't respond to my voice. We called an ambulance, and by the time they arrived Jalisa was conscious, but was still groggy and unstable." Delisa sank back into Jaleel's arms and cried uncontrollably.

Camilla turned to Tim; he was right there waiting for her. He held her tight and planted kisses of comfort on her forehead. She cried into his chest and he gave her the strength she needed.

"Excuse me Mr. and Mrs. Wright, we are ready to take Jalisa into surgery. We normally ask parents and immediate family members to donate blood at this time, so that we can begin some preliminary screening. After surgery, Jalisa will be moved to ICU on the third floor. There is a waiting room up there; that's where we will look for you after surgery. If you don't have any questions, the nurses out front can direct you to where you can donate."

Camilla and Delisa walked hand in hand back to the ER waiting room with Jaleel and Tim trailing behind them. Everyone stood to their feet as they came out, waiting to hear an update. Jaleel informed the family of Jalisa's condition and asked them to donate blood while Paul snatched Tim by the arm and pulled him outside.

"Tim, please don't tell me you slept with Camilla."

"What?" Tim chuckled.

"I don't see anything funny."

"What's funny is, you think who I sleep with is your business."

"Tim, I know your history with women and after you leave here I still have to look these people in the face. I want to be able to do that with a clear conscience. I don't want to dodge daggers because of something

56

you've done."

"Look Paul, I see how much you love them and how much they love you. They are good people; they even made me feel like part of the family. Don't worry. I haven't done anything to jeopardize your relationship with them. We didn't hug, kiss, or anything like that. We just talked."

"Really? Because she is clinging to you like she's known you all her life and I saw the way you handled her when you came in. So, out with it, little brother. Tell me what happened."

"There is nothing to tell. Camilla was upset after listening to Sheena's message and I was trying to comfort her. That's it. Plain. Simple. Innocent."

"Okay, if you say so. I trust you." He trusted that they didn't have sex, but there was nothing plain or simple about what he saw.

They went back into the waiting room and found Linda sitting alone, rocking Adrianna. Linda, Paul, and Tim were not blood relatives and were not required to donate blood. Paul gave her a kiss on the cheek. "Hey Mom why don't you go get some fresh air. We'll take care of Adrianna for a while."

"Thanks, I really need to stretch my legs. I'll be back in a few minutes." Linda handed the baby to Tim while Paul helped her stand.

Paul watched his brother rock Adrianna to sleep. He had never seen him hold a baby, but he looked like a natural. He rocked the baby until she fell asleep then placed her on his shoulder. Adrianna snuggled against his neck. Tim lightly patted her back, making sure she was sound asleep. The rest of the family returned from giving blood and Camilla reached to take the baby from Tim.

"It's okay, baby. I got her. You sit down and rest."

Paul and Sheena looked at each other and smiled. No one else heard Tim call Camilla baby, but they did, and it confirmed Paul's suspicions. Paul watched for Camilla's response to see if she reciprocated Tim's feelings and what he saw and heard told him she did.

Camilla placed her hand on Tim's thigh. "We're going to the third floor to wait for Jalisa to get out of surgery."

"Okay, you grab the diaper bag and I'll carry the baby."

Paul laughed to himself as they all walked to the elevator. He thought about Tim's behavior after Camilla had arrived at dinner and how close and touchy feely they were while playing Taboo. Tim jumped at the chance to go to the store with Camilla, and they were clingy when they arrived at the hospital; it all made sense. His little brother had it bad, and it had happened just as quickly as it happened with him and Sheena. He watched them in the waiting room. They sat off to themselves. Tim, still holding Adrianna in his right arm, wrapped his left arm around Camilla and she rested her head against his shoulder. Tim placed a kiss on Adrianna's head then one on Camilla's. She wrapped her arm around his stomach. They looked comfortable and natural, just like a family.

Paul felt a tinge of jealousy. He wanted to start a family and now that he thought about it, he was surprised Sheena hadn't gotten pregnant. They had been married for months and never used protection.

"Sheena," Paul whispered in her ear. "Have you ever wondered why you haven't gotten pregnant yet?"

"No, I know why. I'm on birth control. I get the Depo Provera shot every few months. I got the first one before we got married. As a matter of fact, it's almost time for my third dose. Why?"

"You never told me that. Why did you get on birth control?"

"You know how shy I was about sex before we got married. I couldn't even tell you I was a virgin. I wanted to ask you what you thought, but I couldn't figure out how to talk about it without telling you I was a virgin. So, I talked to my mom and she told me that it would be smart to use birth control for a while, so we could get to know each other better, and when we were ready I could stop. Are you mad?"

"No, I'm not mad. What if I told you I wanted you to stop taking birth control?"

"Say no more. I'll cancel my appointment. I'm ready to have your baby. I was waiting for you to be ready." Sheena leaned against Paul and rested her head on his shoulder. She closed her eyes and tried to get some rest, but as soon as she got comfortable a nurse walked in.

"I need to see Mrs. Wright." Jaleel and Delisa stood and the nurse walked over to them. "I need to speak to you in private. Will you please follow me?"

Delisa looked around the waiting room, only family was there. "It's okay. We are all family, you can speak freely."

"Well, Mrs. Wright, it's about the blood that was donated. We need a donation from the biological mother and father. We have yours, but we do not have a sample from her father."

"Yes, you do. He gave blood right after I did."

"Okay, Mrs. Wright, I really need to talk to you alone."

"Like I said, we are all family. Say what you need to say." Delisa saw the uneasiness in the nurse's face and couldn't imagine what could have her so nervous.

"We ran a test to determine blood type. It's a quick test that eliminates donors immediately, so we don't waste time screening blood that can't be used. Jalisa is O and so are you. Mr. Wright is AB." The nurse paused with a look of anguish on her face and wished she had more privacy. Better yet, she wished she didn't have to give more bad news to a family that was already dealing with so much. "And with the given blood types, there is no way Mr. Wright is Jalisa's biological father. Jalisa would be type A or B if Mr. Wright was her father."

"Run the test again," Delisa screamed. "He is her father!"

Jaleel's nostrils flared with anger. "There is no need to run the test again I am AB and you're O. You know that. Jalisa is not my daughter. How could you lie to me for four years, letting me believe that she was mine?"

"Jaleel, I did not lie to you. She has to be your daughter. I have never cheated on you." Delisa reached for his arm to comfort him, but he snatched it away.

"I can't believe you!" Jaleel walked around in circles trying to get control of his anger. He stepped toward Delisa and tried to speak, but anger had a hold on his voice.

"Jaleel, please calm down and let me explain."

"I don't want to hear anything you have to say right now." Jaleel stormed out of the waiting room. Delisa sank to the floor, crying hysterically. Her wails could be heard down the hall. Sheena rushed to comfort her. "Paul, go after Jaleel and see if you can talk some sense into him."

"Talk some sense into him? He has every right to be upset. Your cousin has been lying to him for four years and he just found out."

The look on Sheena's face cut him off and she spoke slowly. "My cousin would never do something like that. You are judging her without having all of the facts."

"Sheena, don't get mad at me because you're doing the same thing. You're just judging in her favor."

"I'm not trying to have this discussion right now. Can you just go look for Jaleel?"

Everyone sat around in shock, not fully believing what had just taken place. Tim held Camilla as tears trickled down her cheeks. Sheena's parents silently prayed while Delisa's parents tried to console her. Paul caught up with Jaleel waiting in the hall for the elevator.

"Jaleel, wait up."

"I don't want to talk right now."

"That's fine, because you don't need to talk, you need to listen. I know you're upset. You have every right to be, but Jalisa is going to be looking for her daddy when she comes out of surgery. No matter what a blood test says, you are her father." Paul paused to find the right words to continue. He and Jaleel weren't the best of friends, but they had gotten closer over the past week and he hated to see anyone in so much pain. "Don't make Jalisa pay for Delisa's mistake."

The elevator chimed and the doors opened. Paul and Jaleel stood in silence, neither moved. Then, the doors closed. Jaleel turned to look at Paul with despair and anger etched on his face, and then walked back to the waiting room. He could hear Delisa's cries coming down the hall and he ran to her thinking the doctor had came in with bad news about Jalisa.

Delisa saw him come through the door and jumped to her feet, grabbing him firmly.

"Jaleel, you have to believe me. I was not purposely trying to deceive you. Please, let me explain."

"I don't want to hear what you have to say. For the past month you have made me feel like I wasn't good enough to be with you, and you were the one keeping secrets from me. We will deal with that later. Right now, you need to pull yourself together. Jalisa does not need to see you like this." Delisa reached for him, but he scowled and turned his back on her.

"Jaleel please let me explain."

Jaleel huffed and went to sit on the opposite side of the waiting room. Paul silently sat next to Jaleel, staring at Sheena. The lines had been drawn on the battlefield, and he couldn't believe he and his wife were on opposite sides. Everyone sat on their respective sides of the waiting room; no one spoke and no one moved. They stared into space, some dozed off, and others wrestled with their thoughts.

9

Everyone sat up when the doctor walked in. "I need the family for Jalisa Wright." They all stood. "Jalisa made it through the surgery. We were able to relieve the pressure on her brain and everything looks promising. We put the cast on her wrist and that is expected to heal properly. As for everything else, we wait. Jalisa is in recovery for about an hour. The nurses will let you know when you can see her. Do you have any questions?"

Delisa stepped up. "Is there any permanent damage to her brain?"

"We won't be able to tell right now, but once she wakes up we can run more tests that will give us a definitive answer."

"Thanks for your help, Doctor." Jaleel shook his hand and went back to his side of the room. He sank down into his seat and thanked God for bringing Jalisa through the surgery.

Camilla and Tim went back to their corner and Adrianna began to squirm. Tim checked his watch. It was five in the morning and he hadn't got much sleep. "Baby, do you think Adrianna is ready for a diaper change and a bottle?" He whispered to Camilla, who had already settled against his chest and was falling back to sleep.

She lifted her head and smiled. "I think you're right. What time is it?"

"It's five. I was going to get some coffee. Do you want some?"

"Ooh, that sounds good. Can you get some muffins or something? I am starving."

"Okay baby, is there anything else you need?" Tim whispered against her ear.

Camilla smiled into his eyes as he handed Adrianna to her. "Tim, why do you keep calling me baby?"

"I'm sorry. I hadn't really noticed. Am I offending you?" He lied. He couldn't help himself. Every time he looked at her his feelings overwhelmed him, and when he held her in his arms it felt like she belonged there. "To be honest, you've had me unglued from the time I set eyes on you. You have me thinking, doing, and saying things I never thought I would and I haven't even known you for twenty-four hours. If you want me to back off, I will."

"Well, as you can see, I have a daughter to consider. I can't have a fling with someone who is only going to be in town for a few days."

"I understand… I'll back off." Tim left the waiting room without looking back. Camilla's words had stung. He'd completely forgotten that he was only in town until Saturday.

Delisa waited until Tim was gone then she stood and stared Camilla down from across the room. "All right Cammie, out with it. What is going on between you and Tim?"

"Nothing, Tim is a great guy and we have a few things in common. We're just becoming friends."

"Friends? Well, I'm going to tell you what Jaleel once told me. Friends don't take care of each other the way he is taking care of you." Delisa's speech slowed as she remembered the night Jaleel said those exact words to her.

Delisa gasped. "Jaleel, that night…" She ran to Jaleel and kneeled in front of him. "When we found out I was pregnant…"

Before she could say another word, Jaleel cut her off. He looked down at her with fire in his eyes and with tight lips spoke coarsely. "All this time you made me feel like I wasn't good enough to be with you. I prayed, even got a prayer partner, so I could be right and be worthy of your love. Lo and behold, you have a little secret of your own. I don't want to hear *anything* you have to say. Get the hell away from me." His words echoed through the waiting room, all conversations stopped and every eye was on him.

Delisa sat stunned and broken in front of Jaleel, his words ringing in her mind. She wanted to beg and plead with him, but the words escaped her. How could he believe she would purposely deceive him? She had given her all to him and he was the one whose heart strayed. Delisa reached out to touch Jaleel and he moved away from her, leaving her kneeling in the corner alone. Sheena helped her up, trying to comfort her by reassuring her that Jaleel would come around. He just needed time.

Delisa rested her head in Sheena's lap and sobbed uncontrollably. Camilla sat next to her rubbing her back and cleaning her face. Camilla made eye contact with Jaleel. She didn't know what the truth was, but wanted to run over and slap him for the way he was treating her sister. They eyed each other, neither wanting to be the first to turn away. Jaleel was determined to stand his ground and not allow the family to intimidate him. Camilla wanted Jaleel to know that she was not just going to stand by while he hurt her sister.

"Mr. and Mrs. Wright?" Everyone turned to look at the nurse. "Jalisa is awake and is asking for her daddy. She is only allowed two visitors at a time. She's in Room 312 whenever you are ready." The nurse heaped coals of fire on Jaleel's head. Calling him *Jalisa's Daddy* further fueled his anger and he stormed past everybody as he made his way to Jalisa's room.

Tim walked back into the waiting room just as Jaleel and Delisa were leaving. He tried to pass Jaleel a cup of coffee, but he stormed passed him. Tim saw the fire in Jaleel's eyes and the tears streaming down his cheeks and decided not to press the issue. He passed out muffins and coffee to the rest of the family and everyone was grateful. He had time to think while he was gone, but was no closer to a solution than he was before he left. He knew he had feelings for Camilla, feelings he'd never had for another. He even wanted to get to know her better, but he couldn't give her more than this weekend. She deserved more. Soon he'd be flying home and probably wouldn't return until next year, which led him to the same unwanted conclusion as before: they couldn't be together. She excited him in a way that no other woman had, and he wanted her in his life.

Sheena overheard what Jaleel said to Delisa and Paul's secretive actions suddenly made sense. She pulled Paul to the side. "It's you isn't it? You're his prayer partner. That is what the early morning phone calls have been?"

Before he could answer, Sheena parted his lips with hers and devoured his mouth. Paul broke free of her kiss and looked her in the eyes, "What was that for?"

"You are amazing. I thought you hated Jaleel."

"I did, but the night after our little fight," Paul laughed. "You reminded me that we wrestle not against flesh and blood. It helped me realize that I was going to have to find a different way to handle my conflicts in the future. And then last week when you had Jaleel meet you at the house so you could talk, he asked me to pray with him and help him get on track. I would have told you, but he asked me not to say anything. I am glad you trusted me."

"It wasn't easy. The devil kept trying to tell me you were cheating, but I refused to give in. Now that I know what is going on, I am surprised I didn't notice it sooner."

Paul held her tight, elated their disagreement from earlier was over. "I owe you an apology. You were right I was being judgmental."

"No, you were right. I was being judgmental and I didn't have all the facts, but was siding with Delisa because she is my cousin. Please forgive me."

"Tonight has been crazy and we are all emotional and not thinking straight. I'll forgive you if you forgive me." Paul pulled her close and rested his forehead against hers.

"You're forgiven." She returned his firm embrace, silently thanking God for the strength he gave her to believe in her husband.

Jaleel pulled up in front of his house. He had just left the hospital from visiting Jalisa. Sheena relieved him. It was supposed to be Delisa.

They had arranged to take turns sitting with Jalisa to avoid having to be in the same room with each other for too long. Jaleel was glad when Sheena showed up at the hospital. He was not in the mood to deal with Delisa. But now, as he sat in his car in front of his house, he understood why Sheena came. Delisa's car was there.

Furious, he walked through the front door, regretting not changing the locks. Delisa stood in the foyer and began speaking before he could throw her out. "Jaleel we need to talk. You can't just shut me out. We need each other more now than we ever have."

"Delisa, what part of *I don't want to talk to you* don't you understand? Give me your key and get out." Jaleel put his hand out and waited for the key.

Slowly, Delisa began sliding the key off the ring. Her eyes were red and glossy from all the crying she'd been doing. She desperately needed Jaleel to hold her and tell her everything was going to be all right. Jalisa had been in the hospital for two days and instead of improving, her condition had worsened. Delisa was falling apart.

She was about to hand her key over, but a thought crossed her mind and she pulled her hand back. "I am not giving you this key. This is my house too, and I'm moving back in. Deal with it or you get out." Before storming out, she saw rage swell in Jaleel's eyes and hoped he was not chasing after her.

A flood of emotions washed over Delisa as she raced back to Sheena's house to pack her things. She went from fear, to anger, to determination. She was determined to reconcile with Jaleel, and the only way to do that was to move back home. She packed all her belongings to leave before Paul came home, but as she was loading her stuff in the car, he pulled up next to her.

"Delisa, what are you doing?"

"I'm moving back home." Delisa tried not to make eye contact, hoping he would not get involved.

Paul watched with confusion as Delisa loaded her last bag and ran around to the driver side. "Delisa, I talked to Jaleel last night, and he was still pretty upset. I don't think moving back right now is wise."

Delisa stopped with her back to Paul and mumbled over her shoulder. "Thanks for the concern, but it's really none of your business." She hopped in her car and sped off, not giving Paul a chance to respond.

Paul immediately pulled out his cell phone and called Camilla. "Camilla, I think you need to meet Delisa at her house. She has this brilliant idea to move back in with Jaleel."

"Oh no."

"Right. She packed up all her stuff and is on her way there now. I talked to Jaleel last night. He doesn't want anything to do with her and he's not going to be happy when she shows up. I will meet you there just in case things get out of hand."

"That's okay. I have Tim with me." Camilla saw the look on Tim's face and instantly regretted telling Paul he was with her.

"What? Tim is with you?"

"Yes, I wanted to spend some time with him before he left so I picked him up a little while ago. We were just going to have dinner."

"No need to explain to me. You are both adults, but I think I will meet you at Delisa's, just in case." Paul hung up the phone, laughing at his little brother.

Camilla apologized to Tim. "I am sorry. I didn't know there was a problem with people knowing we were having dinner together."

"There is not a problem. It's just that Paul kind of accused me of sleeping with you the other day."

Camilla gasped. "What?"

"Don't worry. It has absolutely nothing to do with you. I kind of have a history of doing things like that and he didn't want me to hurt you." Tim reached across the table and grabbed Camilla's hand. "I would never hurt you. If you give me a chance, I could make you happy."

Camilla slid her hands away and looked around the restaurant, avoiding eye contact, because she knew looking into his eyes would cause her to give in. "I'm sorry, but I have a history of picking the wrong men. I have more than myself to consider. Long-distance relationships always end in disaster. I can't afford to have my heart broken." Camilla grabbed her purse and headed for the door.

Tim sat for a moment, confused by what he was feeling. He'd extended his vacation for two days just to spend more time with Camilla. He was in unfamiliar territory. Wanting to have a relationship with a woman instead of just sleeping with her was foreign to him. He was hurt and confused as he made his way to the car. He quietly climbed in the passenger side and leaned his head back, trying to clear his mind. He was scheduled to take a flight home in the morning. His heart told him to stay, but his head told him to run and move on.

Paul pulled up in front of the house. Delisa and Jaleel were outside. Jaleel towered over her. Anger and hurt overwhelmed him and he was losing control. With each word he spoke, the volume of his voice escalated. He inched closer and closer to Delisa. She had never seen Jaleel so upset. His hands balled into fists at his sides. His brow furrowed, the veins in temples throbbed, and the muscle in his jaw ticked. The most frightening thing she saw was the rage in his eyes. This wasn't the same man she loved or the man who just a few short days ago had tried to win back her affection. She slowly backed away from him, trying to keep her distance from him. They'd been angry with each other before and had arguments like all couples do. This was the first time she ever feared he'd hit her.

"I can't believe you had the nerve to come back here like everything is okay. I don't want you here!"

Paul rushed out of his car and stood between them. Seeing the fury on Jaleel's face he was glad he followed his instinct to follow Delisa. "Jaleel, let's just go back into the house."

"I am not going anywhere until she is gone."

Delisa tried to step around Paul to make eye contact with Jaleel. "Please just calm down and let me explain everything."

Jaleel pushed Paul to the side and rushed into Delisa's face. "What is there to explain? You let me believe I was Jalisa's father so that I would marry you."

68

"What? You know that is not true. Is that the only reason you married me?"

"I loved you and I accepted my responsibility like a man."

"And you still love me. I'm not going to let you throw away what we have."

"*Delisa.*" Jaleel tried to get a handle on his emotions. He didn't want to think about loving her. "Please, just go."

Camilla finally arrived and instantly tried to reason with her sister. "Delisa, what are you doing?" Camilla grabbed her sister by the shoulders and turned her around to look in her eyes. "I know you're hurting, but this is not the way to work things out. Give him space and time, and then you guys can work things out."

"Camilla, I am not leaving. This is my house. He is my husband, and I am not giving up without a fight."

Paul's phone rang and he signaled for Tim to come handle Jaleel before he stepped to the side to answer. "Hey, baby. What's up?"

"Paul, I need you to bring Delisa to the hospital and pick up Jaleel, too. Jalisa has taken a turn for the worse and the doctors don't think she will make it through the night," Sheena spoke between her sobs. She had been sitting by Jalisa's side praying when the heart monitor started ringing. The room flooded with doctors and nurses. Sheena was simply pushed out of the room and left alone while they worked on Jalisa. She stood by the door as they wheeled her to surgery. One of the doctors stopped to tell her to call the rest of the family because things were not looking good. Just like that, the room was empty and all was quiet. Sheena sat alone fumbling with her cell phone as she tried to call Paul.

"We are all together right now. We'll be there in about twenty minutes."

Paul took a deep breath, slowly moving between Jaleel and Delisa. With authority, he spoke calmly and compassionately. "You guys need to calm down and get yourselves together. Sheena just called. We need to get to the hospital. Delisa, you ride with Camilla. Jaleel can ride with me."

S 10

Sheena paced around the hospital room waiting for Paul to show up, or for one of the doctors to tell her what was going on with Jalisa. Her head was pounding and her stomach was queasy from fearing the worst. She knew God to be a healer, but could not shake the feeling that Jalisa was not going to pull through.

Everyone arrived at the hospital at the same time and rushed up to Jalisa's room to find Sheena leaning against the window, staring at the ground. Paul wrapped his arms around her waist and pulled her head to rest upon him. Sheena released all of her anxiety and tears into his chest. Delisa had called and asked her to sit at the hospital while she tried to work things out with Jaleel. Sheena was all for it. Jaleel and Delisa needed each other, and after what happened, they were going to need each other even more.

Delisa gripped Paul's shoulder and nudged him aside. "Sheena, what is going on? Where is Jalisa?"

"I was sitting here praying and the alarm on her heart monitor went off. Doctors rushed in, then wheeled her out, and the only thing they said was to call the family because it doesn't look good."

Delisa paced around in circles, breathing heavily, and pulling the front of her hair. Her breathing sped up, her fingers began to tingle, and the room started spinning. Delisa felt herself losing consciousness and reached to grab someone, but no one was close enough. Jaleel saw her going down and leaped to catch her. Her body was limp, but he was able to catch her head before it hit the floor. He picked her up, placed her in a chair, and stood next to her so her head could rest on his side.

Camilla went to find a nurse and was back before Jaleel had finished setting Delisa in the chair. The nurse checked Delisa's breathing and pulse, and then looked at her pupils. "What happened before she collapsed?"

Jaleel explained to the nurse how upset Delisa was and how fast she was breathing. As he talked, the nurse wet a cloth and rubbed it on Delisa's face. Slowly, she opened her eyes and jumped when she saw the nurse standing in front of her.

The nurse smiled and handed Jaleel the cloth. "Mrs. Wright, it sounds like you might have hyperventilated and passed out. I know you are under a lot of stress right now, but you have to relax. Make sure your wife sits here for a while. Keep wiping her head with this cloth. If she is feeling light-headed again, you know where to find me." The nurse walked out, Jaleel rolled his eyes, passed the cloth to Camilla, and walked out behind the nurse.

Jaleel sat in the waiting room trying to clear his mind. His heart had crumbled when he thought something was seriously wrong with Delisa. Just that quick he forgot how furious he was with her and all the love he had for her prevailed. He knew it would be hard to get over her, even harder to live without her, but he couldn't trust her. Jaleel rubbed his hands across his head as he tried to sort through the mess in his mind.

"I saw that." Paul stepped into to the waiting room and sat next to Jaleel.

"You saw what?"

"I saw how all that anger you had toward Delisa vanished when you thought she was hurt."

Jaleel sank back into his chair and leaned his head back. "Was it that obvious?"

"Of course it was. I think you better stop playing games and get over this anger before you lose a good woman."

"I am not playing games. Delisa had to know there was a possibility that I was not Jalisa's father. If she slept with two guys around the same time, why lead me to believe that I was the father."

71

"Jaleel, you are asking the wrong person. You need to talk to Delisa."

"I can't. I don't think I can forgive her for deceiving me. I know I'm not perfect, but what she did is unforgivable."

"I hear you. If the shoe was on the other foot, I would probably be just as upset as you are. But, what you need to decide is, are you willing to live without Delisa? If the answer is no, then get over this and get over it quick. There is no need spending weeks in misery."

Jaleel nodded. "I hear you." He had a lot to think about, but Paul helped him find some clarity. Jaleel had a hard time forgiving Delisa because his father loved his mother and all she gave him was heartache. His mother intentionally deceived his father, and time and time again he forgave her.

His mother was about fifteen years younger than his father. She had a rough life and had been used and abused by many men. She was thirty years old when they met and had never had a man care for her they way he did. They fell hard for each other and were married within a year. Things were great for the first ten years. He showered her with expensive gifts, showed her what it felt like to be a woman, and rebuilt her self-esteem. She made his house a home and gave him a child. There was nothing he wouldn't do for her.

When Jaleel turned fourteen, he watched his mother tear his father apart with her acts of deception. She started staying out late and would come home saying she stopped for a drink with some of her co-workers. His father would stay up late, looking out the window and praying for her to make it home safely. Jaleel wanted to tell his dad to stop praying and let her go, but his father was God-fearing and believed that prayer changed all things.

Those long nights turned into days. She would stay gone for days, and when his father questioned her, she simply said she needed her space and he would forgive her. One time, Jaleel confronted his father. His mother had been gone for two days and his dad was sitting by the phone, occasionally checking the dial tone. Jaleel told his dad, "You ought to change the locks so she can't get in. She's a tramp and she doesn't deserve you."

His father slapped him so hard he fell to the ground. He helped Jaleel up and told him, "She is your mother and I don't ever want to hear you disrespect her again."

From that day forward, Jaleel vowed that he would never let a woman hurt him the way his mother did his father. Every girl he met, he treated like trash and the more his mother deceived his father the worse he got. Then, one night he woke up in the middle of the night to use the bathroom and overheard his parents arguing. Apparently, his mother had contracted some sort of STD and passed it on to his father. She swore she didn't have any diseases and accused him of cheating on her. She squeezed out some tears, slapped him across the face, and stormed out.

The next day, Jaleel came home from school and his key would not work in the door. He banged on the door, rang the doorbell, and stood there for five minutes before his father answered. Jaleel walked in the house and his father offered no explanation; he simply handed Jaleel a new key, went in his room, and locked the door.

Jaleel never saw his mother again. She called a few times begging Jaleel to give her a copy of the key. She never said she missed him or wanted to see him. She just yelled about not having a place to live and needing all of her things. Finally Jaleel told her, "We are through letting you hurt us. Now, I will pack your things and sit them on the porch. Pick them up this weekend, or I will throw them away."

His father slipped into a deep depression and wouldn't get out of bed for days at a time. His job called and demanded he come back to work or he would be fired. Jaleel talked to his father's boss and explained that his father was really sick and might not make it back for awhile. The boss said, "I like your father. He has been a good friend, but there is nothing I can do to save his job. My boss is coming down on me. What your father could do is request early retirement. He's of age, after all. They should approve it." That's exactly what he convinced his father to do.

Eventually, his father recovered and moved on with his life the best way he could. His mother stopped calling and disappeared, but Jaleel was never the same. He avoided serious relationships and when he did meet a girl that made him feel something, he quickly shut her out. Jaleel viewed women as the enemy who seemed nice in the beginning, but would eventually turn on you. That is how he viewed Delisa when he first met her. He couldn't help but think he was right.

Tim sat on the edge of the bed. He had finished packing and Paul was waiting downstairs to take him to the airport. He sat there battling in his mind whether he was going to leave or not. Everyone was still at the hospital. He and Paul left so he could make his flight.

Convincing himself that Camilla didn't need him and that she had plenty of family she could lean on for support, he gathered his suitcases, hopped in the car, and headed to the airport.

"Thanks for inviting me out, big brother." Tim was trying to break the silence in the car.

"Anytime, little brother. I really wish you would reconsider moving out here. You are all I have, and I wish you were closer." They always enjoyed each other's visit and became real emotional when it was time to say goodbye.

"That's not true. You have Sheena and her entire family. They love you. You don't need me."

"None of them will ever replace you. Sheena and I are getting ready to start a family, and I want my children to know their uncle."

Paul waited for his response, but there wasn't one. Tim just stared out the window with a blank expression on his face. Paul wanted to ask him about Camilla, but it wasn't his place to say anything. Tim had to figure this one out on his own.

After a dreaded goodbye, Tim now sat on the plane preparing for takeoff. He sat in an aisle seat out of habit, but today he had no desire to continue his routine of trying to catch the eye of beautiful women seated around him or flirt with the flight attendants. Tim's life was full of beautiful women and people who called themselves friends, but this past week was full of acceptance and the unconditional love of family, something he had never experienced. Tim put on his headphones, laid his head back, and shut his eyes to ignore the women who were trying to play his usual game. He tried to prepare his mind for a mundane existence among so called friends and a multitude of inept lovers.

The plane taxied down the runway and lifted into the air with ease. Tim tried to relax, but was more on edge than he'd ever been on a plane. His lungs seemed to cave in, causing his breathing to become shallow. He sweated profusely, but shivered with chills. His fingertips tingled and his body became weak. Anxiety and fear gripped him. Tim placed his head in his lap, taking slow deep breaths to calm down. The thoughts of his life, Paul, and Camilla were unraveling him and he was relieved when he heard the flight attendant nearby offering drinks. Tim ordered two scotches, instantly guzzling the first and savoring the second.

Tim stepped off the plane and immediately reached for his cell phone to call his brother. "What's up, big brother?" Tim's tone did not match his light hearted greeting. "How is Jalisa?"

"It's not looking good. She's been in and out of consciousness and has started having seizures. Her breathing is shallow. The doctor said she does not have much longer. They will not let anyone besides her parents in to see her, but we are praying, believing that God is going to bring her through."

Tim sighed, wishing he had stayed. "Well, I am not much of a praying person, but I will do my best. Please keep me posted."

"I will. How was your flight?"

Tim heard the flat tone of Paul's voice and knew his brother's mind was consumed with his family. Not wanting to further burden him, he lied. "It was good. I'm not going to hold you. Get back to your family and call me if you need me."

"All right, talk to you later."

Tim hung up and called Camilla. She checked the caller ID and smiled. "Hey, I'm glad you called."

Her voice made his heart flutter. "I just talked to my brother and..."

"Yeah, I heard him and hoped you would call me. Was your flight okay?"

"It was good, seemed a little longer than usual. The cold weather out here is a shock to my system after being out there." Tim finally found his car in the long term parking lot and hopped in.

Camilla giggled. "This is America's Finest City."

"You sound like my brother. If I had a dollar for every time he has said that to me, I would be a rich man. He's always trying to sell me on San Diego."

"You should listen to him. Living here wouldn't be so bad."

"All right, all right." Tim had to change the subject before she had him packing his bags, quitting his job, and relocating. "How are you holding up?"

"I am good considering what's going on. I think Adrianna misses you. We've been at the hospital for hours and I can't get her to sleep the way you did."

"You say the word and I am on the first plane back to San Diego."

"Thank you, but that's not necessary. I know you have to work." Camilla really wanted to tell him: *Yes, I need you. I can't make it through this without you*, but she didn't want to intrude on his life. "I will be fine. Pastor Hawkins and some of the ministers are on their way here to pray with us."

"All right, keep your phone near you. I am going to call later to check on you. I love you and I'll talk to you later." Tim hung up the phone, wanting to kick himself. He couldn't believe he told Camilla he loved her. He didn't understand how he could have such strong feelings for a woman he had just met and why he continued to throw himself at her when she obviously did not want him.

Camilla held the phone to her ear for moments after they hung up. Had she heard him correctly? Did he say he loved her? The words replayed over and over in her mind, and she came to the conclusion that he

76

couldn't have said those words. They barely knew each other.

Tim lay on his bed, staring at the ceiling. Camilla leaned back in the chair at the hospital. Both tried to rest, but sleep escaped them both as thoughts of each other raced around their minds. They needed each other more than either of them understood.

Delisa walked into the waiting room crying hysterically. She ran to her father and collapsed in his arms. "Daddy, she's gone." The room erupted with wails and Delisa cried out, "Lord, why did You take her from me?" Her wailing echoed through the halls. Sorrow of a grief-stricken mother gripped the hearts of the nursing staff and families in the rooms nearby. Everyone wanted to console her, but were so overtaken with their own grief they couldn't find the words.

Jaleel quietly spoke. "They are giving us all an opportunity to say goodbye before they take her away." He placed his hands over his face trying to conceal his grief. "So, if you want to come with me, I will take you to her room."

Pastor Hawkins arrived while they were being taken to see Jalisa. Paul informed him that Jalisa had passed away and the pastor's optimistic look turned into one of mourning. He came to pray healing, but would end up praying comfort instead. He, himself, knew the pain of losing a loved one and knew the road ahead of them would be a long, tiresome, and trying journey where their faith and sanity would be attacked.

Pastor Hawkins immediately began praying as they walked into the room. *"Father, whose Name is Jesus, we need You to come into the midst of us. Your children are hurting and there is no one who can comfort them the way You can. You are the beginning and You are the end. You are the giver of life and He that gives can also take it away. It is not for us to understand, but for us to trust that You have everything under control. Give this family strength to stand in this hour of bereavement. Keep them in the right frame of mind, and allow them to move forward. We rebuke depression and anger. We declare peace and joy in the midst of sorrow."*

The room was filled with so much grief that even the pastor had trouble controlling his emotions. The hour was getting late, but the pastor waited and prayed until everyone went home. After they left the hospital, Delisa needed to go for a drive. Everyone was convinced she shouldn't drive, so she waited until they were asleep and snuck out like a teenager breaking curfew. Delisa drove around for a while and eventually made her way back to Sheena's house. She sat outside in her car, tears slowly rolling down her face. She tried to talk to the Lord, but couldn't find the words. She felt so alone. She had lost her child and her marriage was falling apart. She needed Jaleel and his strength. Hoping he needed her, she started the car and drove to her house. She unloaded her bags and stood on the porch, debating whether to ring the doorbell or use her key. Deciding that just walking in would anger him, she rang the door bell and waited. Jaleel opened the door and stared into her eyes. Her eyes were just as red and glossy as his. Without saying a word he stepped aside to let her in, then grabbed her bags and took them upstairs. Jaleel crawled back into bed signaling for Delisa to join him and without hesitation she slid next to him and buried her face into his chest. He wrapped his arms around her, pulling her as close as he could then buried his face in her hair, and they both cried themselves to sleep.

11

On Tuesday morning, Camilla was awakened by her door bell ringing. She tried to ignore it, but the person on the other side was persistent. When she mustered up enough strength to stand, the blood rushed to her head and the room began to spin. She stretched out her arms to steady herself. Her body was drained from hours of crying and lack of sleep. Using the walls for support, Camilla slowly walked to the front door. She yanked the door open without checking to see who it was and tears she thought had dried up hours ago flooded her eyes again.

Tim's heart ached as she fell into his arms sobbing. Paul had called to tell him what happened, and that Camilla had gone home alone. He got her address and took the first flight back to San Diego. Tim lifted Camilla and carried her back to bed. After making sure she was comfortable, he grabbed a glass of water for her and checked on Adrianna. Tim ran his hand across Adrianna's face and watched her squirm.

He returned to the bedroom to find Camilla lying on the bed, still sobbing into the sheets. He pulled her close resting her head on his chest. "Baby, I'm here now. I'm going to help you get through this."

"Tim," she cried. "You shouldn't have come back. What's going to happen with your job?"

"My job will be there when I get back. I couldn't let you go through this alone." He actually didn't know what was going to happen with his job. It was the furthest thing from his mind. She was his only concern at the moment and he would stay as long as she needed him.

Sheena and Paul kneeled together on the side of their bed and prayed. They knew the days ahead would be rough and sought God for strength. "Father, You know the pain and grief that my family is suffering right now, and we will not make it through this without You. Strengthen us and keep our faith from wavering." They were overtaken with emotion and hoped God would understand their tears.

Sheena got up, called Camilla, and was surprised when Tim answered the phone. "Tim, what are you doing here? I thought you left yesterday."

Tim explained how he turned right back around to comfort Camilla.

"Well, I'm glad you're there with her. She needs you. I was calling to tell her to meet me at Delisa's house in a couple of hours for breakfast. Will you make sure she gets there?"

"Delisa, isn't with you?"

"No. She called and said she was going to be with Jaleel. Apparently, things went well, because she never came back."

"Okay, I'll get Camilla there."

They ended their call and Sheena ran into the bathroom to talk to Paul. "Why didn't you tell me your brother flew back to be with Camilla?"

"What are you talking about?"

"You don't know? I just called Camilla and Tim answered the phone. He said he talked to you."

"No, I called him and told him about Jalisa. He asked how Camilla was doing and I told him she insisted on going home alone. He asked for her address to send her flowers." Paul laughed. He should have known his brother was up to something. "Are you mad? If so, I'll tell him to back off."

"No, I saw them together. They hadn't known each other for twenty-four hours and it was obvious he had feelings for her, but stay out of it. We don't want either of them mad at us if it doesn't work out.

Neither one of them have a good track record when it comes to relationships." Paul agreed. If Tim and Camilla were going to be together, they would have to find each other on their own.

Paul and Sheena were getting out of the car when Tim and Camilla pulled up. They would've been there sooner, but they dropped Adrianna off at her grandparents' house. Paul did not hesitate to start in on Tim. "Sending flowers... Yeah I think that's what you said," Paul smiled.

Tim dropped his head as he got out the car. "Yeah, I wanted to deliver them personally. Don't make this harder for me by teasing and laughing," he pleaded. "You know I have never been in this situation before. I can't get her out of my mind and I don't know what to do."

"Wasn't it just last week when you told my wife not to introduce you to any women in her family because you weren't ready to be hemmed up? I hate to point it out little brother, but, you look pretty hemmed up to me."

Paul bent over laughing and Sheena playfully punched him in the arm.

"Stop, Paul. Do I need to remind you that not too long ago you were in the same boat?" Paul's laughter stopped. Tim's and Sheena's began.

"Thanks." Tim kissed Sheena on the cheek.

"Don't mention it."

Paul jokingly whispered in Sheena's ear as she walked by, "Traitor."

Tim helped Camilla out the car and headed toward the door. After several knocks with no answer, Camilla used her key to enter. The house had an eerie quiet and everyone feared what they might find. Sticking closely together, they made their way up the stairs. They knocked on the door to the master bedroom, but there was no answer. They tried the knob and it was locked.

"I called Jaleel. He said they would be here. Camilla, call the house phone. Maybe they're sleeping." Sheena tried to conceal her concern.

81

Camilla was just about to call when the front door opened. Jaleel stepped into the house. "What are you guys doing?"

"Looking for you and my sister. Is she with you?"

"No, I ran to the store to get food for breakfast. She said she was going to take a shower."

"Oh God, Jaleel come unlock the door," Camilla screamed, fearing the worst.

Jaleel dashed upstairs, burst into the room, and went straight for the bathroom. Delisa sat on the floor with the shower running, her head resting on the bath tub. She looked so frail and distraught. They all crowded into the bathroom. Jaleel sat behind Delisa, wrapping his arms around her. Camilla and Sheena kneeled in front of her with Paul and Tim standing behind them. Without hesitating, Sheena prayed. *"Send strength, oh God. Strengthen Jaleel and Delisa. Strengthen us all."* Sheena continued to pray with power and authority and the power of God filled the room.

Paul looked over and saw Tim crying and trembling from the power of God he felt. He reached out and grabbed Tim when his knees buckled under the presence of God.

"Tim, I know you don't understand what you're feeling, but God is trying to give you a great gift. All you have to do is praise Him for being God. Now open your mouth and thank Him." Tim collapsed to his knees as the presence of God intensified. Paul knelt with him and they praised God together. Tim felt warmth wrap around his body, and without fight or struggle he received the gift of the Lord.

They all sat back, watching Tim speak to the Lord. They marveled at God's timing and how He worked in mysterious ways. It brought peace to Delisa's mind to know that her daughter's passing brought a soul to Christ. She leaned her head against Jaleel and praised God for His greatness.

After Tim regained his composure, he sat up wiping his face and leaned against the bathroom cabinet. He looked around. Everyone was smiling. Their once grief-stricken faces were now glowing with joy.

Besides weddings and funerals, Tim had never really been to church, and he was really confused about what just happened and why everybody was so happy about it.

"Okay." Tim stood to his feet. "Who is going to tell me what just happened to me? That was crazy. Stop looking at me and start talking because I'm freaking out!"

Paul spoke up first. "Let's go downstairs. Somebody grab a Bible."

Sheena and Camilla prepared breakfast while Jaleel tended to Delisa. Paul and Tim sat at the table talking. Paul let Tim read John 3:5 and Acts 2. Tim sat for a while contemplating what he read, what he experienced, and the things he heard coming out of his mouth.

"I'm...saved. Wow."He got up and hugged his brother. "Why would God choose me? I've done lots of things I'm not proud of. How can He forgive me?"

Paul hugged him tighter. "He loves us despite what we've done. It's His love for us that took Him to Calvary." They hugged, crying and praising God. There was not a dry eye in the kitchen.

It was the morning of Jalisa's funeral. Family members from across the country had flown in to pay their respects. Jaleel and Delisa started their day early with prayer and headed to the mortuary to have their last private moment with their daughter. The strength God had given them throughout the week was amazing. They still had their weak moments and times were they questioned God's plan, but their faith in Him never failed. The past few days had drawn them closer. The problems in their marriage seemed to have dissipated. Their lives had been in turmoil for the past month and they hoped laying their daughter to rest would be the end of the tumultuous storm that loomed over their life and the sun would shine with the dawning of a new day.

They stood together beside their daughter's casket. Neither of them spoke. Delisa caressed Jalisa's face, adjusted the lace on her little white dress and straightened the satin bow in her hair. Jalisa always liked having bows in her hair. She wanted to wear them all the time, and when Delisa wouldn't put them in she would find Jalisa hiding in her room trying to put them in herself. Jaleel kissed his little girl on the cheek like he did just about every night. After all the bed time stories and all her attempts to stay up later, the last thing he did was kiss her good night before he walked out the room. If she spoke or made a noise, he had to come back and give her another kiss. She would giggle each time he came back and when he said one last kiss she knew it was time to go to sleep. He felt so ashamed that his stupidity had robbed them of their good night kisses the entire month before she passed. He would never again be able to tell her one last story, give her one last sip of water, or one last kiss. The fact he wasn't her biological father no longer crossed his mind. She was and forever would be daddy's little girl.

On the way back home, Jaleel's emotional dam broke. He had suppressed his grief trying to be strong for Delisa and it all flooded him at once. He pulled the car over because his tears were clouding his vision.

"I miss her so much," he cried. "The house seems so empty without her. I woke up last night and I was really groggy. I thought I heard a noise and I went in her room to check on her... I could barely breathe when I saw her empty bed."

"Honey, we just have to take this one day at a time. There will be good days and bad, but as long as we have each other and the Lord we can make it." Delisa repeated almost word for word what he had told her several times throughout the week. She brushed her hand across his brow then down his cheek, wiping his tears away. He cupped his hand on the side of her neck and traced her lips with his thumb. She kissed his thumb and closed her eyes to enjoy his touch. When she opened her eyes, their eyes met and they sat on the side of the road engrossed in each other's presence. Their kisses were soft, slow, and restorative. Each kiss further confirmed their reconciliation. Although there were still unanswered questions and unresolved issues, love prevailed. Caught up in the moment, time slipped away from them and a cell phone ringing brought them out of their trance.

"Delisa, I'm at the house. Where are you?" Sheena spoke before Delisa could say hello.

"Oh my goodness, Sheena. What time is it?"

"It is ten o'clock. Is everything okay? Where are you?"

"We went to see Jalisa and had to pull over for a while. We lost track of time, but we are on our way back."

Tim and Camilla proved to be a great team throughout the week. They shared the cleaning and the cooking; he watched Adrianna while Camilla went to school and studied. They even alternated Adrianna's early morning feedings and diaper changes. Every night they crawled into bed together and Tim would hold her close. Some nights she cried herself to sleep, sometimes they talked, but they never discussed their feelings for each other. He was the strength she needed and being with her was all he needed.

Tim and Camilla lay in bed talking. "Camilla, have you been filled with the Holy Spirit?"

"Yes, I have, but after I graduated high school I kind of went buck wild and got involved in a lot of unholy stuff. I found myself so far away from God I couldn't find my way back. I go to church on occasion, but I always feel so judged, like people are staring, whispering behind my back. I always wind up leaving early."

"I've been thinking. There has to be a reason God chose me, and if you have His Spirit, there has to be a reason He chose you, right?"

"Yeah, I guess you're right."

"Well, I want to find out what that reason is. Will you go to church with me?"

"I'll go with you, but aren't you leaving soon?"

Tim sat up. He had been dreading the conversation about him leaving, but since she brought it up, he decided to be honest. "I got a call from my boss a couple days ago. He demanded that I return to work. I told him what was going on, and he said Jalisa is not my family and if I didn't return immediately I was fired. I told him I wasn't coming back until next week and he let me go."

Camilla gasped. "What are you going to do once you go back home?"

He hadn't thought about going home. Anything that didn't involve being with her was pushed to the back of his mind. He thought about her question and decided to get everything out in the open. "Camilla, why do you think I'm here?"

"I don't know. I ask myself that every day. You showed up unannounced at a time where I really needed you. I wouldn't have made it through this week without you."

"Do you have feelings for me? I told you how I felt before I left last week and you kind of blew me off."

Camilla paced around the room. "Tim, it's not that simple for me."

He stood behind her, caressing her shoulders. He whispered in her ear. "Why does it have to be complicated? What does your heart say?"

"I have followed my heart too many times. It has always led me to heartache. After I had Adrianna, I told myself I had to start using my head and be more responsible."

"So, you're just going to ignore what you feel for me?"

Camilla walked into the bathroom then turned to look him in the eye. "I'm not saying I feel anything."

She closed the bathroom door and rested her back against it. She'd followed her heart before, committing herself to a man who was never fully committed to her. He cheated on her several times, and when a woman knocked on their door claiming to be pregnant with his baby, Camilla had finally had enough. She packed his bags, put him out, and changed the locks. The pain of betrayal nearly made her lose her mind, and she couldn't risk that type of instability with Adrianna around.

Tim stood for a moment, not fully believing that she was pushing him away. He had never wanted a woman the way he wanted her, but he loved her enough to respect her wishes. He would back off. Tim packed his bags and dressed for the funeral. When Camilla exited the bathroom, she saw his bags and her heart sank.

"So, you're leaving?" She asked, trying to hide the sadness in her voice.

"Hey, I'm not going to push myself on you. You made it clear that you aren't interested in anything more than friendship. If that is all you are offering, I will accept it. But I can't stay here pretending to be a family and holding you every night. Why torture myself?" His heart was broken. The past week had felt so right, so perfect. "I will be here through the funeral, but tonight I will sleep at Paul's. I'm sorry for pressuring you. It won't happen again."

Tim walked out of the room to piece together what was left of his ego. He had been with many women, but never loved any of them. He pursued many women and none ever rejected him. Camilla was his first for both. He had given all he had to her in such a short time and all she offered was friendship. He felt like a fool and vowed to stick to his old ways, steering clear of love.

The family lined up outside of Zion Pentecostal Church, everyone adorned in black, preparing to say their final goodbyes to a precious loved one whose presence would be greatly missed. The men stood as strong pillars to support their women. They walked in two by two, heads held high. They came to remember and celebrate Jalisa's life. All of their mourning had been done during the week and they wanted this day to be full of the love they all had for her.

The sanctuary was surprisingly full. Who knew a child so young had affected so many lives? The casket was surrounded by a beautiful array of fresh flowers and a few enlarged portraits of Jalisa. Delisa and Jaleel opted for a closed casket. They wanted everyone to remember her with a smile on her face.

The service was a beautiful tribute to Jalisa's life. The pastor encouraged the family to keep believing in God even when they didn't understand Him, and even the soloist sang a song of encouragement. The most moving part of the service was the slide presentation. Sheena had collected pictures of Jalisa from the entire family. Since Jalisa had been the only baby of the family until Adrianna was born, everybody had quite a few. There were pictures all the way from her birth up until that

Thanksgiving, the day of her tragic accident. Though they still shed some tears, Jaleel and Delisa left the church on that day with peace.

Camilla drove Tim to his brother's house. They sat outside, neither speaking until Adrianna started crying in the backseat. Tim grabbed her out of her car seat. "Hey, what's the matter?" He tried to stop her from crying.

Camilla watched as he worked his magic on Adrianna, getting her to calm down almost instantly. "You are going to have to teach me your trick. I can't get her to calm down so quickly."

"There is no trick. I just have that affect on the ladies."

She rolled her eyes, and he immediately regretted his attempt at humor.

Camilla calmly and gently took Adrianna and placed her back in her car seat. "I don't mean to rush you, but I've had a long day and I need some rest." She avoided making eye contact. She had to ignore the force that was drawing her to him and listen to her head that was screaming for her to leave before it was too late to resist him.

Paul opened his front door to see Tim standing on the porch with his bags. "What are you doing here?"

"It is a long story and I'm tired." Tim walked pass his brother, not giving any explanation for his sudden appearance. He lay in bed that night trying to determine his next move. Should he go back home with no job, no family, no real friends, or should he stay in San Diego?

Morning came and with it came Tim's decision. He would go home, try to get his job back, and find a church. He knew living in San Diego would cause him to see Camilla often and he wanted to give her space. He called a cab and headed to the airport, leaving a note for his brother to avoid the dreaded goodbye and unwanted questions.

Jaleel walked upstairs toward his bedroom. All their guests had left, and he finished locking the doors, checking the windows, and turning off the lights. Delisa had gone upstairs earlier to lay down. He was proud and amazed at the strength she possessed. His wife had walked into their daughter's funeral with her head held high and laid Jalisa to rest without faltering. That day in the bathroom seemed to be her turning point. God had sent His Spirit in full force, taking her from suicidal to peaceful within minutes. Everyone expected her to be emotionally destroyed and overtaken with grief, but when God gave peace it surpassed all understanding. Delisa had a peace that not even she understood.

Jaleel walked into the room where Delisa was standing in the doorway of the bathroom. The shower was running and she was smiling. "Honey, I was just about to take a shower, you want to join me?" She walked away not waiting for his response, but left the door open for him to decide.

He slowly followed her into the bathroom; his heart was beating out of control. They had not been intimate in over a month, and a part of him feared they'd only reconciled because Jalisa passed away. Her offer, even though a simple gesture, gave him a secure hope that she had forgiven him for his wandering eye, but could he forgive her for deceiving him?

Easing behind her, he looked in her eyes through the mirror and whispered against her ear. "Do you love me?"

They held each other as they showered, and tears ran down Delisa's face mingling with the stream of water from the shower. "Jaleel, thank you for being here and sticking by me through all of this." Her tears intensified.

"Where else would I be?" These sudden bursts of emotion had become the norm since Jalisa's passing.

"You have to know that I really thought you were Jalisa's father. Yes, I was still sleeping with my ex, but after that night we spent together I cut him off. I always used a condom when I was with him, so when I came up pregnant I was certain you were her father. I was not trying to trick you. It honestly never crossed my mind that he might be her father."

Jaleel did not allow her to finish. "Jalisa was my daughter. Nothing will ever change that. Is that why you came home; because you felt guilty about the blood test?"

"No, honey. I love you and want to be here. Don't you know that?"

They finished their shower and continued their conversation in the bedroom. "My thoughts and emotions have been so out of control this past week, I really don't know what to think about us."

"Well, for starters, just know that I love you. Anything outside of that we will work on." They climbed in bed and for the first time in days, sleep was waiting for them. They slept close and held each other—this time out of desire, not comfort.

In the weeks that followed, everyone tried getting back into their normal routine. All out of town guests returned home, Camilla completed her finals and prepared for graduation, Sheena returned to work and prepared for the end of the grading period, and Paul returned to his office to find a mountain of paperwork and tons of messages.

Jaleel returned to work at the same hospital where his daughter passed away. Each morning it was a struggle for him to walk through the doors, but he always mustered up enough strength to make it through the day. Delisa returned to the daycare. On her first day back, she sat in the car for twenty minutes trying to build enough courage to walk through the doors and pass the class where she usually dropped Jalisa off every morning to get to her office. Finally, she called her assistant, said she couldn't do it, and went to Camilla's house. The days following weren't any different, and eventually, Delisa handed in her letter of resignation.

12

Sheena decided to keep her appointment for her birth control shot, but would decline the shot and discuss her chances of becoming pregnant. The doctor did a complete physical, drawing her blood to check cholesterol and blood sugar, and then did a pelvic exam. They discussed her menstrual cycle, ovulation, and the appropriate time to take a pregnancy test. Sheena was so excited after her visit to the doctor that she went directly to Paul's office.

Sheena entered the lobby of Paul's office building and was stopped by the receptionist. "Excuse me, but you can't just walk through here. You need to stop and sign in." She condescendingly picked up the pen and mimicked writing on the line. "You can have a seat over there and I will notify them that you are here."

Sheena smiled. *If this little receptionist doesn't watch it she might find herself in the unemployment line,* she thought. Sheena considered dropping her name to inform the receptionist to whom she was speaking, but decided that the expression on her face would be more rewarding when Paul came out and greeted his wife.

Sheena signed in as instructed. "I'm here to see Paul Matthews."

"Do you have an appointment?"

"No, I don't, but—"

"Ma'am, our lawyers are very busy and do not like a lot of interruptions. In the future, can you make sure you schedule an appointment before you stop by?"

"Just tell him Sheena is here to see him." Sheena took her seat, not giving any further response to the receptionist. She could not believe how rude this woman was. She didn't know Paul had hired a receptionist, but would definitely speak to Paul about the woman's professionalism.

Just as Sheena settled into a seat in the lobby Ellen, Paul's secretary, walked out. In spite of her brusque interaction with the receptionist, Sheena couldn't help but smile. When they'd first met, Ellen had pulled Sheena to the side and admonished her to not let Paul's overbearing authoritative behavior run her off. She explained that he was a good person who sometimes had a hard time separating his business persona from his personal life. Sheena stored the warning in the back of her mind. Yes she'd seen that authoritative side, but everything else she saw captured her heart.

"Sheena, how are you? It has been a long time since you visited." They skipped workplace formalities and embraced.

"I'm great. I've just been really busy. I only stopped by to talk to Paul for a minute."

"Did you check in with Lillian, our receptionist?"

"Yes, I did."

"Good, she will be able to locate him quickly so you don't have to walk around looking for him. I was just on my way out to get his lunch. Will you be staying? I'd be glad to get you something as well."

"That sounds good. Thank you so much." Ellen walked off and Sheena turned toward Lillian. She shook her head and pulled her cell phone out of her purse. She didn't know what this woman's problem was, but she was not going to let it ruin her good mood. "Paul, I'm in the lobby. Can you meet me at the receptionist's desk?"

A few minutes later, Paul strolled into the lobby. Sheena's mouth went dry. She could watch him walk all day. His graceful stride oozed confidence and sensuality that never ceased to make her heart flutter. She glanced to her right, trying to compose her wayward thoughts and barely comprised lust all over Lillian's face. The look on her face explained everything. Lillian wanted her husband and didn't like women showing up to see him unannounced. Sheena looked from Lillian to Paul and smiled.

She had nothing to worry about. Lillian may have had eyes for her husband, but her husband's were on her. *That's all that matters.* She turned her back on Lillian, blocking her out of her sight and her mind. "What are you doing here? Is everyone okay?" Paul placed his hand at the small of her back to lead her into his office. Once inside, he pulled her to him and nuzzled her neck.

"I went to the doctor this morning and..."

Paul spun her around to look in her eyes. "Are you feeling all right? What's the matter?" He placed his hand on her forehead and neck checking for a fever.

Sheena leaned in to him, taking advantage of his touch. The past few weeks had been so hectic they hadn't been intimate, and the sensation of his hands was melting her. Her breathing was heavy and voice full of desire. "I'm fine. I stopped birth control..." Paul slid his hand down her spine, making her body tremble so fiercely that she could not form a sentence.

Paul laughed inside. He knew exactly how she felt. He had watched her get dressed for work that morning and hadn't been able to get his mind right all day. He locked his office door and led her to the chaise.

Sheena gasped with excitement and fear. "Paul, what are you doing? We can't do this here." She tried to stop him from undressing her, but his warm breath against her bare skin intensified her yearning and desire for him took over.

Before she knew it they were panting heavily as their bodies connected. Being caught up in their lovemaking, they forgot about where they were and lost track of time. Sheena vaguely heard Ellen's voice through the intercom. "Honey, we have to stop. Ellen is back with lunch."

Paul was determined to have his fill. He sat up, pulling her to straddle his lap and pressing down on her hips, he entered her again. Sheena moaned and threw her head back as he pressed her hips down then pulled them up over and over again. In unison, their bodies quaked with pleasure, and after their moans subsided the only sound was the panting of their breath.

Sheena stood and tried to get dressed, but every time she picked up her clothes, Paul would snatch them from her. She saw him scanning her body from head to toe. "Is there a problem, Mr. Matthews?" She teased.

"Yes, there is Mrs. Matthews. I can't seem to get enough of you."

"Well, what are you going to do about that?"

Without warning Paul stood and lifted Sheena. Wrapping her legs around his waist, he whispered against her lips. "Let me show you what I'm going to do about it."

Again, her body succumbed to his advances. He took his time loving her, kissing, and caressing every place he had so hastily neglected the first time. When they finally parted, their bodies were exhausted with satisfaction and sleep fell over them.

The phone rang and Paul jumped out of his sleep, waking Sheena in the process. "Hello?"

Paul watched Sheena scrambling around the office for her clothes, barely listening to the person on the phone. The corners of his mouth tilted up. She knew him well. If she was still naked when he got off the phone, it would be a few more hours before they went home. Glad that the caller was brief, Paul quietly hung up the phone.

"Where do you think you're going?"

Sheena stopped mid-stride, eyes as wide as a child who'd gotten caught stealing cookies out of a cookie jar. "Honey, it's four o'clock. I can't believe we've been in this office for over four hours. I only came here to tell you about my doctor's appointment." Sheena finished putting the rest of her clothes on.

"Okay, tell me about it. Don't leave. I like it when you come here."

"Obviously, you like it a little too much." Sheena looked at her husband's still naked gorgeous body. "I would love to tell you about my appointment, but you have to get dressed so I can think straight."

Paul laughed as he seductively put his clothes on, never breaking eye contact. "Is that better?"

No, Sheena thought, *this man could wear a pair of raggedy sweat pants and still look good.* Sheena smiled, "You think you're sexy, don't you?"

Paul laughed, "No, I don't, but it's obvious that you do."

They laughed and talked for a while, then, realizing they hadn't eaten, they decided to skip the sandwiches from lunch and go to a nice restaurant. Sheena felt a little embarrassed when they stepped out of the office. Her hair was tussled, her clothes wrinkled, and when Paul stopped at Ellen's desk to inform her he was leaving for the day, Sheena couldn't look her in the eyes. Paul saw the shame on Sheena's face and laughed.

Sheena could not believe he was laughing at her. "It is not funny."

"Yes it is. This is my office and I can do whatever I want, including make love to my wife."

Sheena gasped and looked at Ellen who tried to pretend she hadn't over heard their conversation. "Paul, stop trying—" Before she could yell at him, he covered her mouth with his, making her forget the awkwardness.

They enjoyed some much needed alone time away from their house and family. They set the past few weeks aside and focused on being newlyweds. They made it home late that night and fell into bed, exhausted from a long day, but rejuvenated from their time together.

13

Camilla sat on her bed dressed for church, contemplating whether she was going or not. She promised Tim she would go with him and last Sunday she had this same battle. She wanted to go and figure out why the Lord saved her. She wanted to change her life, but last Sunday she lost the battle. She didn't want to face all the stares and whispers, but this Sunday she woke up with a determination, and though she contemplated, her determination was much greater.

Walking into Zion, Camilla scanned the congregation. Jaleel stood up front next to the pastor. He was one of the lead deacons assigned to assist the pastor. Paul sat in the fourth row on the end with Sheena and Delisa sitting next to him. Camilla wished she had arrived when the choir was singing so she could slip in unnoticed, but the church administrator was at the podium reading announcements and no one was listening.

Slowly, Camilla walked down the aisle. She could feel the stares. The whispers were no longer whispers, but in her mind sounded loud enough for the whole church to hear. She felt like running out and never coming back, but she made eye contact with Jaleel and his smile helped her down the aisle. She stopped next to Paul and in unison the three of them stood each kissing and hugging her as she walked passed them to take her seat. They were elated to see her, but also shocked as no one had asked her to come. She just showed up on her own. Camilla tried to calm her mind and block out her suspicions, but they poured in stronger and louder. Although she had never heard the whispers and no one ever confronted her, she felt like everyone knew her lifestyle and her many indiscretions.

The choir started singing and tears instantly fell from Camilla's eyes. The sound of Hezekiah Walker's, *God of a Second Chance,* echoed through the sanctuary. The soloist's voice ministered the words and they came across with comfort and restoration.

"Lord, I need to feel the touch of Your hand, Your will for my life. I want to understand. Lord, forgive me like only You can, for You're the God of a second chance." Her voice was smooth and powerful.

The song spoke to Camilla's heart; it also touched many others in the congregation. People were standing on their feet, their hands in the air and tears in their eyes. Camilla looked at everyone crying and for the first time in a long time she didn't feel like an outsider.

The soloist's voice came back in and spoke the sentiments of Camilla's heart. *"Lord, I'm tired of the way that I am. In Your love I want to live and stand, to adhere to Your every command, for You're the God of a second chance."*

The choir sang the chorus as Pastor Hawkins went to the podium. They sang softly behind him as he encouraged the people. "There's many of you here today who thought you had messed up so bad that God would never forgive you. You walked away from Him years ago and have been living a life contrary to the word of God. You have done things that you are ashamed to admit, but today God is offering you a second chance."

He stepped off the pulpit and walked down the aisles, speaking to the people. "You can be forgiven, you can be free, and you can be made whole. You just have to come back to Jesus. He is waiting on you. Will you come?" He returned and stood at the altar with his arms stretched out to the congregation.

Without hesitation, Camilla stood, passing Adrianna to Delisa. She made her way to the altar. The power of God engulfed her as she walked. She fell to her knees and cried out, "Lord, forgive me. I'm sorry. I want to come back."

The altar was full of people crying out for repentance, and those in their seats cried out for those at the altar. The service was full of emotion. Friends and family members stood and rejoiced as they watched their prayers being fulfilled. When Camilla finally went back to her seat, she felt changed and had a new outlook on life. The remainder of the service strengthened and fortified her resolution to serve the Lord. When she left the church, she vowed not to walk away from God again.

Tim sat on his leather sofa reading the invitation to Camilla's graduation over and over again. He hadn't been able to forget about her since he left. When he closed his eyes to sleep at night, he saw her face; he could even smell her perfume. He hadn't talked to her since he left, but not a night went by he didn't have to make himself not to call her. He tried to continue his same life style, but he felt out of place. The clubs he frequented had lost their flavor, the women had lost their appeal, and even the music seemed to be different. He had gone out one night and wound up at some woman's apartment, but couldn't engage in his usual acts without Bible scriptures and Camilla's face popping up. He did all he could to get over her and nothing worked.

Thoughts of her haunted him at night, and when he couldn't sleep, he would read the Bible. Though he didn't understand much of it, he continued to read. Christianity was quite new to him. The more he read, the more he wondered if he would be able to live up to the standard. The majority of the things he enjoyed seemed to be completely against the Bible, but his experience at Delisa's house encouraged him to keep reading and attending church. In the short time he had been home, he found a church to attend Sunday morning worship and a new convert's class.

Staring at the invitation in his hand, he knew his response to the invite would have a major affect on his life. If he accepted, he'd probably never get Camilla out of his system. If he declined, she'd probably be so upset with him she'd never want to see him again. Deciding that he had to have her in his life, he picked up the phone and once again he made flight reservations to San Diego. This, time he purchased a one way ticket…

Tim wasn't able to convince his boss to rehire him and hadn't been able to find a new job. He had plenty of money in savings and would be fine financially for a while, but he was saving to open his own accounting firm and refused to see his dream fade away. The invitation in his hand was the last push he needed to make him move to San Diego. He called Paul to inform him of his decision. Paul was so ecstatic, he instantly offered to find Tim an apartment. Tim declined, stating he had to see it himself before moving. Paul didn't argue, but offered him a bed in his house for as long as he needed. They talked for awhile about Tim's accounting firm and how he could help Paul's law firm. They scheduled a time to meet to go over pertinent details.

Tim was just about to end their call when Paul slipped an unnerving question in. "So what are you going to do about your feelings for Camilla?"

"What feelings? We hung out for a while. I was feeling her, but she wasn't feeling me. I've moved on."

"Whatever, little brother. I told myself I was not going to get involved, but I saw you with her. Her pain was your pain. You barely knew Jalisa, but when you saw how bad Camilla was hurting, you mourned with her. You did everything you could to support her, including risking your job to be by her side. I don't care what you say, feelings like that hit men like us hard and it is even harder to get over them." Paul laughed remembering his own struggle with Sheena.

"I know exactly what you're dealing with. Sheena tried to shake me loose several times when we first met. She was a Christian pretty much from birth and I had only been to church for funerals and weddings. Needless to say, she was brought up with the belief that Christians could not marry unbelievers, but I wasn't having it. Just like you, I was in love with her the first day I met her and was willing to do whatever it took to have her."

"Who said I am in love with Camilla?"

"It doesn't need to be said. Be honest with yourself before you miss out on the only woman you have ever cared for. Do whatever it takes to make her accept her feelings for you."

Tim spoke softly. "You are right. I do love her, which is crazy. I barely know her and we have never been intimate. I thought you were crazy when you got engaged to Sheena after knowing her just six months, and here I am a few weeks in and would marry Camilla today if she'd have me."

Paul laughed. He was shocked that Tim had already considered marrying Camilla. Tim was an adamant bachelor and had denounced the idea of marriage at a very young age. "This cannot be my little brother talking marriage. This coming from the same man who once said marriage and monogamy are for men whose testicles never descended."

"Why do you have to bring up old stuff?" Paul was laughing so hard Tim wanted to hang the phone up in his face.

"Aww, I'm sorry little brother. I'm just happy to see you changing your ways. I was worried about you for a while."

"Well, do you have any suggestions to help me persuade Camilla?"

"No, I have already gotten involved too much. You are on your own. I am going to get off this phone before Sheena hears me. She told me not to get involved."

Tim felt more assured about his decision to move and racked his brain trying to figure out how to approach Camilla. He was never one for being subtle or playing games, and it was obvious Camilla's heart had been broken by men who, just like him, liked lots of women. At least he was always upfront about his intentions... If a woman claimed he broke her heart, it was only because she'd ignored his intentions, hoping to be the one to catch him. Tim knew he had to make Camilla realize he was not as bad as she thought.

Tim spent the next couple of days putting an end to the lifestyle he had grown accustomed to. He had grown up in this city, came back after college, and established himself. As he drove around, he reminisced about his childhood. He drove past his elementary school which was in the heart of what some people called the ghetto, but to him, it was home. Looking back on things, Paul must have known how dangerous the neighborhood was, because he walked Tim to school every day and would walk two blocks past his own school just to make sure Tim made it safely.

Tim got out of the car and walked around. He remembered how he used to hate school and the trouble he caused in the classroom. It wasn't that school was too hard; he always scored the highest on tests. He hated school because he never had a parent who showed interest. His mom was dead and his dad didn't care. He never attended open house or parent teacher conferences, but Paul always came. When Tim was in the fourth grade, Paul attended his open house, and for the first time, Tim's teacher gave Paul the whole story. All the teachers in the past held back a lot of information because Paul wasn't the parent, but not Mrs. Olson. Paul had walked to Mrs. Olson, shook her hand, and introduced himself like the adult he was forced into becoming. At only fourteen-years-old, life and unforeseen responsibility had matured him. Tim sat at the table with Mrs. Olson and Paul as they looked through a packet of Tim's work, assignments he'd scribbled through, math work he'd guessed on, and book reports he hadn't completed. Then they talked about Tim's behavior, how disruptive he was, how he bullied the other children, and how he was very disrespectful. Paul gave Tim a look he had never seen before and Tim knew he was in trouble.

When they arrived home, Paul grabbed Tim by the shoulders, looked straight into his eyes, and spoke softly. "Tim, it's just me and you. No one is coming to rescue us from this neighborhood; we have to get ourselves out. Don't you hate living here, living likes this? Don't you want to be able to eat dinner every day or even play outside and feel safe? The way you are acting in school is going to keep you stuck right here. Those same people out there that make us scared to go out after dark didn't take advantage of the opportunities given to them and now they are stuck. Tim, I know I am not your father, but you have to make some changes. You are very smart. I saw your test scores, but you just have to put more effort into your class work. Will you promise me you will try harder?" Tim made Paul a promise that day and changed his outlook on school. He wasn't perfect, but day by day, year by year, he got better. By the time he graduated from high school, he was accepted to college with a math scholarship.

As Tim drove around the city, he reflected on how he and his brother had accomplished exactly what they set their heart on: getting out of the ghetto. They'd come from not knowing whether there would be food for dinner to being able to eat dinner in fine restaurants every night. His drive ended at one of his favorite restaurants where he was meeting some friends for a farewell dinner. Although his relationship with his friends had dwindled since he returned from San Diego, he would miss them. They had some good times together, but moving away would also put the distance between them that he needed to further his relationship with Christ.

Jaleel had taken the day off from work to spend with Delisa. He wanted to surprise her with breakfast in bed followed by a shopping spree, but he was surprised to find out she had a job interview. She hadn't mentioned anything about working since she quit her job. He supported her decision to quit and preferred for her to stay home longer. Lying in bed, he watched as she frantically scampered around the room getting dressed. She changed outfits twice and was now walking around in a black bra and panty set. Her hair was pulled into a bun and she wore her black eyeglasses. It had been months since their last intimate encounter and the sight of her half-dressed made him feel like the sex-obsessed teenager he was when they first met. He grabbed her, pulling her onto the bed to straddle him.

His aggressiveness was a shock. She hadn't noticed he was watching her, "Jaleel, what are you doing?" She tried to look into his eyes, but they were busy scanning her body. "You're going to make me late for my interview."

"Why are you going to this interview? I make more than enough to take care of us. You don't have to go back to work."

The pressure between her thighs and the heat from his hands on her back made her voice tremble. "What do you expect me to do? Stay home to cook and clean?" Delisa gasped as his hands slid to the front of her body cupping her breasts.

"No, what I am saying is you don't have to rush back to work. If you choose not to go back at all, I'd be happy." Jaleel unsnapped her bra and she didn't protest, "Are you going?"

Delisa thought for a few moments then stood, grabbing her bra. "I have to go. I don't want to miss this opportunity."

Jaleel's head sank and without making eye contact he half-heartedly resigned. "I understand. I'll be here when you get back." He wanted to prove to her he was a changed man. The man he used to be would have left her feeling insecure and unwanted, but he realized how much of a fool he was and regretted every moment he made her feel uneasy.

Delisa continued dressing without saying a word. She avoided eye contact because the initial look of disappointment on his face was unsettling. She was very independent and took pride in the fact she didn't need a man to take care of her. She'd gone to college, got a degree, and had landed a nice paying job on her own. She finished dressing, kissed Jaleel on the cheek, and left. Sitting in the car in the driveway, Delisa was conflicted. One of the reasons she had worked so hard in the past was because she was unsure of Jaleel's commitment to her and wanted to be able to support herself should he decide to leave her. The feelings she knew he had for Sheena always made her feel like he could leave at any moment, but now he was a changed man. It reflected in the way he looked at her, talked to her, and touched her. He was all hers, and now she was confident in his commitment to her.

Deep down, she knew she was not ready to go back to work at another daycare where she would be surrounded by so many children and reminded of her own loss. She really wanted a career change. She was not the type of woman to sit around doing nothing, but more time off to figure some things out was appealing. She jumped out of the car and ran back into the house. As she entered the house, Jaleel was headed toward the kitchen and he stopped in his tracks.

"Did you forget something?"

She ran and practically jumped into his arms. He stumbled back from the force of her body, but quickly he gained his footing, lifted her, and wrapped her legs around his waist as she planted kisses all over his face, eventually resting on his lips. He effortless carried her upstairs and placed her on the bed. He undressed her and his lips visited every portion of her body, becoming reacquainted with her feel, smell, and taste. There was desperation in the passion of their lovemaking, and the fire that burned within them was exacerbated by every touch. When the fire was quenched, they lay in peace resting in each other's arms.

"Jaleel, are you sleep?"

"No, what's on your mind?"

"I was thinking of going back to school to get my Master's. Do you think you will be able to pay all the bills as well as my tuition and books?"

"Of course I will. I have enough in my savings right now to cover your tuition, so you can get started right away. As a matter of fact..." Jaleel grabbed his laptop. "If you enroll now, you should be able to start spring semester." Jaleel got online, and within a couple of hours, he had applied for admission to several graduate programs. Delisa watched as he took charge; she snuggled up next to him, occasionally kissing his muscular arm as he typed in all the required information. A few times, her kiss took his breath away and he stopped typing to enjoy her affection. There had been a great change within him. His concern for her and interest in her goals was an aphrodisiac. When he finished typing, he couldn't close the laptop fast enough before she assaulted his lips with hers, reassuring him of her love and desire for him. They resolutely sealed their reconciliation.

Jaleel and Delisa finally made it out of the house. He surprised her with a shopping spree. He followed her around the mall into every store, never complaining about the time or the money spent, but sat back and enjoyed as she modeled each outfit for him. Jaleel even picked out a few outfits that Delisa really liked. Afterward, he proudly walked to the register, paid for her items, and then carried her bags while she went to the next store. She made each purchase based on his look of approval when she came out the dressing room. She was dressing for him and wanted to catch no one's eye but his.

Delisa was never one to spend long hours shopping, but she was having such a good time. It wasn't really the shopping, but more so the attention Jaleel was giving her that excited her. He gave her his undivided attention, ignoring cell phone calls and friends they saw in the mall. Normally when they went to the mall, Jaleel would give her the credit card and tell her to call if she ran into problems. He would then head straight for the food court. When she would finish, she'd have to carry her bags around the mall looking for him. When she finally found him, he would never offer to carry her bags to the car. She watched him as he sat on a bench trying to reposition the bags he was carrying to make the load lighter. She tried to grab a few bags, but he gave her a stern look and told her to put it down.

Ten stores, twenty bags, and five hours later, Delisa's shopping spree was over. She walked into the house, feet aching and back hurting. Jaleel had carried all the bags and seemed to have more energy left than she did.

Jaleel saw Delisa sitting on the bottom of the steps and was instantly concerned. "Are you okay?"

"Yes, I am just tired. I'm trying to build up enough strength to climb these stairs."

Jaleel put the bags down, picked Delisa up, and carried her upstairs, placing her on the bed. Then he carried all the bags upstairs. When he returned to the room, Delisa was getting up and he firmly told her, "Sit down."

Delisa smiled at him and playfully said, "You have been bossing me around all day."

Jaleel put the bags down, picked Delisa up, laid her back on the bed, and massaged her feet. "I would not call it being bossy. I am just taking care of my woman. Now, you lay here while I run you some bath water."

"I will only take a bath if you join me. You had more of a work out today than I did. You need to relax."

"Of course I'll join you." Jaleel went into the bathroom and Delisa jumped off the bed.

Jaleel ran back into to the bedroom when he heard Delisa scream. She was standing next to the bed with all of her receipts laid across the bed. "Oh my goodness, Jaleel, why did you let me spend this much money?" Delisa always reviewed all her receipts after shopping then added up her totals. She almost always felt buyer's remorse and took something back.

Jaleel reached around her, wanting to kick himself for not taking the receipts out the bags, and grabbed all the receipts. "Don't worry about how much we spent. I got it covered."

"Jaleel, I spent almost three thousand dollars..."

"Look at it like this. I spent three thousand dollars on a gift for my wife and since it was a gift, you can't take anything back. To be completely honest, it doesn't even come close to the amount I set aside to spend on you today." He took the receipts put them in the bathroom sink and burned them.

Delisa stood with her mouth hanging open, unable to believe she had gotten so caught up in the moment that she actually spent that much money and Jaleel wanted her to spend more. She walked toward her bags, and again Jaleel was bossy. "Take a bath first, then you can sort through your new things."

Delisa smiled, and gave him a playful salute. "Yes sir." She followed him into the bathroom.

14

Camilla frantically ran around her apartment getting dressed for her graduation ceremony. With everything she had gone through this past year, she could not believe the day was finally here. She was a bundle of nerves and Adrianna was not being cooperative. Adrianna lay on the bed screaming at the top of her lungs, and Camilla could not figure out what was wrong. She changed her diaper and fed her, which was the reason she was not dressed. Adrianna spit up all over her clothes and Camilla had to change her. The doorbell rang and Camilla used it as an opportunity to take a break from Adrianna.

Camilla looked through the peephole and smiled as she opened the door. "Tim, what are you doing here?"

"You know I would not miss your graduation. I came by to give you a ride. From the sound of things, you could use a little help."

"Yes I could! Please go work your magic on Adrianna. She is driving me crazy."

Tim had another motive for coming by her apartment before the graduation and wasn't going to allow a screaming baby to deter him. He purposely brushed his body against hers. He sensed the affect it had on her, and it gave him the courage he needed to go ahead with his plan.

"Camilla, baby, I have missed you. I've been miserable these past few weeks and I don't want to live without you. I know you feel the same way and for whatever reason you are fighting it, but I am not going to let you push me away again." He brushed his lips across hers and walked into her bedroom, leaving her standing at the door.

Camilla stood at the door, not knowing whether to be furious with him for being so forceful or feel flattered that he missed her. She followed him into the room to give him a piece of her mind, but when she saw him holding Adrianna and both of them smiling, her heart melted. "How do you get her to calm down so easily?"

"Maybe she understands what I am trying to get you to realize. I love you and we belong together. I have never felt like this before, and I will not let you get away." Tim continued playing with Adrianna while Camilla watched. "If you don't finish getting dressed, you are going to miss your own graduation." Tim smiled. He knew he was getting to her and Adrianna was helping him every step of the way.

Tim and Camilla arrived at the college. Her other guests had not yet arrived. "Tim, I told Delisa to meet me right here to take Adrianna. Will you wait for her while I get ready?"

"Camilla, I can watch her. I am going to be her daddy one day." Tim rubbed his nose against Adrianna's and she tried to bite him.

"Tim, I know you can watch her," Camilla tried to ignore his comment about being Adrianna's daddy. "I just don't want Delisa to be standing out here waiting for me."

"Okay. I will wait for Delisa and we'll meet you right here after the ceremony." He leaned in and kissed her before she walked away. The rest of the family arrived shortly after Camilla left. Everyone greeted Tim and they went to find their seats. Paul pulled Tim to the side. "Little brother, I am starting to think you love Camilla more than me. This is the second time you came into town and went to her house before coming to see me."

"You're not going to make this any easier for me are you?"

"No, just consider it pay back for how you treated me when I was dating Sheena."

They caught up with the rest of the group and took their seats as Tim passed Adrianna to Delisa. Before Tim could get comfortable in his seat, Adrianna started crying. Delisa tried talking to her and bouncing her, but nothing worked. Felicia, Adrianna's grandmother, and Sheena tried as well, but none of them could calm her. The people close by were getting frustrated and were mumbling rude comments. Delisa grabbed the diaper bag and was going to take Adrianna outside, but Tim Jumped up. "I'll take her." He reached out and grabbed Adrianna before Delisa could protest. Adrianna's cries instantly stopped.

All three women looked at each other then looked at Tim. They watched as Tim and Adrianna smiled and cooed at each other. No one could understand why Adrianna was so attached to him. She barely knew him and he had been gone for weeks. Sheena silently laughed. She knew more than the other two ladies. They didn't know Tim slept at Camilla's house for a whole week after Jalisa passed away. It was Tim who took care of Adrianna while Camilla studied for finals. It was Tim who helped Camilla cope with the loss of her niece. In that short time, they bonded as a family, and even Adrianna felt the strong connection they shared.

When the ceremony concluded, Tim waited for Camilla at their designated spot with everyone else. When Camilla finally walked up, they all screamed, congratulating her on her success and saying how proud they were of her for not giving up. Camilla was overwhelmed with praises from her family and tears of joy flowed down her face. When her dad wrapped his arms around her, she cried uncontrollably.

"Cammie, I am so proud of you. So many young ladies give up when faced with the things you have encountered, but you didn't quit." He kissed her forehead, almost getting choked up himself.

Tim and Camilla drove home in silence. She thought about the comments he'd made and his feelings for her. How could he be so sure about them being together? She had strong feelings for him. His connection with Adrianna made those feelings stronger. She loved him, but after all of the hurt she experienced in her past, she vowed never to tell a man she loved him. Camilla toiled over whether she should take a chance and love him the way her heart wanted to or run away.

Camilla paced around her room; her decision was made. She waited for Tim to finish putting Adrianna in her crib. He walked into the room and Camilla started rambling. "Tim, I think you are a great guy and you are great with Adrianna. I know you have a past and so do I. My past has taught me to stay away from men like you. I don't know what all of this means, but I love you. I know you live in another state, but maybe we could work something out. You just have to promise you won't cheat on me. If you lose interest, let me know and I will handle it. Just don't cheat on me." Camilla finally took a breath and looked Tim in the eye.

"Camilla, I love you and will never hurt you. You are the only woman I have ever loved. I have always been upfront with women the same way I have been with you. If you really love me, we can make it work."

"Tim, I have loved you since that day at Sunset Cliffs and it scares me. We hardly know each other. How can we be in love so quick? How can we be together when you live so far away?"

Tim pulled Camilla closer to him. "Tell me I'm your man and I will tell you how it's going to work."

Camilla smiled and wrapped her arms around his waist. "You are my man. I wouldn't have it any other way."

"I am glad you said that, because we are getting married next week…"

Camilla interrupted. "What do you mean getting married next week? We live in two different states, and we have only known each other for a few weeks. How can we get married so soon?"

"You said you loved me, right?" Camilla nodded her head yes.

"Then that is how we can get married so soon. I can make you happy and there is no other woman for me. So why wait to be together?"

Camilla stepped out of his embrace to think. Every time they were together, everything seemed perfect. She also felt empty when he left, but was that enough to build a marriage? The short time he'd stayed with her, they felt married and had bonded without sleeping together.

"Okay, I will marry you under one condition. We keep it quiet for a while. I'd like to enjoy being married before I have to deal with my mom and sister. When they find out I've married a man I just met, they aren't going to be happy. It shouldn't be hard to keep our relationship a secret because we will not be living together."

"I'm sorry. I have no problem keeping it quiet, but if you think you are going to be my wife and live in a different state you are sadly mistaken." Tim smiled. He wanted to see if Camilla was willing to move to be with him.

"Okay, how soon do you want me to move? If you help me with the cost, I can be packed by the end of next week." Camilla saw the smirk on his face, "What is so funny?"

"All that won't be necessary. I just wanted to see if you were willing to move with me. I already moved here. I came straight here from the airport this morning. All of my things should be delivered by the end of next week."

Camilla's smile spread across her face. "Really, Tim?" She could no longer contain her excitement. She jumped up and down screaming. "We are getting married." She wrapped her arms around his neck and for the first time, she kissed him with all the passion she had for him.

Tim broke their kiss. "Camilla baby, you cannot kiss me like that. At least not until we get married." His heart was racing and he doubted whether he could take another kiss like that without losing control.

Camilla breathed heavily on his neck. "I'm sorry. I just got a little carried away. So what do we do next?"

"Let's go out and celebrate. We need to get out of this house before we make a mistake." His erection was throbbing against his zipper. The Bible talked about temptation, but he never thought about how temptation would manifest.

"We can't. Sheena is having a graduation celebration for me at her house. Are you coming?"

"Of course I am, especially since that is where I am going to be staying."

"What? You're not staying here?" Camilla whined.

"I would love to, but I am really trying to do this Christian thing. Sleeping in the bed with you is a temptation that I would not be able to resist." Tim leaned in, kissing her softly. "After we're married, I'll move in until we find a house, but right now I have to go."

"Please don't leave. I'll behave. I've actually been going to church

111

and trying to live right, too." Camilla walked to the couch and Tim followed. "It was really hard at first. I dressed up and wound up not going. The next Sunday I made it to church and God was there waiting for me. I vowed to live for Him. It hasn't been long, but I've been doing pretty well."

Tim slid his leg behind her and pulled her between his legs. They laid on the couch talking and getting to know each other. They discussed their childhood, laughed about their college experiences, shared their goals and dreams, argued over who missed the other more, and even prayed that God would bless their marriage. Tim held Camilla tight, placing small kisses on her temple. He couldn't believe she had agreed to marry him. He had prepared himself for weeks, maybe even months of wearing her down, convincing her to give him a chance. Her eagerness assured him that she loved him. Camilla relaxed in Tim's arms. The man she was afraid to trust suddenly felt safe. She kissed the arm wrapped around her chest and sank deeper into his embrace.

Camilla arrived at Sheena's shortly after Tim. The house was already full of her family and friends. Camilla's stomach bubbled with anxiety over having to be in the house, pretending that Tim's presence had no affect on her. Camilla walked into the house. Her eyes immediately found Tim and a scowl of disgust spread across her face when she saw her friend. Latrice, who was known to be loose and ready to sleep with any man with a pulse, was grinning in Tim's face. Camilla ignored all greetings and praises that were thrown her way; her mind was set on busting Latrice's bubble.

With the fakest smile possible, Camilla handed Adrianna to Tim and turned to Latrice. "Hey Latrice, I am glad you could make it. I see you have met my boyfriend."

Tim choked on his soda and almost dropped Adrianna. Her calling him "boyfriend" was a total shock. Tim grabbed Camilla by the arm and pulled her to the side. "Baby, what are you doing? What happened to keeping things quiet?"

"I'm sorry. I saw her talking to you and I forgot my own plan."

"You don't have to apologize to me. I want everybody to know that we are together... Don't tell me you actually thought I was interested in her?"

"No, but I know how Latrice is. I wanted to set her straight before she got any ideas. So, change in plans, because I know Latrice is off running her big mouth somewhere. We tell everyone we are together, but not about us getting married... Okay?"

"Sounds good to me. Does that mean I can do this." Tim leaned in and softly kissed her lips.

"Excuse me." Delisa's voice interrupted their kiss. "Tim, what are you doing to my little sister?"

Tim turned around and was relieved to see a smile on Delisa's face. "You should be asking your little sister what she's doing to me, because I cannot think straight whenever she is around."

"You guys look good together. Please take care of her. If you hurt her, we are going to have a problem." Delisa patted Tim on the shoulder.

Camilla stepped up to defend Tim. "Delisa, I am a grown woman and can take care of myself. Besides, Tim is a good man; he stood by me and took care of me and Adrianna when Jalisa was in the hospital."

"Camilla, I don't want to argue with you tonight. Actually, I wasn't even upset. Why do you act like this whenever I show concern for you?"

"Because you are only three—"

"Camilla, this is not the time, nor the place. Enjoy your party and deal with this later." Tim stepped between them to stop the argument from escalating. He placed his arm around her waist and escorted her to another room.

Sheena walked up in time to see Delisa still fuming. "What's wrong?"

"Camilla! She makes me want to scream sometimes." Delisa explained what happened and how Camilla overacted.

"Look Delisa, you know how Camilla is. She has always gotten upset when you try to be her mother. You have to let Camilla and Tim

113

figure everything out alone. That is what Paul and I decided—"

"What? You guys knew and didn't tell me?"

"How can you see the two of them together and not know? If it makes you feel any better I think they just recently made it official." Sheena really didn't know; she was just going off of what Paul had told her.

"I guess I have been preoccupied with Jalisa. It's just that Camilla and I have a good relationship until I give her advice."

"Come on, Delisa. Don't do this to yourself. You know Camilla has never liked you bossing her around. She used to always say, *Who said you're the boss?* You would always respond, *God did when He made me the big sister.*" Sheena and Delisa laughed.

Delisa bossed Camilla around from the day she started crawling. By the time Camilla was seven, she'd had enough. From then on, Camilla always did the opposite of what Delisa told her. This got her into trouble most of the time, but Camilla refused to do anything Delisa told her.

Tim followed Camilla around the house as she introduced him to the rest of her friends. He was ecstatic that he could be openly affectionate with her and was just about to kiss her when Jaleel and Paul walked up. Tim rolled his eyes and prepared for the jokes.

"What's up, little brother?" Paul chuckled. "Someone asked me if I've met Camilla's new boyfriend and had to run over and see who they were talking about. So, is there something you want to tell me?"

Jaleel burst out laughing. "Yeah Tim, the last time we had a conversation like this you said you didn't want to be hemmed up, and from the looks of things…" Jaleel was laughing so hard he could not finish his sentence.

"What is so funny? Don't make me get my sister and cousin to put you two in your place," Camilla jumped in to give Tim some relief.

"Go ahead," Paul and Jaleel said in unison.

"Okay, act bad if you want to." Camilla walked off to find Delisa and Sheena; both were sitting in the same place she'd left Delisa. "Can you guys come get your husbands? They are giving Tim a hard time."

The three women walked into the other room to find Jaleel and Paul bent over laughing. Tim was not amused.

"Do you remember when Tim came out for Thanksgiving? You came home and I kissed you? Then Delisa came home and kissed Jaleel. Tim was so full of jokes, telling you not to introduce him to any of the women in your family because he was not ready to be hemmed up?"

Camilla gasped. "Tim, you didn't say that did you?"

"Yes he did," Paul answered for him. "Then, Thanksgiving day you came in and Tim's mouth was hanging open. He couldn't keep his eyes off of you. Then he lied, saying he was jetlag when I asked him what was wrong."

"Oh Tim," Camilla laughed. "Baby, I am sorry, but that is hilarious." She was laughing, but knowing that she'd changed his heart about love strengthened her desire for him.

Everyone had a good laugh at Tim's expense; eventually he was laughing, too. He had to admit meeting Camilla made him do a complete turn. She had him going from hardcore bachelor to lovesick fiancé in just a few weeks. He didn't care how it happened or why; he was just excited she finally accepted him. He was going to do everything he could to make her happy.

"Camilla, can I talk to you for a minute?" Their laughing was interrupted by Latrice.

Camilla walked away with Latrice, knowing she needed to apologize for being rude. "Latrice, I am sorry for the way I approached you earlier. Please forgive me."

"Girl, I'm not tripping. I just wanted to let you know that the reason I was talking to him. He looked so familiar, and I was trying to figure out where I know him from."

"Latrice, he is not even from here. He visits once or twice a year, so the possibility of you knowing him is very slim."

"I don't know. You know, I never forget a face. Just give me some time. I'll figure it out." Latrice walked away leaving Camilla's mind wondering. She knew both Latrice and Tim had slept around, and she

115

hoped they hadn't slept together on one of his visits.

The party was winding down and the majority of the guests had left. Tim was upstairs checking on Adrianna when he felt a hand slip around his waist. It startled him for a second, but he relaxed when he realized who it was. Camilla slid her hands up and down his back. She was getting ready to go home and didn't want to leave him. She wrapped her arms around him and rested her head on his back. Neither were used to their new lifestyles. When they partied, they partied hard which usually involved lots of drinking. Both of them were terrible when they were drunk and usually woke up hung over in unfamiliar places. Tim, with strange women, and Camilla always woke up with shame for getting so drunk. Now it was a little after midnight and the party was done. No one was passed out on the floor and everyone got in their own cars and drove home without being under the influence.

Slowly, Tim turned in Camilla's arms to face her. "Are you getting ready to leave?"

"Yes, I was just coming to get Adrianna..." Camilla paused, trying to decide how to word her next sentence. "I know we can't sleep in the same bed, but maybe you could sleep on the couch? I just don't want to be away from you another day of my life." Camilla nervously bit her bottom lip as she waited for his response.

Tim thought her offer was tempting, but he didn't trust himself. "I can't, but let's do this... Meet me at the courthouse Monday at noon. I have a meeting with Paul that morning, but we can get married right after. Are you sure you want to marry me, because this is going to be forever. We will communicate and work through the hard times, no separation or divorce."

Camilla looked into his eyes and saw his sincerity. "Tim, I love you. I know I pushed you away at first, but I want forever with you. I am willing to do whatever it takes to be with and stay with you. So, I will meet you on Monday." Camilla smiled and gently kissed him.

Tim held her tight. He wanted to take his woman and child home, but he knew if he came close to her apartment they would make a mistake

116

they could not take back. "Camilla, you need to head home it is already late. Why don't you leave Adrianna here with me? I will bring her in the morning when I pick you up for breakfast."

Adrianna had only slept away from home a few times. Each time, Camilla was a nervous wreck. Tim had never taken care of a child by himself and that made her even more nervous. He was going to be the only father Adrianna would ever know, and he would always be alone with her. Camilla rushed downstairs to get her spare key from Delisa and gave it to Tim. She then drove home, leaving Adrianna sleeping on Tim's bed.

Morning came quick and Tim was at Camilla's apartment bright and early, letting himself in with his key. He crept into Camilla's room with Adrianna in his arms and planted small kisses on her face to wake her.

"Tim, what are you doing here? I thought you weren't going to spend the night? Is Adrianna okay?" Camilla spoke without opening her eyes.

"Well, I'm glad to see you trusted me with Adrianna enough to get a good night sleep, because it is eight o'clock in the morning." Camilla jumped up and looked around the room. She couldn't believe she had slept through the night without worrying about her baby. "Adrianna slept well, too. She didn't wake up at all."

"What do you mean didn't wake up? She has never slept through the night."

Tim laughed. "Don't be jealous that she just likes me better than you."

"I am really starting to think so, but since she likes you better, you shouldn't mind giving her a quick bath. All of the stuff is in her room. You can use the kitchen sink."

"Camilla, you know I don't know what I am doing."

"It's okay. I didn't either my first time. Use the baby wash, lotion, and a towel off the changing table, grab a diaper and an outfit and you're good to go." Camilla walked into the bathroom laughing at Tim's facial expression. Tim tried his best, but found it extremely difficult to hold on

117

to a wet, wiggling baby with one hand and wash her with the other. Adrianna splashed water all over the place and kept grabbing and sucking the wash cloth when he tried to wash her. Tim placed Adrianna on the counter to dry her off and put lotion on her. He didn't realize he should have put her diaper on first and Adrianna 'went potty' all over the counter and on the clothes she was going to wear for the day.

"Are you having a little trouble?" Camilla unsuccessfully tried to contain her laughter.

Tim laughed at himself. "I never thought giving a bath would be this difficult. I guess I have a lot to learn."

"Don't worry, it happens to the best of us. I gave her a bath last week and she pooped in the water."

They laughed as they walked to the room to dress Adrianna and leave for their day out as a family. Before going back home, Tim took Camilla to purchase their wedding rings. Her reluctance surprised him, but once he assured her that they would not wear them until she was ready to announce their marriage, excitement took over. Camilla tried on every engagement ring in the store. Then, they shopped for a dress and a suit for their wedding.

15

Paul and Tim were up bright and early Monday morning putting the final touches on their presentations. Tim was very excited about opening his own business. His years of hard work and saving were finally paying off and he wanted to set a precedent for excellent service. He couldn't slack off just because the client was his brother. Both men walked into the meeting room and greeted each other with a firm handshake. Paul presented the law firm's goals and financial history then he laid out what he needed Tim to do for his company. He concluded his presentation with estimates from three different accounting firms for the same service. Tim was not intimidated by his brother and was confident in his accounting skills. He presented his company's motto and outlined the services the company was capable of providing then compared his estimate with the three Paul presented and explained the extra services he provided which made his estimate a little higher.

Paul was surprised and well pleased with Tim's presentation. He had thought of things that would be essential to maintaining the account that Paul hadn't. He knew his brother was good with numbers, but his professionalism and business sense were surprising. They finalized the terms of their contract, agreeing upon services provided and price. Then, Paul brought in two lawyers who worked for him who also needed personal services. Tim was unprepared, but his knowledge of the field enabled him to answer all questions. By the end of the meeting, Tim had two additional clients. The meeting came to an end and Tim vowed to send over the three finalized contracts by the end of the week.

Paul sat back in his chair and smiled at Tim. "Are we out of business mode?"

Tim nodded yes.

"Good. I am proud of you, little brother. You came in here, did your thing. It was top of the line, much better than all the other presentations I have received."

"Thanks man, I appreciate you treating me as a business associate and not your little brother."

"Well, I have something to show you. Just remember, we are in brother mode, so don't get mad." Paul pulled out a manila folder filled with information about office buildings that were available. He presented each site to Tim along with his own pros and cons.

Tim silently reviewed the information. He separated the stack by price, then picked out the two he liked within his price range. "How far are these two from here?"

"They are about five to ten minutes up the road." Paul tried to conceal his excitement. He loved his brother, and even though Paul had married into a nice family that accepted him, he still missed his brother. "I thought you would like those two. I liked them, too. You want to run and look at them real quick?"

Tim looked at his watch. He was getting married in an hour. "Sure, but we have to make it quick. I have to be somewhere in an hour."

"Where are you going?"

"I am going to the most important meeting of my life." Tim wanted to shout and scream *I am going to marry the most beautiful women I have ever known.*

"What is more important than starting your business?"

"Man, you are nosy."

"I guess it's just the lawyer in me. I get paid big bucks to be nosy." Paul laughed.

They went to look at the office buildings. The first one didn't spark any interest, but when they walked into the second one, Tim's eyes widened. The entrance was a perfect size for a reception area, there was a conference room, and three mid-size offices. The best part was the rent being cheaper than what he originally thought. With the fees Paul's firm would pay, the two personal accounts, and if the three other law firms that Paul referred to him decided to come on board, he'd be able to cover all expenses, hire an assistant, and have enough money left over to live nicely.

Tim was so caught up envisioning what his office would look like that he lost track of time; it was already ten minutes until noon. "Sorry, big brother. I have to go, but let me meet with the other firms. If they decide to sign on, I most definitely want this one." Tim ran out of the office hoping he would make it to the court house on time. He should have asked Paul for the fastest way to get there, but didn't want to deal with all the questions that would come with it.

Tim arrived at the courthouse and had to drive around to find a parking space. He regretted choosing lunch time to meet because traffic was terrible. By the time Tim got out of his car, he was fifteen minutes late.

"Tim, where are you? You said noon. If you didn't want to do this why play games? I am standing here waiting on you looking like a fool for believing you loved me. I am leaving!" Camilla rambled into the phone as soon as it clicked on.

"Wait!" Tim's heart was racing, and his feet joined in trying to catch her before she left. "Baby, don't do this! I am here now; just wait for me, please."

"Tim, if you really wanted to marry me you would have been here on time. So I am letting you off the hook. You don't have to marry me." Camilla's chest was heaving as she tried to contain her emotion.

"Camilla, please let me explain." His plea was answered with a click.

Camilla hung up the phone. Tears filled her eyes as she looked down at the dress Tim bought her. She felt like a fool for allowing love to hurt her again. She started walking toward the bus stop, inwardly regretting her decision to take the bus so she could ride home with Tim. As she stepped up to the crosswalk, she pushed the button to cross and when she looked up, Tim stood on the other side. Camilla's hurt turned to anger as they stared each other down. Tim was glad he caught her before she left. He was not going to let her leave without a fight. Camilla didn't want to face Tim, so she turned and walked in the other direction. Tim lost all sense and ran after her. He dodged in and out of traffic as horns blew and tires screeched, causing Camilla to turn around. Her heart sank when she saw Tim almost get hit by a bus.

As he stepped up on the curb, she ran and threw herself into his arms. "Tim, you are crazy? What would possess you to run through traffic like that? You could have been killed."

"I saw you leaving and I couldn't let you go without explaining what happened. I love you and want to marry you. I know there is no excuse for me being late. I am so sorry. Please marry me, Camilla. If you don't, it would have been better if I got hit by that bus because I don't want to live without you." Tim saw the resistance in her face and refused to accept it. "I had a meeting with Paul this morning. He is hiring my company to manage his company's finances. He brought in two other lawyers that hired me. He referred me to three other firms and took me to see a couple of office buildings. I didn't realize how long it would take me to get here and find parking." Tim saw Camilla's face soften and paused to give her an opportunity to speak.

Suddenly Camilla felt foolish for being so angry. He was only fifteen minutes late, and she was going to throw their future away without letting him explain. "Sorry, I should have let you explain before I got upset. I guess I already broke our agreement to communicate."

"It's okay. We are not perfect. I should have called to let you know what happened. Let's go get married."

Tim and Camilla walked in and, surprisingly, there was no line. Their hands shook and stomachs did flips as they completed their application for a marriage license. They held each other tightly as they waited for their names to be called. Camilla would have loved to have a big, traditional church wedding with all her family and friends present, but she loved this man and wanted her life with him to begin immediately. Her last serious relationship destroyed all her dreams of happiness, marriage, and a house with a white picket fence. Tim popped up when she least expected and turned out to be everything she needed.

Finally, their names were called. The ceremony was quick and to the point. There was none of the pomp and circumstance of a traditional ceremony. Despite the harsh tone in the voice of the Justice of the Peace and a ceremony that seemed more like a merger than a marriage, Tim and Camilla's eyes were filled with tears and their hearts with joy when they were finally allowed to kiss as husband and wife.

They walked out of court house and embraced each other, holding tightly. They didn't want to let go. Tim lifted her and kissed her passionately. Their tears mingled and hearts raced as their kiss intensified.

Reluctantly, Tim ended their kiss and looked in her eyes. "Are you ready to go home, Mrs. Matthews?"

"No, I am not..." Camilla had made some plans to celebrate her wedding even if she wasn't going tell anyone what was going on. "I made plans for lunch. I told Sheena and Delisa to meet me for a couple's lunch at one thirty. Paul and Jaleel are supposed to be there. This will be our reception. I also made arrangements for Delisa to pick up Adrianna from daycare since we can't go on a honeymoon just yet. I made us hotel reservations for tonight." Camilla smiled at the delight that showed on Tim's face.

"Sounds good. Let me walk you to your car so we won't be late."

"I rode the bus, so I could ride home with my husband."

Tim escorted Camilla to his car he was shocked at how much thought she had put into this day. The only thing he thought of was bringing his clothes with him so he wouldn't have to go back to Paul's house after they got married. He helped her into the car and rushed around to the other side. He paused before starting the car. "Baby, are you really happy? I don't want you to have any regrets."

"Of course I'm happy. Please be confident in my love for you and I will do the same. I have no regrets."

Camilla slid her hand up Tim's chest and caressed the muscles she'd longed to touch since the day she met him. Tim watched her hand as it traced each muscle, then slid to his chin pulling him to meet her lips. Each kiss was slow and intense. The longer each kiss lasted, the more they become familiar with each other's taste. The burning desire that had been kindled between them for months was finally being quenched with each stroke of their tongues. Their hands roamed all over each other's bodies as time slithered away from them.

Camilla broke free from the trance Tim's kisses placed on her. "Honey we can't do this here. Everyone is waiting on us."

"I know, but do we have to go to lunch? We could just go to the hotel," Tim breathed deeply, trying to calm down.

"Baby, I would love to, but you know if we don't show up they will call us all night. Besides, we have the rest of our lives to be together."

Tim groaned and started the car. Their kissing episode in the car made them twenty minutes late to lunch. They walked into the restaurant trying to act normal, but every touch from each other, be it purposely or accidental, sent chills up their spines. All eyes were on them when they stepped up to the table and everyone burst out laughing.

"What's so funny?" Camilla's face glared in confusion.

"Cammie, don't look so confused. You know why we are laughing. You are always late." Delisa chuckled. "We thought you would be on time since they had to take off from work to meet you, but you stayed true to form arriving fashionably late."

Camilla smiled as she spoke. "For your information, Tim is the reason why we are late."

Tim's jaw dropped. "So you're just going to throw me under the bus?" Tim leaned in and whispered against her ear. "And if my memory serves me correctly, that wasn't entirely my fault."

Tim's deep voice and warm breath against Camilla's bare skin sparked a fire within her and she sat through the entire lunch hoping no one saw the flames. Every time the heat would begin to rescind, Tim would rub his hand down her leg, brush a stray hair out of her face, or just smile, and the flames would skyrocket. She hardly participated in conversation because she couldn't focus on what everyone was discussing. Tim knew exactly what he was doing and loved every minute of it. He watched her squirm and it egged him on. If it were up to him, they would have blown off lunch and gone straight to the hotel where they'd be entangled in each other's sheer desire. Since she'd made him come, he decided to torture her. He wanted to keep her mind focused on who she had just became and her body focused on what she was going to receive later…

When lunch was over, Delisa and Sheena pulled Camilla to the side. "Cammie, are you feeling okay? You seem kind of scatterbrained."

"I am fine. I am better than I have been in a long time." Camilla tried to walk away to avoid giving to much information, but Sheena stopped her.

Sheena smiled at Delisa. "I know what is wrong with her; it's Tim. She's in love with him."

"What? That is crazy! She barely knows him."

"I don't care how long she has known him. It happened to me. Now it's happening to your sister, and no matter what you say, I believe it happened to you, too. Something about the type of women we are and the men they are. We all love hard without ceasing. When you meet the one, it doesn't take long for your hearts to connect."

Camilla didn't say a word and was glad when the men came to take their women home.

Tim and Camilla spent the rest of the evening in the hotel. The consummation of their marriage had at last sealed their vows. They were no longer two, but one. For the first time, Tim had made love to a woman he loved. He took his time loving Camilla and she let down her guard to receive all that he offered. Their lovemaking lasted well into the night, and when they woke the next morning, they continued their discovery of each other.

Delisa gathered Adrianna's toys and placed them back in her

overnight bag. Having a baby in their house awakened so many emotions which she'd thought were gone. It had been almost a month since she laid her daughter to rest. She handled it all better than anyone expected, but taking care of Adrianna brought back memories. Memories of Jalisa's birth, her rolling over, sitting up, her first tooth—all the stages of development flooded Delisa's mind and a haze of depression loomed over her. She tried to pray and ask God for strength, but the words escaped her and tears flooded her eyes. She missed Jalisa more than anyone knew, and the pain of losing her began to eat away at her heart. When the doorbell rang, Delisa drug herself to the door, stopping by the bathroom in an attempt to clean her face. She opened the door, hiding the emotional turmoil that plagued her.

She didn't realize how late in the day it was until she opened the door and the light from the sun burned her eyes. She had been hiding in the house still dressed in her night clothes, waiting for Camilla to pick up Adrianna. Delisa stood, resting her body against the door, allowing Camilla and Tim to enter. She barely had enough energy to walk back to the family room where Adrianna laid on the floor playing with a toy. Camilla and Delisa were both so caught up in their own emotional state they didn't recognize the joy or depression overcoming the other. Delisa watched as Adrianna kicked and squealed with excitement when she saw her mother and tears rolled down Delisa's face. She quickly wiped the tears away hoping no one saw, but Tim did. He saw her tears and decided not to say anything, but placed his arm on her shoulder letting her know he was there for her if she needed him. Delisa grabbed his hand letting him know she was grateful for the gesture. Tim excused himself from the room and called Jaleel. "Hey Jaleel I think you should head home. We are here picking up Adrianna and Delisa doesn't quite look like herself."

"She was up late taking care of Adrianna. She's probably just tired."

"I think it is a little more than being tired. It looks like she has been crying. She seems really weak and depressed."

"All right man, thanks for calling. I'll come check on her in a few minutes. Can you guys hang around until I get there?"

"Sure, I'll see you in a few minutes." Tim went into the kitchen and made Delisa and Camilla a cup of tea. Camilla drank her tea, still unaware that her sister was hurting. Her mind was so full of thoughts of her new husband and the life they were beginning. By the time they finished their tea, Jaleel had arrived. With one look at Delisa, he knew exactly what was bothering her. Tim quickly took his family home, allowing Jaleel to take care of his wife. Once they left, Jaleel slid next to Delisa and tried to wrap his arms around her, but her body stiffened and she pulled away from him.

"Delisa baby, talk to me. You need to talk about it."

"I'm fine. I just want to be left alone. Go back to work. I'll be all right." Delisa went up to her room, locked the door, and remained there for the rest of the day. Trying to muffle her anguish, she wailed into a pillow.

"Delisa honey, unlock the door." Jaleel banged on the door, but there was no answer. He rushed downstairs to find his key, but when he entered the room, Delisa insisted she would be fine. The more he tried, the more adamant she became. Over the next few days, her mood grew worse. With the holidays approaching, everyone expected the worst.

16

On Christmas morning, everyone woke in different homes in different locations, and in different state of minds. Christmas can bring out the fondest of memories and fill the day with smiles and laughter. It can also solidify grieving for lost loved ones with the same consuming memories. Christmas can bring a person to the highest point of joy or the lowest point of depression.

For the first time, Sheena awoke on Christmas morning in her husband's arms. She planned to spend the whole day enjoying his presence and anything that interfered with that had to go. She turned around to see if he was awake and surprisingly his eyes were wide open.

"Good morning, Mr. Matthews."

"Good morning, Mrs. Matthews." Paul kissed her forehead. He was also excited about their first Christmas together and had been waiting for her to wake so he could give her the gifts he'd purchased. Sheena had begged him all week to give them to her, arguing that she was not a child and shouldn't have to wait until Christmas morning, but Paul refused to give in to her pouting and whining. He retrieved her presents from one of the guest rooms. When he returned, Sheena was gone.

Paul searched the house for Sheena and finally found her in the garage bent over a box talking to herself. "Sheena, are you all right? Why are you in this cold garage half-naked without shoes?"

She jumped in surprise. She was hoping to make it back into the house before he noticed she was gone, but the gift she had purchased for him was not cooperating. "I came out here to get your gift." She turned around and placed a black little puppy in his arms. "I had a hard time finding a gift for you. What do you give a man who has everything and has enough money to buy himself anything he wants? Then the more I thought about it I realized I could get you something you have wanted your whole life, a dog."

Paul had always wanted a dog, but his parents always told him they couldn't afford to take care of one. He would play with the stray dogs in the neighborhood. After his mom died, he brought one of the strays home, hid it in his room, and fed him scraps from dinner for three days before his dad realized there was a dog in the house. That was when the horrible beatings started. His dad had spanked him before, but that night he beat Paul hard and long until the skin on his bottom split.

Paul grabbed his puppy with excitement. He was surprised at Sheena's choice of dog. She didn't pick a cute, small dog, but gave him a black lab. He thought if they ever got a dog she would want something like a dachshund. "I can't believe you bought me a dog."

"Do you like it?"

"Of course I do. There is only one thing I wanted more than a dog."

"Really, what is that?"

Paul smiled that sexy smile that always melted Sheena's heart and caused her to give in to his every desire. "I want a baby. Have you asked the doctor why it is taking so long?"

"Paul, it has only been a few weeks. We have to give the birth control a chance to get out my system. There is nothing I want more than to have your baby, but we have to be patient. So, enjoy your puppy for right now."

"Baby, I'm sorry. I love the puppy. I don't want you to think I don't like it. You know how much I've wanted a dog."

"You don't have to apologize. I know you love the puppy, and I also know how much you want a baby." Sheena leaned in to kiss Paul, but was licked on her cheek by the puppy instead.

Paul laughed. "It looks like he loves you as much as I do."

"Do you know what you are going to name him?"

"When I was a kid, I said if I ever had a dog I would name him Roscoe. Roscoe it is." Paul loved his wife. She always gave him her undivided attention and he knew she was dying to open her Christmas presents. "Sheena baby, your gifts are on our bed. Go ahead and open them while I bring in Roscoe's things."

Sheena took off running to their room while Paul brought in feeding bowls, dog food, leashes, a travel cage, a doggy bed, shampoos, and chewing toys. Sheena had thought of everything. Paul had just finished bringing everything in and was headed upstairs with Roscoe following behind him when he heard Sheena screaming. Paul laughed, knowing exactly what was going on. He bought Sheena three designer handbags with matching shoes. Paul walked into the room and Sheena jumped all over him. She scared poor Roscoe so bad that he ran back downstairs and stood at the bottom trying to bark.

"Thank you, thank you, thank you," Sheena squealed as she planted kisses all over Paul's face. "I love them! They are beautiful. I already know what outfits I'm going to wear with them."

"I knew you would love them. I'm just grateful for an opportunity to spend some money on you. I still don't understand why you don't let me buy you things." While they dated, Paul had tried to shower her with expensive gifts, but she would never accept them. Even during the few months they had been married, she wouldn't allow him to buy her things.

"I just don't want you to think I married you for your money."

"You keep telling me that and I still don't understand why you think I would feel that way. You knew the first day we met that I was pretty well off and I had to practically force you to date me. Even then, you wouldn't accept the jewelry and things I tried to impress you with. Only the Lord knows the next time you are going to allow me to give you something, so I went a little overboard. You have another gift coming, but I couldn't hide it here. We have some guests coming for breakfast and they will bring it with them. So go get dressed before they get here."

"I don't want any guests. I want to get back in the bed and make love all day until it is time for dinner."

"Sounds pretty tempting." Paul picked Sheena up and wrapped her legs around his waist. "How about I make love to you right now and we can do the all-day thing tomorrow."

Paul crawled onto the bed with Sheena's legs still wrapped around him, laid her on the bed, and was just about to remove what little clothing she had on when the doorbell rang. They both groaned. Paul hoped it was her gift and ran off to answer the door. Roscoe sat patiently at the door waiting.

Jaleel woke up Christmas morning to find Delisa sitting alone inside Jalisa's room. She had surrounded herself with all of Jalisa's favorite toys. It had been a month since Jalisa passed away, and this was the first time Delisa had come into her room. She had decorated the room to make her daughter feel like a princess. Jalisa had every toy and doll a little girl could want and had treated every doll like it was special. She'd take them out of the box and comb their hair while talking to them then place them back in the box. They always thought it strange how a four year old could be so compassionate toward her dolls. Delisa would often help comb the dolls' hair, but Jalisa would only let her touch certain dolls. Then, she would give instructions on how she wanted it done. They would spend hours playing dolls.

Jaleel watched his wife take each doll out of the box and comb the hair. Silent tears slowly rolled down her cheeks and met beneath her chin. He wished there was something he could do to take away her pain, but every time he tried to comfort her, she would push him away. He prayed from a distance, hoping that giving her space to grieve would help. He dealt with his own grief by keeping busy. Every time he thought about Jalisa, he would find something to occupy his mind. He would read a book, go jogging, pray, or do some work on the computer. He took the computer apart, put it back together, searched for viruses, upgraded software, uninstalled unused programs, downloaded music, and made CDs. He did all he could to keep from slipping into the same kind of depression his wife was dealing with.

Jaleel left Delisa alone in Jalisa's room while he took a shower and dressed for the day. When he returned to the room, Delisa was asleep on the floor, still surrounded by the dolls. He picked her up to carry her to their bed, but as he lifted her, she woke up. He saw the fury that came into her eyes and he put her down.

"Jaleel, what are you doing?" She huffed and her nostrils flared.

"I just thought you would be more comfortable sleeping in bed." He was confused and didn't understand why she was angry.

"I want to be in here where I can remember my little girl. It may be easy for you to forget her, but it is not that easy for me. I guess since she wasn't your real daughter you don't care." Delisa regretted the words as they came out of her mouth, but she said them and there was no taking it back. She watched as tears filled Jaleel's eyes and he backed away from her, leaving her standing alone in their daughter's room. She stood in silence until she heard the front door open and slam shut then she fell to her knees and cried uncontrollably.

Jaleel, although not dressed for it, ran in an attempt to release his anger and grief. Not once had he thought about not being Jalisa's father. He was there when she was born and had raised her. He loved her, missed her, and hated ever finding out he was not her biological father, but he refused to focus on the negative, choosing rather to put all his energy into other things. Jaleel ran hard and when he got tired, he pushed himself even further. He ran farther than he ever had and still his mind was in turmoil. Before he realized how far he had run, he was two blocks from Paul and Sheena's house. He pushed himself the last two blocks rang, the doorbell, and then collapsed on the porch.

Paul stood with Roscoe by his side. He looked through the peephole, and when he didn't see anyone, he turned to go back upstairs and continue making love to his wife, but something told him to open the door. He opened the door and saw Jaleel kneeling on the porch, his chest was heaving as he labored to catch his breath. His face and clothes were drenched with a mixture of sweat and tears. Paul helped him to his feet and took him to the kitchen to get some water. Sitting in silence, Jaleel rested his face in his hands, and Paul sat waiting patiently for Jaleel to explain what was going on.

Finally catching his breath, Jaleel spoke slowly and softly. "I have tried to be there for Delisa and help her get through this, but she pushes me away. I love her and I know she is hurting. It hurts me to see her like this and not be able to comfort her. But, I don't think I can take it anymore." Jaleel let his tears flow freely. He normally prided himself on being a strong man and didn't want anyone seeing him cry. He cried when Jalisa passed, but had kept every emotion bottled up since the funeral. He felt a hand slide across his shoulder and turned to see Sheena standing behind him with fear on her face.

"Jaleel, is everything okay? Is Delisa all right?" Sheena's heart ached for Jaleel.

"She is at home torturing herself, going through Jalisa's things."

"And you left her alone?" Sheena's expression turned to one of anger and she turned to leave the kitchen to go to Delisa's house, but the sharp demanding tone of Paul's voice stopped her.

"Sheena, sit down." Paul had rarely taken that tone with his wife, but in the short time they had been together, he learned that when it came to the well-being of her family she reacted before she got the facts.

"Paul, she should not be alone right now." Paul gave her a stern look and Sheena sat down.

Jaleel continued explaining what had happened. He even explained how he had been dealing with his own grief. When he mentioned how Delisa threw him not being Jalisa's father in his face, Sheena closed her eyes and shook her head. She knew her cousin had to be hurting badly to be so hateful.

"So, what did you do after she accused you of not caring?"

"I left, started running, and kept running until I got here."

Paul whistled, not fully believing how far Jaleel had run. "You ran from your house to here?" You could look at Jaleel and tell that he was in excellent physical condition, but they lived over ten miles apart with lots

133

of hills. "Jaleel, I know you are hurting and you have handled this whole situation better than I would, but you know Delisa loves you. She is just hurting. When you are angry and hurting, you say things you don't mean. She is just trying to make sense of everything. All I can say is she needs you. You guys need each other more now than you ever have. Don't let her push you away."

Sheena began fixing breakfast while Paul and Jaleel continued their conversation. She brought them each a cup of coffee and smiled with pride at her husband. She was surprised at how much he had grown spiritually over the past few months. She had always been the spiritual rock of the family. When she was going through, she never had anyone to turn to for advice. Now, she had Paul to support her with prayer and encouragement and had no problem stepping back and letting him lead her. She listened as Paul quoted scripture after scripture, and before long, he and Jaleel erupted in praise. Sheena watched in amazement and almost burnt the bacon getting caught up in her own praise. She marveled at the power of God and how He could take a man distraught with grief and then rejuvenate him with joy.

The doorbell rang and Paul, assuming it was Sheena's Christmas present, opted to answer it instead of allowing Sheena to get it. Paul returned to the kitchen and, to everyone's surprise, Delisa was with him. She had driven around their neighborhood looking for Jaleel and when she couldn't find him she hoped he had gone to Sheena's. She walked into the kitchen with barely enough strength to stand. Her appearance was an obvious contrast to the atmosphere of praise that was in the kitchen. Her hair was disheveled, eyes red from crying, and her pale skin made her frame look fragile.

Jaleel grabbed her and held her tight speaking what everyone else saw. "Baby, you have to snap out of this. The devil is trying to consume you with grief... Don't let him win."

Slowly, Delisa lifted her arms and wrapped them around Jaleel's waist which was more than she had done all week. She relaxed in his embrace and Jaleel warred in the spirit for his wife, praying that she found the strength to push pass this rough spot and live again. She went limp in his arms, and he placed her in a chair and knelt in front of her continuing his prayer.

"Jaleel…" Delisa's voice was raspy from hours of crying. "Why would God bless us with a child only to take her away a few short years later?"

"Baby, I don't know, and it is not my job to try to figure out why God does what He does. I am just going to serve Him and trust that He has everything under control. The more we focus on *why,* the angrier we will become, because we will never be able to figure out why." Jaleel lifted her head to look in her eyes. "Just let Him, and me, love you through this."

"Jaleel, why don't you take her to one of the guest rooms? I'll bring you guys some food and some sweats so you guys can shower. Please stay as long as you need."

Jaleel carried Delisa to the guest room while Sheena continued cooking breakfast, and Paul ran to answer the door.

"Hey, little brother, I thought I was going to have to hunt you down. What took you so long?" Paul overlooked the heated kiss he caught Tim and Camilla in when he opened the door, but he was worried his brother was headed down the wrong path. No matter how much Tim tried to convince him that he and Camilla weren't sinning, Paul knew it was just a matter of time before their desire for each other overrode good sense.

"I had to take care of some things before leaving the house, but we are here now and Sheena's gift is here safe and sound."

"Good. Thanks for helping me, and you are actually here on time. Delisa and Jaleel are here. Things got pretty bad between them this morning, but God is working it out…" Paul was getting ready to explain to Camilla when he heard Sheena heading toward the door.

"Paul, who's that at the door? The food is getting cold." Realizing it was Tim and Camilla, Sheena's disposition brightened. "Come in you guys. Don't stand out here in the cold."

"They will in a minute. They came to bring your gift." Paul dangled a set of keys in Sheena's face.

"What are these for?" Sheena grabbed the keys and when she noticed the BMW symbol she dropped the keys on the ground. "Paul, you can't buy me a car."

Paul rolled his eyes. "I can and I did." He picked the keys up and placed them in her hand.

"My car is fine. I don't need another one, and it's paid for. I don't want to burden you with another bill."

"This car is paid for, too, and does it look like I am burdened with bills? I hid the keys to your old car. If you plan on going anywhere, you have to drive this. So, take the keys and go check out your new car."

Camilla couldn't believe Sheena didn't want the car. "Sheena stop being silly and…" Tim nudged her and told her to stay out of it before she could finish her sentence.

Sheena laughed at Camilla's facial expression. "Girl, get over it. Paul is a bossy bully, too. I thought it was because he was a lawyer, but now I see it runs in the family." Sheena kissed Paul's cheek. "But they only do it when they are looking out for you." Sheena grabbed Paul's hand and went to check out her new car.

As they walked away, Camilla punched Tim in the arm. "Tim, don't treat me like that. I don't like being dismissed, and I don't like being bossed around."

"Camilla, I was not bossing you around. I just asked you to stay out of it."

"No, you didn't ask me. You told me and you didn't even look at me. You just barked out a command."

"You are really overreacting." Camilla walked into the house and slammed the door in his face, leaving him standing on the porch still carrying Adrianna.

Tim marched into the house ready to explode with anger. "Camilla, why are you getting so worked up over something so simple?"

"Why can't you respect how I feel and apologize? My ex used to order me around and manipulated me into staying with him."

"I am not your ex. I am your husband. You were getting ready to say something you shouldn't have and I stopped you. I hope you would do the same for me, and if you are waiting for me to apologize, you are going to be waiting for a long time, because I never apologize unless I am wrong." Tim was done arguing with her. It was their first argument and he didn't like it one bit. He grabbed her and kissed her before she could protest.

Camilla resisted at first, but eventually she opened for him and accepted his entire kiss. "Tim, you hurt my feelings."

"Baby, I was not trying to hurt you. I'm sorry. You have to realize you are dealing with a real man now. I am going to lead us to what is right. Sometimes you may not like it, but it is only to benefit us."

"I am sorry for being such a brat." Camilla slid her hand up Tim's chest and around his neck pulling him down to meet her lips. She pressed her body against him and a low moan rolled out of his mouth. He adjusted Adrianna in his arms and was ready to capture Camilla's mouth when Paul and Sheena walked in.

"You guys need to be careful." Sheena walked past them to prepare plates for everyone to eat. "You keep telling us that you are not sinning, but kisses like that eventually lead to the bedroom."

"Sheena, I know you are concerned, but I am a grown woman…"

"Camilla, don't go there with me. I have never treated you like a child. I am concerned that all of the progress you have made with the Lord is going to be wasted. You guys are already living together, which I am totally against. I don't want to see you guys mess up."

"Please just trust us. We are not sinning. We are both trying to build a relationship with the Lord. That is all you need to know."

Sheena relented and dropped the subject. She took food and clothes to Jaleel and Delisa, fed Roscoe, and then joined the others at the table. Everyone ate silently until Adrianna's agitated crying broke the tension. They were all relieved that there was something else to focus on besides the previous conversation.

Camilla left the table to change Adrianna's diaper and Tim followed closely behind her, waiting until they were alone to speak.

"Baby, I don't know how much longer we can keep this from them. I don't think they will be upset. They are more upset about us living together than I think they will be about us being married."

"It's about more than them being upset. They have always tried to control me, telling me what to wear, how to act, how to raise my daughter, and I don't want them telling me what kind of wife I should be."

"Sometimes they do that out of love. They don't want you to make the same mistakes they did. Paul does it to me all the time, and I'm thirty years old. He is probably going to call me tomorrow and we're going to have the same conversation you and Sheena had."

"Honey, please don't tell him. Let me enjoy the peace for a few more weeks, and then we can come clean."

"All right, I won't say anything, but I know they are going to be more upset that we kept this from them than they will about everything else."

They finished changing Adrianna, made her a bottle, and then returned to their breakfast. The mood at the table was a little lighter. Adrianna became the center of attention. Everyone watched as she drank her bottle then laughed at how fast she had finished. She drank every last drop and whined when she was done.

"I've been trying to get her to eat baby food, but she doesn't seem to like it." Camilla passed Adrianna to Tim to search the diaper bag for the jar of carrots she packed. "If she is still hungry, these carrots are the only thing she is going to get." Camilla shoveled a spoonful of carrots in to Adrianna's mouth, they came right back out, and ran down her chin. Camilla tried several times, but Adrianna kept spitting the food right back out. "I guess she doesn't like it."

"It's not that she doesn't like it." Delisa's raspy voice caught everyone by surprise. "She just doesn't know how to use the spoon yet. She was born with the instinct to suck, but the spoon is something she has to learn. Do you mind if I try?"

Camilla got up to let her sister sit down. The sight of Delisa looking so weak and fragile brought tears to Camilla's eyes. She hadn't seen her sister in a week and didn't realize the extent of the depression that was plaguing her. Under normal circumstances, Camilla would have told Delisa no and to stop being so bossy, but sympathy for her sister took over and she stepped aside.

Delisa scooped a little bit of baby food on the spoon and placed the spoon on Adrianna's bottom lip. Adrianna sucked it right off. "The trick is to not put so much food on the spoon. Her little mouth can only take so much, just barely put the spoon in her mouth, and let her suck the food off." For the first time in days, Delisa smiled as she watched her niece. "See, she likes it. We just have to help her get it in there." Delisa stepped away to allow Camilla to finish feeding Adrianna. She followed everything her sister told her and was able to feed Adrianna the whole jar of carrots with very little mess. Camilla hugged her sister, thanking her for the advice. She regretted being so selfishly caught up in her own life that she hadn't taken the time to check on her sister.

Later that day, they all joined each other again for dinner, exchanging gifts and wishing each other a merry Christmas. Delisa's mood had picked up some, but it was obvious she still wasn't herself; however, she did manage to tell Camilla and Tim to be careful several times. Camilla let it slide because of Delisa's mental and physical condition, but her anger was noticed by everyone. Tim praised her for letting it go and not making a scene. The night ended early. Everyone was exhausted from their long emotional day. Each couple retreated home and went straight to bed. They brought in New Year's Day as a family, praying that the pain of the year past would be gone and that joy would be tripled. Jaleel, Paul, and Tim formed a prayer team and vowed to meet once a week to pray for their families. They confided in each other, sharing their fears and their goals. They formed a bond that would stand the test of time. They were brutally honest with each other and checked each other when they got out of line. They tried to talk about Tim and Camilla living together, but it was a sensitive subject that Tim refused to talk about. The new year brought promises of change which everyone readily accepted.

17

It was late January when Tim finally moved into his office building. He had finally convinced the other law firms to hire his company to manage their finances. He paid the lease for six months and bought brand new furniture for each room. Camilla spent long nights at his office decorating, making sure everything was perfect. She went to his office directly after work and worked there until she could barely keep her eyes open. Some nights she was even too tired to pick Adrianna up from her parents. She spent most of her time on Tim's office and the reception area; she wanted it to look professional, but not stuffy.

Tim left for the office early, but went back home to retrieve the office supplies he left behind. He was surprised to see Camilla still home. She didn't go to work the day before because she was not feeling well, but was feeling much better last night.

"Camilla." He rubbed her back to wake her up. "I thought you were going to work today."

"I am going to work. I wanted to take another day off, but when I called in to see if I could, they said that since I was still in my probationary period they would fire me if I didn't show up today."

"Well honey, I hate to be the one to break it to you, but it is almost eleven o'clock."

Camilla gasped and jumped up to put her clothes on, but was overcome with nausea and had to run to the bathroom before she ruined the carpet.

Tim helped her back in bed. "Don't worry about work. If they fire you, we will deal with it. You are staying in bed today. If you are not feeling better within the next couple of days, I am taking you to the doctor." He made sure she was comfortable then grabbed the things he came home to get. "Baby, call me if you start to feel worse and I will cancel the rest of my appointments."

"That isn't necessary. I probably have a stomach virus. It should pass in a day or so. You take care of business and I will see you this evening. Sheena dropped Adrianna off at daycare. Will you be off in time to pick her up?"

"Yeah, I will pick her up. You get some rest." Tim went back to his office, hating to leave her while she was feeling sick, but he had appointments with potential clients and didn't want them to have a bad first impression of his company.

Tim returned home later that evening to find Camilla still in bed sleeping. He could not tolerate seeing her so miserable and decided to take her to the urgent care clinic. After convincing Camilla she needed to see a doctor, he dropped Adrianna off with Sheena since her house was on the way.

Camilla started feeling better as they sat in the waiting room. The doctor ordered lots of lab work and they waited for the results. "Tim, let's go home. We have been sitting here for an hour. I feel better and we can call for the lab results."

"No, I won't be able to work tomorrow. I have to know that you are okay." He wrapped his arm around her and pulled her close.

"Mr. and Mrs. Matthews?" The doctor stepped up to them. "I have your results. Do you want the good news or the great news?"

"Let's start with the good news." Tim kissed the crown of Camilla's head and hoped for the best.

"The good news is all of your labs look fine there are no infections or anything to be concerned about."

"Then why am I vomiting so much?"

"Well that leads me to the great news. You're pregnant." The

142

doctor saw her facial expression and thought maybe his news wasn't so great. "I brought you some prenatal vitamins and a list of doctors who are associated with this hospital."

Camilla's mouth hung open as she watched the doctor walk away. She felt like such an idiot for not taking birth control. She'd been so caught up in their relationship, she hadn't thought about birth control. They had never discussed having children and she didn't know how Tim was going to respond. She had several pregnancy scares in the past, and the men always got upset. Immediately, they would demand she get an abortion—even before she was one hundred percent sure. "Tim, I am so sorry," was all she could mutter as she ran out to the parking lot.

The ride home was long and quiet. Both were afraid to speak and afraid to hear what the other had to say. They walked into their apartment, uncertain of how this was going to affect their relationship and the tension almost brought Camilla to tears. They stood on opposite sides of the room watching and waiting for each other to speak.

"Tim, I am such an idiot. I should have been on birth control. Please don't be upset. We can work through this. I am so sorry."

"Camilla, calm down. I knew you weren't on birth control. Did I complain? I wanted you to get pregnant. The timing is not great..." Tim chose his words carefully. "I know you just had a baby and this is probably the last thing you wanted, but I am excited. Our whole relationship has moved really fast. I know it probably scares you, but I am not going anywhere. I want this baby and many more."

"I am so relieved you feel that way. I thought you were going to come in here and pack your bags. I don't know why I was thinking like that. You have proven yourself to be a man I can depend on. I know you would never leave me." Camilla closed the distance between them. "I want to have your baby... The *many more* we can discuss later, but I want this baby more than anything."

"That's good. There is one problem though. Your family is going to hate me if we don't tell them that we are married. There is only so long you can hide a pregnancy."

143

Camilla bit her lip in deep thought. She knew Tim was right and the sooner they told the truth the better it would be for everyone. "You're right. If I had known I was going to get pregnant so fast I would have told them a long time ago. So, how do you want to do this?"

"What do you mean how do I want to do it? I am keeping my mouth shut and letting you do all the talking."

"You are just going to leave me hanging like that? Please Tim, help me tell them."

Tim laughed. "All right, since it was your idea to keep our marriage a secret, you tell them we are married, and I will tell them we are having a baby."

"No, that is not fair. I have to get everybody all upset then you get to make everybody happy about a baby."

"So you want everyone to be all upset and mad at me?"

"No, let's come up with a way to tell them and minimize the shock. Maybe we could send everybody letters with a copy of our marriage license." Camilla laughed at the thought of Delisa and her parents beating down her door after reading the letter. Tim joined her laughter, lifting her off her feet, and spinning around the room.

"You know what baby? I am so excited to finally be able to love you in public without our family thinking I'm a bad person that I will tell everyone. But first, I want to celebrate our baby." Tim laid her on the sofa and started removing her clothes.

"It's all of this celebrating that got us in this situation."

Tim laughed but continued his pursuit, taking his time to make sure she received all she needed before releasing his own satisfaction. He continued to lay on top of her, playing in her hair as she drifted off to sleep. When her eyes closed, he kissed her, waking her up again. Each time she smiled, enjoying his playfulness. Tim carried her to their room, so they could be comfortable as they slept. Briefly Tim stared at her, wanting to make love to her again, but decided to let her rest. His life had changed so much since he met her. He never imagined being a husband or a father, but since he'd met her he wanted nothing more. In just a few months she had become the center of his world, and he finally realized how empty his life used to be.

Delisa and Jaleel sat in the waiting room at the therapist office. Delisa's depression wasn't any better, and he finally convinced her she needed to see someone. There were plenty of capable therapists in the hospital where he worked who would've helped him for free because of the many times he saved them by fixing their computers. But, he also wanted a therapist who was Christian. It was a long process met with much opposition; most doctors felt that religious beliefs had nothing to do with their skill and refused to tell him. But he finally found one who was proud to proclaim she was a Christian. When dealing with clients who were Christians, she incorporated prayer and the bible into therapy sessions.

Dr. McCall stepped out of her office and invited Delisa in. Jaleel followed behind her, but the doctor stopped him. "She has to do this on her own. When there is someone else in the room some patients aren't completely truthful or will not be as open as they would if they were alone."

Jaleel looked the doctor up and down, then thought for a moment. "I understand," was all he could say. He wanted to argue with her and demand she let him in, but in the end, all he wanted was for Delisa to get better. If being in the room hindered the process, he would set his ego aside and allow the doctor to do her job.

Delisa walked into Dr. McCall's office looking around. The office didn't look at all how she had imagined. The African art on the walls accentuated the contemporary furniture and the family pictures on the desk helped Delisa relax. Knowing that the doctor was both a mother and a Christian made her feel more comfortable with the whole situation. Delisa headed for the sofa where she assumed her session would take place. That is where they'd taken place in all the movies she had seen. She was just about to sit down when Dr. McCall stopped her.

"You are more than welcome to sit over here." The doctor was sitting behind her desk pointing to the chairs in front of her. She shook Delisa's hand as she sat down. "Your husband tells me that you are a Christian, so I would like to begin our sessions with prayer. I want you to pray out loud and pray for whatever is on your heart."

Taking a deep breath, Delisa slowly began to pray. It had been weeks since she prayed and momentarily found herself at a loss for words.

"Dear Heavenly Father, I thank you for being my savior. I thank you for loving me and thank you for being with me even when I feel alone. I thank you because the power of life and death is in your hands. I may not understand your purpose, but I have to trust that you know what is best. I ask that you help my family, especially my sister, who seems to have gotten herself into a terrible sinful situation; give her a way of escape. I ask that you mend our relationship and give us a better understanding of each other. Remove all of the hatred she has toward me and let her see how much I love her. Bless Sheena and Paul in their efforts to conceive a child; you are the giver of life."

Once again, Delisa's emotions spun out of control.

Dr. McCall was taking notes on what Delisa prayed for, her emotion, and tone, also noting that she hadn't prayed for herself. "Delisa what do you think about life and death?"

"Life is a blessing and death is something we all have to experience. God controls the longevity of life and the time of death."

"How does that make you feel?"

"I try to believe that God knows what's best and that He gives us enough time to do what we were created to do, but…" Delisa paused, and for the first time, made eye contact with Dr. McCall hoping she had an answer. "How do you explain the death of a child who was not given enough time to really live?"

Delisa stared at the doctor hoping for an answer, but what she got instead was more questions. The questions continued throughout the remainder of the session and when her hour was up Delisa left feeling more confused and angry about God taking Jalisa from her. She was so

146

upset that she brushed pass Jaleel in the waiting room without even speaking. By the time he caught up to her, she was getting into the elevator. He watched as she paced around the elevator. When the doors opened, she rushed out almost knocking someone over who was waiting to take the elevator. Jaleel apologized for her rudeness and quickly caught up to her, abruptly halting her frenzied pace.

"Delisa what is wrong? You almost knocked that lady over." He watched as her chest heaved and her eye swelled with tears.

"This is a waste of time. She can't help me! All she did was ask questions. She didn't have any answers."

"Honey, she is not supposed to answer your questions. She is going to help you work through your grief. Please just give her a chance to help you."

"No, and I don't want to discuss it anymore." Delisa stomped off to the car.

Jaleel rolled his eyes as he slowly walked behind her. He needed relief from her depression and mood swings before he lost his mind. He didn't know which he preferred: her not getting out of bed crying all day, or her yelling at him arguing over simple stuff. He was trying to be there for her, but his patience was wearing thin. Jaleel no longer argued back, he just let her rant and rave while waiting for the next emotion. He prayed and prayed, but nothing seemed to change. He wanted the old Delisa back—the one whose fire and passion brought him to his knees, the one who was full of life and loved the Lord, and who'd never questioning His authority. He drove Delisa home in silence vowing to do whatever it took to get her back to herself.

He sat quietly in their bedroom as she undressed, took a shower, and hopped in bed throwing the covers over her head. Seeing her get in bed naked confirmed what he needed to do. Jaleel showered and joined her in bed moving quickly before she could fight him off. He felt awkward being so aggressive with his wife, but it had to be done. He grabbed both her arms pinning them above her head and restricted her legs with his all in one quick smooth movement.

"Jaleel, what are you doing? Get off of me!"

He responded with kisses to her neck and breasts. Her body tensed as she struggled beneath him. Tears filled his eyes as she pleaded for him to stop. He covered her pleading lips with his, hoping she would return his kiss, but she resisted. He caressed her body doing all he could to arouse her. When he felt her wet lips and warm breath on his ear, he knew he had her where he wanted her. He let go of her arms and legs, and she eagerly opened to receive him.

Her nails dug into his back as her body shuddered in ecstasy. She bit his shoulder, trying to muffle her cries of pleasure. The pain of passion she inflicted egged him on. It was the middle of the day, but they made love like it was late at night, exhausting each other until they had no choice but to sleep.

A few hours later, Delisa woke up feeling more relaxed than she had in a long time. She reached for Jaleel and he was gone. Putting on her robe, she searched around the house for him. She found him in the kitchen with no clothes on making a sandwich. "Jaleel, what are you doing? That is not sanitary," Delisa chuckled.

Her voice startled him, but hearing her laugh was music to his ears. He smiled at her as she laughed at him. "Do you want me to make you a sandwich?"

Delisa started laughing even harder. "No, I prefer my cooks to have clothes on." She admired his gorgeous body as she stepped close to him. "Give me this sandwich. I will make you some real food while you go put some clothes."

"You keep looking at me like that and I am going to lay you across the table for round two."

"You mean round four." She smacked his butt as he walked away.

By the time he returned, Delisa had whipped up a shrimp salad with garlic bread. Jaleel tore into it, not wasting a crumb. Delisa finished her food and looked at Jaleel with crossed eyes. He tried to figure out what was on her mind, but her expression was not forth telling.

"Delisa, what's wrong?" He reached out and grabbed her hand

hoping that her mood wasn't shifting. He was enjoying the playful side of her and didn't want it to end.

"I was just thinking..." She leaned in close enough for her lips to brush his ear when she talked. "What would you have done if I didn't give in to you? Were you really so confident in your skills that you knew I would give in?"

The softness in her voice sent chills down his spine. "Actually, I hadn't even thought it through that far. I knew I wanted you and you needed me. That was motivation enough. You did have me worried for a second. I felt like I was assaulting my wife, but I felt you soften. I knew I had you then."

"Wow, you sound really arrogant, but I will let it slide. I'm sorry that you felt you had to be so aggressive in order to make love to me. I know I have been a handful lately, and you have been great. I promise to put more effort into getting better. I will not go to therapy, but I will go to church. I know God is greater than anything I am dealing with, and He will help me."

"Okay, we will not go back to the therapist only if you promise to come to me for therapy at least three times a week." Jaleel held her to every word she said and patiently waited for the Lord to heal her mind.

18

Sunday morning came and with it a late winter storm. The rain fell in a melodious rhythm on the roof. Sheena laid in bed watching the rain trickle down her window. She had been laying there for some time and couldn't muster up enough strength to get out of bed. Rainy weather always had that effect on her, but she rarely had the opportunity to stay in bed all day. Today was no exception. Forcing herself to get up, Sheena tiptoed to the shower trying not to wake Paul. She let the warm water from the shower gush on top of her head and run down her body.

The sound of the water filled her ears and she didn't hear Paul step into the shower behind her. He stood there admiring her beauty. Her beautiful black hair flowed down her back as water trickled down her flawless skin enhancing every curve. He silently wished she'd turn around so he could taken in the fullness of her beauty, but when his wish was granted it was not the response he expected. Sheena turned around and opened her eyes. The sight of someone standing behind her frightened her. She let out an earsplitting scream and ripped down the shower curtain trying to get away. Paul had to grab her by the waist to keep her from stumbling out of the bath tub onto the floor.

Sheena playfully slapped him across the chest, "What are you doing in here? You almost scared me to death." Her heart was still racing. She could not believe he snuck up on her. "I thought you were still sleep."

"I was, until you got out the bed. I was going to let you shower alone until I looked at the clock and saw how late it was. I figured I better join you or we would be late for church." Paul grabbed her soap and washed her body and she did the same for him. It took all their strength to get out of the shower and get dressed. They knew that one kiss or touch would cause them to skip service.

They arrived to the church late and had to pray in the car to get their minds in the right place. By the time they walked in, the church was already having a high time in the Lord. The praises were going forth. They took their seats in the back and joined in.

Sheena looked around and saw her family praising God. Tim and Camilla were on the left side standing together with their hands lifted. Delisa and Jaleel were four rows in front of Sheena doing the same. Sheena's heart overflowed with joy. After all they had been through in the past few months, it was good to see that everyone still had a praise for God. Delisa's praise turned to a wail; Sheena rushed to her side. It wasn't long before Camilla joined her. They pulled Delisa to the altar and she fell to the floor worshipping and crying out to God. The women kneeled beside her, praising and praying together. Delisa released all the anger she'd felt toward God and He comforted her mourning heart.

Pastor Hawkins sermon seemed to be sent from God just for Delisa and Jaleel. "Sometimes what you have lost seems greater than what you have left. The weight of what you have lost makes it hard to breathe. Sometimes it is so hard you want to just stop." He paused and looked around the congregation, "We don't want to admit it, but depression and suicide are in the church. If we took a survey, I'm sure we would find a least one person on each row who has entertained the thought of suicide. We may even find a few who have attempted to take their own life." The pastor spoke with power, delivering God's word to a hurting people. He took his time speaking with clarity to make sure everyone got an understanding. "Some have lost loved ones, friendships, marriages, or even jobs. We spend so much time focusing on why God did it that we get angry and upset with God because we don't understand what He is doing. But sometimes it is not for us to understand. The Word of God says that His ways are not our ways and his thoughts are not our thoughts." Delisa cried through the entire sermon. Jaleel tried to be strong and choke back his tears, but his attempts were unsuccessful. With his closing remarks, Pastor Hawkins grabbed their hands, leading them to the altar. "The trying of our faith worketh patience. Let patience have her perfect work, that ye may be perfect and entire wanting nothing and after you have been tried in the fire you shall come forth as pure gold." Pastor Hawkins prayed ministering to Jaleel, Delisa, and others that joined them at the altar.

Paul had planned to take Sheena home immediately after service to finish what they had started, but after the benediction all he could think of was his family. He invited them over and ordered takeout. Jaleel and Delisa pulled up to the house right behind Paul and Sheena. They expected Tim and Camilla to show up right away, but they didn't. Thirty minutes had gone by, the food had arrived, and still no Tim or Camilla. They decided to eat without them figuring Camilla probably had to run home and change Adrianna.

They were just getting into their meal when Paul's cell phone rang. Paul answered the phone on speaker. "What's up, Tim? You could not grace us with your presence for lunch?"

"We were on our way there and some fool ran the red light. Camilla is banged up pretty bad, and I am freaking out. The car hit us on Camilla's side. She was in so much pain when I pulled her out of the car. I really need you guys right now. They took Camilla to get a CAT scan. She has no one with her because I am with Adrianna."

"Oh my God, Tim! Is Adrianna okay?" Delisa picked up Paul's phone and yelled in to the receiver.

"She's crying a lot and the doctors are afraid she may have some internal bleeding, so they are running all kinds of tests and taking X-rays. Please hurry and get here." They hung up the phone and everyone grabbed shoes, coats, purses, and rushed out of the door.

The ride to the hospital was quiet as everyone remembered the fate that awaited them the last time they were at the hospital. Paul wondered how much more one family could take. During the short time he and Sheena had been married, family relationships had been on the line, marriages were in jeopardy of failing, a loved one had been lost, and now this. He drove his car as fast as he could, praying for both safety and to not get a ticket.

Delisa sat in the back seat practically holding her breath. She could not bear the thought of losing someone else she loved. Her relationship with her sister was rocky, but she loved her and would never want anything bad to happen to her. Her love for her sister was the reason their relationship was shaky. She wanted Camilla to be happy, but the choices she made always brought heartache. Now it seemed liked she was headed down that same road with Tim. Camilla always gave her all to men, moving in with them, having these serious relationships which had no foundation. Subsequently, things always ended with her heart broken. Tim seemed like a great guy with genuine feelings for Camilla, but Delisa questioned his motives for moving in with her so soon.

Walking into the ER, Delisa didn't know what to expect. She prayed that her sister and niece would pull through. "Hi, we are here to see Camilla Walker. I believe she came in an ambulance from a car accident." They all watched as the nurse searched the computer for Camilla's name.

"I am sorry, we do not have a Camilla Walker checked in. We do have an Adrianna Walker."

"That's her daughter, so Camilla should be here too."

"I'm sorry. Adrianna is the only Walker we have checked in. Let me go get her father."

They sat in the waiting area feeling a little confused and frustrated. Why would Tim say they were at the same hospital if they weren't and why would the ambulance take them to separate hospitals? They tried to come up with an explanation, but came up with nothing. Almost an hour went by and no one had come out or said anything to them. Delisa had begun to pace the room and was ready to complain to the nurse when she saw Tim enter the waiting room with Adrianna. Adrianna was resting her head on Tim's chest as she sucked on her pacifier. She had big tears in her eyes as she looked around. When she recognized the familiar faces, her head popped up. She spit out her pacifier trying to talk as if giving her account of all the events that took place. Delisa laughed and cried relieved that her niece was okay.

"Tim, where is Camilla? The nurse said the only Walker they had checked in was Adrianna."

Tim's head dropped and he sank to his seat. He looked around at all the curious expressions staring back at him. "Camilla is here," he wanted to lie and tell them maybe someone typed her name wrong, but he knew lies were tangled webs. He didn't want to get caught in one. "It's just that... Her last name is not Walker." He held his breath as he waited for his words to sink in.

Sheena was the first one to figure it out and chuckled at the revelation, "So why don't you tell us what her last name is." She placed her hands on her hips and watched as Tim squirmed trying to explain himself.

"Well, just like you and Delisa have your husbands' last names, Camilla has her husband's last name."

Delisa gasped and was getting ready to tell Tim off, but Sheena cut in. "Just so we are clear, who would that husband be?" Sheena was enjoying this too much and Paul had to elbow her to get her to stop laughing.

"Well, little sister just so we are clear..." Tim stood, placing one hand on Sheena's shoulder and the other on Paul. "That husband would be me, and if you don't mind watching my daughter, I have to get back to my wife." Tim rushed off hoping that by the time he returned the shock and anger would have worn off and maybe they would be happy for them.

Tim walked into Camilla's room and the nurse was putting stitches in the gash on Camilla's head. "So, how is she doing?" Tim asked as he took a seat next to the bed.

"I was telling your wife that she is one lucky lady. When she came in, she looked pretty bad with all the blood dripping from her head and nose, but all her X-rays are fine. She is going to have a splitting headache and some muscle stiffness, but all in all, she is fine."

"Tim honey, where is Adrianna?"

Tim heard the anxiety and concern in Camilla's voice. "Relax, she is fine. All her X-rays were clear—no scrapes, bruises, or broken bones. She is with Sheena and Delisa in the lobby." Tim let out a deep breath, knowing he had to prepare Camilla for what was going to happen when they left. "Just so you know, I had to tell them about us."

"What?" Camilla tried to jump up but was quickly pinned down by the nurse who told her to hold still.

"They came here asking for Camilla Walker. The nurse said they didn't have a Camilla Walker, and they questioned me. I could not lie, so I decided to come clean. Besides, we had already agreed to tell them because of the baby…" Tim hadn't even thought about their unborn baby. "Is the baby okay?" He sat up and placed a hand on her stomach.

"Yes, the baby is okay. God must have really had his hand of protection on us." Camilla smiled as Tim rubbed his hand across her belly.

"All right, Mrs. Matthews, I am all finished." The nurse cleaned up her mess. "I will prepare your discharge papers and get you a prescription for pain medication. Then you can be on your way."

Camilla waited for the nurse to leave before she turned her aching body toward Tim. "So how did everyone take the news about us?"

Tim breathed deeply, "I really didn't hang around long enough for anyone to say anything, but from what I could tell Paul and Jaleel were shocked, Sheena thought it was hilarious, and Delisa seemed furious."

"Great, leave it to my sister to stay true to form. You would think she would be happy that I am finally happy."

"Camilla, give your sister a chance to get over the shock. I am sure she will be happy for us."

"I hope you're right, but history has taught me not to hold my breath when waiting on my sister to be happy for me."

"Well, prepare yourself, because we are all riding home together. We will be confined to a small space with no way out," Tim laughed as Camilla's face scrunched at the thought of having to endure her sister's wrath without being able to walk away. "Don't worry, I have your back."

Paul stood outside the hospital with Sheena who was still amused at the whole situation. "Sheena, what is so funny?"

"Your brother, sitting there squirming like a sixteen-year-old boy talking to his date's father. You Matthews' men are something else. The way you guys love is incredible. You run from it all your life until you run into that one woman you can't ignore. Then, you refuse to let her go. What's so funny is, for men who were once so adamant about not being tied down, when that love shows up y'all accept it so freely, even before the woman knows what hit her."

"Are you complaining?"

"Not in a million years." Sheena kissed his lips, "Your love is exactly what I need, just like Tim is exactly what Camilla needs."

"I agree. Camilla has changed my brother. She got him to settle down and move out here. I don't agree with how they handled everything, but I think they will make each other happy for a very long time." Paul pulled Sheena into his arms. "Just as happy as we will be."

Sheena rested her head on Paul's shoulder as they embraced, both remembering how love had swept them away, consuming their every waking moment with thoughts of each other. Once Paul started going to church, Sheena let all her guards down allowing love to lead her and when he proposed after only five months of dating, she willingly accepted. Their engagement met some opposition, but when everyone saw how in love they were; opposition turned to support.

"You could have at least brought the car around."

Sheena turned to see a smiling Camilla being wheeled to the curb. "Camilla, how are you feeling?" Sheena had expected to be at the hospital all night and was shocked to see Camilla being released so early.

"I am fine. I see my being in the hospital doesn't stop you two from being all hugged up." Camilla laughed.

Sheena laughed right back, "That's what love will do to you and from what I hear you know all about that."

Camilla gasped, upset at herself for opening the door to ridicule and scrutiny, but decided to take a stand. "As a matter of fact I do and

156

since we are on the subject, I do not want to be bombarded with questions about Tim and I being married. It is our business and we don't have to explain ourselves to anyone." Camilla stared at Delisa, making sure she understood. When Delisa shook her head in agreement, they all walked to the car.

The ride home started nice and peaceful, but quickly changed when Delisa decided she had a question. "So how long have you guys been married?"

"Delisa, don't start…"

"Don't start what? I just asked a simple question."

"Well, here is all you need to know. We have been married for a few months…"

Delisa cut in. Her blood was boiling and she could no longer contain her anger. "That means you guys got married before Christmas. He had just barely moved here."

"So what? And to be completely honest, we got married a couple of days after my graduation. Do you remember when I invited you all out for a couple's lunch?" Camilla waited for everyone to think. She was tired of being treated like a child and tired of hiding like one. She was ending this game once and for all. "Well, that was the day we got married, and lunch was our way of celebrating with our family."

"Don't you think it would have been more of a celebration if we knew about it? And I can't believe you kept it from us for so long, had us praying to the Lord for you get out of a sinful situation. You were married the whole time."

"No. You prayed because you didn't believe us when we told you we weren't sinning, and I kept it from you because you never support me in anything. You are the first to tell me I am making a bad decision and the first to say I told you so when things go bad. I didn't want to deal with that. I asked Tim to keep quiet, so we could enjoy being together before you tried to ruin it."

Camilla's comment shut Delisa up. She sat back in her seat and didn't say anything else. Camilla made her seem like some sort of tyrant raining terror on everyone's life, controlling and manipulating until they did what she wanted. Delisa always felt like she was a good sister who wanted the best for her little sister, but for the first time, she realized that what she had done out of love, Camilla saw it as an attempt to control her.

Delisa was trying to formulate her apology when Camilla spoke up again, "And just to get everything out in the open I am pregnant."

Delisa, Jaleel, Paul, and Sheena all sang in unison, "What?"

"Yes, she is pregnant, and I am not going to sit here and let anyone make her feel bad about it. This discussion is over. If any of you have any more questions, you can direct them toward me later. My wife has been through a lot today and doesn't need the added stress. It is a blessing that she, Adrianna, and the baby are fine. Can you guys just be thankful for that and leave everything else alone?" The rest of the ride home was quiet. Tim's tone had silenced all the speculating whispers.

19

Jaleel sat in Dave & Buster's restaurant waiting for Paul and Tim to show up. It was their first time getting together since the accident and they didn't want the tension between Camilla and Delisa to destroy the relationship they had built. Tim waited in his car until he saw Paul pull up. He didn't want to face Jaleel alone just in case Delisa sent a message with him. Once they were seated, Jaleel was the first to speak.

"Tim, we are brothers in Christ, and I would like to think good friends. Whatever is going on between our wives is between them. I don't plan on getting involved."

"I'm glad you said that. I don't want it to affect us either, but I think we have to do something to get them talking to each other. They are sisters and should not be acting like this."

"I agree." Paul had been praying for the women all week hoping that everything would blow over and all would be forgiven. "But let's not discuss it tonight. Everything is good between us, so let's order and have a good time."

"Sounds like a plan. Since Camilla hasn't been working or going to school she's been trying to do the housewife thing and have my dinner ready when I get home, but the woman must have been absent when the Lord handed out cooking skills."

The table erupted with laughter, "Man, we could have told you that. Why do you think we never have dinner at your house? My wife and Sheena refuse to let her cook. They offered to teach her and she said, 'No,

I am just going to have to marry a man who likes to cook.' Tim, brother, please tell me you can cook. If not, you better have takeout on speed dial."

"I can cook, but she doesn't want me to work all day then have to come home and cook, especially when she is sitting at home all day. So needless to say, I am going to enjoy dinner tonight." Tim ordered an appetizer and two entrées with sides. Paul and Jaleel watched as he ate hot wings, potato skins smothered with cheese, bacon, and sour cream, onion rings, and a big cheeseburger with bacon and avocado. Tim went from plate to plate devouring everything except for the celery that came with the hot wings.

Paul gave Tim a hard time with each bite, "Tim, you better slow down before you choke. You said she couldn't cook you didn't say she wasn't cooking; you're eating like you haven't eaten in weeks."

"You are full of jokes," Tim mumbled through a mouth full of potato skins. "I bet it wouldn't be so funny if your wife couldn't throw down they way she does."

"You are right, but I would not be sitting here with sour cream on the side of my face, smacking and licking my fingers."

Jaleel laughed and threw a napkin at Tim, "Clean yourself up so we can play some games before your heart stops from all that grease you just ate."

"Jaleel, I don't know why you are in such a hurry to get this but whoopin'." Paul and Jaleel came here often with Sheena and Delisa. Every time they played hoops, Paul beat Jaleel badly.

"I am hoping to beat Tim since he has all that food weighing him down."

"Big brother, you better school your boy. Let him know that even on my worst day I don't lose. I hope you brought your *A game,* because Paul can't even beat me." Tim was talking mad trash. He stepped up to the hoop, made the first five shots, and got a cramp in his side.

Jaleel laughed hysterically, "That's what you get now step back, so I can beat you." Jaleel definitely brought his *A-game,* beating Paul and Tim. They demanded a rematch and Jaleel beat them again. "I bet you guys will think twice before you call me computer nerd again."

They were in Dave & Buster's for hours playing games, cracking jokes, and having a good time. Before leaving, they sat down to plan how they would handle their wives. When everyone agreed on the terms they went their separate ways.

Paul was halfway home when he decided to talk to Tim before they met with their wives. He was mad at himself for not calling his brother all week, but was also mad that Tim didn't confide in him about being married. They were usually honest and upfront with each other. Sheena had asked him not to take sides and allow Camilla and Delisa to work things out, which he also used as an excuse not to call. Paul turned his car around and headed to Tim's house.

Tim had just finished checking on Camilla and Adrianna when Paul rang the doorbell. "Hey little brother, we need to talk." Paul walked into the apartment before Tim could invite him.

"Okay, what is so important that you had to follow me home to talk?" Tim led Paul to the couch, so they could be more comfortable. He could tell from the look on his face that this conversation was going to take a while.

"I want to apologize for not calling you this week. I was upset that you didn't confide in me about being married. We have never kept secrets from each other and I took it personal."

"You have to know that it was not my idea to hide anything. I couldn't care less about what everyone had to say about us getting married so soon, but Camilla was convinced that her family would try to interfere."

"I know that now. It took me a few days to get over myself and I am sorry. I do want you to know that I was never mad at you for getting married. I am glad that you saw what you wanted and you went after it. I know how it feels to love a woman so much you can't think straight until she is yours. Sheena and I would have gotten married sooner if she wasn't tripping about me not being a Christian."

"I never thought I could love a woman like this." Tim paced around the living room trying to come up with the words to explain his

161

feelings.

"You don't have to explain it to me. I know exactly how you feel. The day I walked into Sheena's office, she had my heart doing flips with her beauty, professionalism, and innocence. She tried to shake me loose, but I was not having it. In my line of work, I meet some beautiful professional women, but they are a little wicked. With Sheena, I could see her innocence when she tried to hide her attraction to me. She seemed almost ashamed or embarrassed about how I made her feel."

"For me, it was Camilla's strength and determination. I know you have never really been into the nightclub scene, but I have met some pretty pathetic women at the clubs. They have the potential to be someone great, but settle for being a baby's momma, on welfare, waiting for their child support check, or are looking for a man to pay their bills. Camilla was dealt the same hand some of them were, but she rose above it, finished her degree, stopped clubbing, and sacrificed her own desires for her daughter. No matter how hard it got she never gave up." Tim turned around to look at Paul and he was laughing. "What is so funny?"

"I was just thinking, now you are my brother and my cousin. Our kids will be first cousins and third cousins. We are a Jerry Springer episode waiting to happen." They laughed so hard they woke Camilla.

Camilla stood in the hallway for a few seconds before they noticed her. "Paul, as your sister-in-law, is this what I have to look forward to, you and Tim waking me up in the middle of the night?"

"Baby, I'm sorry. Paul just needed to talk." Tim rushed to Camilla and whispered in her ear, "I didn't mean to wake you. I promise as soon as he leaves I will help you get back to sleep."

"Don't hurry on my account. I will wait for you. I want to talk to you about my friend, Latrice that you met at my graduation party. She called saying she finally remembers how she knows you. She sounded pretty hysterical, so I agreed to meet her tomorrow for lunch, but we can talk later."

"I am going to let you guys have some privacy." Paul got up to put on his jacket. "Tim, I will talk to you in the morning; I just came by to let you know that I am happy for you. Besides, I don't want to get on my little sister's bad side so soon." Paul kissed Camilla on the cheek. "I will let myself out."

Paul hopped in the car and checked his cell phone. He had three missed calls from Sheena. He immediately called her back not wanting to have an argument about her not being able to reach him. Sheena answered the phone on the first ring. "Paul, honey I need you to come home now."

The excitement in her voice startled him and he pressed down on the accelerator. "What is wrong? Are you all right?"

"I am fine I need to show you something." Sheena was interrupted by sirens blaring in the background. "What is that noise?"

"Baby, let me call you back. I am being pulled over by the police." Paul hung up the phone, sliding it down his cheek trying to hide it from the cops. He pulled to the shoulder of the road and rolled down his window. He turned off his vehicle and sat quietly praying as he waited for the officer to approach. Being an attorney, Paul knew many people who could make his ticket disappear, but being a Christian he never felt comfortable taking advantage of the system. He paid his tickets just like everyone else.

"Good evening, sir." The officer looked into the window and shined his flashlight in Paul's face. "Do you realize how fast you were going?"

"No officer, I don't." Paul hung his head, hoping the officer hadn't seen him talking on his cell phone. Paul had plenty of money and could pay any ticket he received. It was just the principle and a little bit of male ego that made him feel foolish for getting a ticket.

"Do you know that it is now against the law in the State of California to talk on the phone while you are driving?"

Paul shook his head, "Yes, I do know that." With every question the officer asked Paul felt more and more idiotic. The whole situation could have been avoided. He had his Bluetooth in his center console, but hadn't connected it. Paul kept his hands on the wheel, nodded, and answered the officer's questions. When it was all over, he pulled away from the curb with a fat ticket in his hand and a splitting headache.

Sheena was waiting for Paul in the doorway when he finally got home. She had already drawn him a hot bath and escorted him straight to the bathroom. She wanted to relieve all of his stress before she showed him her surprise. She washed his body from head to toe, stopping to deeply massage his neck and back. Sheena could barely contain her excitement. She had been waiting for him to get home for hours.

"Okay, Sheena spit it out. You have been smiling since I walked in the door. What is going on?" Sheena walked into their room and Paul followed behind her. "Baby, where are you going?"

"I was just coming to get this." Sheena handed him a zip lock bag with a home pregnancy test inside.

"What is this?" Paul looked closely at the bag and when he realized what it was he grabbed Sheena lifting her into the air, "Please tell me it was positive."

"Yes, it was, but don't get too excited these tests are not 100 percent accurate. I need to make a doctor's appointment to get a blood test."

Paul put Sheena down trying to contain his excitement but couldn't, "Can you go tomorrow for the test?"

"Paul, tomorrow is Saturday. I will go first thing Monday morning."

"I can't wait that long. Get dressed." Paul grabbed his cell to call in a favor.

"What? There is nothing opened this late."

"Get dressed." Paul smiled and walked away.

Sheena wondered what he was up to, but didn't bother to question him. She learned that when he was in bossy mode it was best to just do what he said because it was usually for the best.

About thirty minutes later they pulled up in front of Sharp Hospital's emergency room. "Paul, no; it is already midnight. I am not going to wait all morning in the ER for a pregnancy test."

"Sheena, get out of the car." Paul walked around to her side of the car and helped her get out.

"Paul, this is silly. Stop being impatient. We can wait until Monday."

Paul pulled her close and kissed her deeply. "I don't want to wait. Please do this for me. I promise we will not be here all morning."

"How can you promise that?"

Paul smiled and walked up to the check-in counter. "I am Paul Matthews."

"Welcome to Sharp Hospital. You and your wife can follow me."

The nurse took them straight to the lab where they took a blood sample and urine sample to run a pregnancy test. They remained in the lab while they waited for the results. Less than thirty minutes later, the results were ready, confirming that Sheena was in fact pregnant. Paul was so excited he was high fiving the lab technicians and the nurse. He apologized for the inconvenience and thanked them for all their help.

As soon as they walked out of the hospital Sheena turned to Paul, "Okay, how did you do that?" Paul smiled and tried to walk away. "Paul, stop smiling and tell me what you did."

"The only thing I did was make a phone call." Paul tried to kiss her hoping to change the subject, but she pulled away.

"Who did you call?"

Paul knew she was not going to let it go without an explanation. "Well, you know your man is very well-connected. The hospital administrator is a client of mine who happens to owe me a very big favor. Let's just say his debt is cleared."

Sheena knew he was well connected and since he'd become her husband she noticed that he had the power and authority to persuade anyone do what he wanted. That power exuded in his voice, in his walk, and in the way he handled his business. His omnipotent authoritative demeanor was a turn on that made it hard for her to resist him.

Paul rushed Sheena to the car and before opening her door, he pressed her up against it; lifting her legs around his waist while he consumed her mouth.

"Stop before someone sees us," Sheena mumbled through his kisses.

Reluctantly, he put her down and helped her into the car. Before Paul made it around to the other side, Sheena noticed she had four missed calls from April, her sister, and immediately called her back.

April's hysterical voice came through the phone muffled and distorted by her crying. "April, calm down I can't understand a word you are saying." Sheena's heart raced with fear. She hated early morning phone calls. They always meant something horrible had happened. Since the call was from her sister, it could only mean one thing: something had happened to her parents.

April took a few deep breaths to calm herself, "Sheena, mom needs you here. Dad had a heart attack."

"Oh my God, April!" Sheena hung her head and sobbed into her lap. "Tell Mom I am on my way."

Sheena hung up the phone and turned to Paul to tell him what happened, but he was already on the phone with his secretary having her make arrangements for them to take the next flight to San Antonio. Paul hung up with his secretary and called Tim, informing him of everything. Tim told Camilla, Camilla called Delisa, and Delisa called her parents.

Paul watched as the family rock, which was Sheena, seemed to crumble before his eyes. She was always the strength for everyone and now she couldn't pull herself together long enough to pack her clothes. Paul picked her up and laid her on the bed, "You rest. I will finish packing for you." He finished packing, and they made it to their gate at the airport just before the first boarding call.

They stood in front of the window as they waited for their group to be called. Sheena felt a hand on her shoulder and turned to see Tim and Camilla standing behind her. "What are you guys doing here?" Sheena didn't wait for a response. She leaned into the embrace that Camilla offered and released more of her tears.

Paul pulled Tim to the side. "I am glad you are here. You didn't have to come, but I am glad you guys are here." Paul watched Adrianna sleeping on Tim's shoulder and couldn't help but smile. "So, are you excited about being a daddy?"

"You know what it is so funny? I am excited about the baby, but I am already so connected to Adrianna that it feels like I already have a child."

"You guys do have an amazing connection. Do you know Camilla's due date?"

"It should be some time around October. I just hope we have a house by then."

"You should let me help you with that. At least let me give you the down payment. We could consider it a late wedding present."

"I just might take you up on that. So what's up with you? Your wife is obviously upset, and you seem to be suppressing some kind of excitement."

"Is it that obvious?" Paul rubbed his hand across his face trying to wipe away the smile. "Well before we got the news about Sheena's father we had just found out that she is pregnant."

"What?" Camilla over heard their conversation. "Why didn't you tell me?"

Sheena looked at Camilla, "I could ask you the same question. I just found out a few hours ago. How long did…" Sheena stopped herself mid-sentence. "I'm sorry. I know you had your reasons and I'm not going to dwell on it. I am happy that you are happy. Tim is a good man." She placed one hand on Camilla's stomach and the other on hers. "It looks like our babies are going to grow up together."

The announcement finally came for them to board the plane. Camilla held on to Sheena as they boarded the plane while Paul and Tim carried the bags.

20

Linda sat on the side of her husband's hospital bed nodding in and out of sleep. April had curled up in a chair and went to sleep hours ago, but Linda could not relax long enough to sleep soundly. James was her life. They had grown closer since their kids were now grown. They took long walks every evening, vacations across the world, and really learned to enjoy each other's company. The thought of losing him was more than she could bear.

James made it through the surgery, but had yet to wake up from the anesthesia. The doctors said that it was unusual for a patient to be out this long, but assured Linda that it was still possible for him to wake up. They monitored his vital signs and everything looked normal. All they could do was continue waiting until James was ready to get up.

"Mom, how are you holding up?" Sheena asked, stepping up to the bed.

Linda was surprised at how fast Sheena had arrived in San Antonio. It was at least a four-hour flight and April had called only seven hours ago. "How did you get a flight so fast? I was not expecting you until later this evening."

"I don't know. Paul handled all of the arrangements."

"Was he able to come with you?"

"Yes ma'am. He is in the waiting room along with Tim and Camilla."

"Camilla is here?" Linda had heard about Camilla's marriage from Felicia and wanted to fly to San Diego to whoop Camilla's behind for hurting her mother. Without a second thought, Linda jumped up and

168

rushed to the waiting room with Sheena trailing behind begging her to let it go. Linda walked in to waiting room and before Camilla could greet her, Linda swatted her across the rear end.

"Ouch Auntie Linda, what was that for?"

"I talked with your mother. I can't believe you hurt her like that."

"I am sorry, but I love him. Why spend years and years dating when you know from day one that you can't live without him?"

"Camilla, No one is upset that you married him. We are upset that you didn't have more faith in us and allow us to share the experience with you. Do you really think that little of us?"

"No, Auntie, it's just..." Camilla was at a loss for words. She looked to Tim for support and he stood behind her caressing her shoulder, but said nothing.

"We have always supported you through every failed relationship and in your decision to have Adrianna, we all stood by you 100 percent. We may voice our opinions, but when it boils down to it, whether we agree with you or not we are there for you."

"Yes you are, but I just didn't want to hear the negative."

"In my opinion, there would not have been anything negative to say about a man falling in love with a single mother and making her his wife. Tim could have easily taken advantage of you, used you to satisfy his needs, and went back home never seeing you again. But, the man left his life to be with you. The worst anyone would have said was *wait until you know him a little better.*"

Camilla hung her head in shame, "I'm sorry... I should have told everyone."

"Mrs. Walker?" The nurse stood in the doorway. "Your husband is awake."

Linda took a deep breath, "Thank you Jesus!" She rushed back to James's room with the rest of the family following close behind. They walked into the room as the doctor was removing the breathing tube. April stood close behind them watching in disgust. Sheena placed her hand on April's shoulder, turning her around to embrace her. "Hey, it is good to see you. How are you doing?"

"I am doing a lot better now that dad is awake…" April squeezed Sheena tight. "…And now that you're here."

April and Sheena didn't have a close relationship because of their age difference, but they loved each other. Now that April was a young adult, they still didn't have much in common, but she often called Sheena whenever she needed to talk. Sheena was always the non-judgmental listening ear. Sheena listened and gave sound advice even when the conversation went against her Christian beliefs. April had called Sheena a few months before turning eighteen, confiding in Sheena that she was considering giving her virginity to her boyfriend. Of course Sheena was stunned because she was twenty-five and still a virgin, but she advised Camilla of all the risks, informed her of the different birth control methods, instructed her on what the Bible said, and ended by telling April to think long and hard before giving away such a precious gift. When April called her back a few months later telling her that she had in fact lost her virginity, Sheena supported her decision, told her to be safe, and to call if she ever needed to talk. James could barely talk after the doctors removed the tube, but was so excited to see Sheena he strained his voice to call her to his side. "How's my baby doing?"

Sheena kissed his forehead and cupped his cheek with her hand. "I should be asking you that question. You gave us all quite a scare."

"I am going to be just fine. How long are you going to be in town? I miss you so much I want to be able to spend some time with you before you leave."

"You just worry about getting better, because we need you to be around for a long time. If you leave us who are we going to call for advice on raising your grandchild?" Sheena watched as a tear fell from her father's eye. "You are going to be a grandpa, so start taking better care of yourself."

Linda rubbed her hand across Sheena's back, "Congratulations baby."

"Yeah, congratulations. I know you are going to be a great mom.

Do you know your due date?" April stepped in to hug her sister again.

"No, when I called you last night, I had just found out, but I can't be too far along…" Sheena paused when the nurse walked into the room.

"I am sorry, but we cannot allow this many visitors at one time. Two of you can stay, but the rest will have to go to the waiting room." The nurse quickly excused herself before anyone could protest.

"April, drive mom home so she can shower and rest. Paul, why don't you guys check in to the hotel and I will call if there are any changes."

"Sheena, no one is staying at a hotel. You all are staying at the house with us. I don't want to hear otherwise." Linda grabbed her purse and headed toward the door with April following behind.

"If anyone needs to rest it is you and Camilla. You guys ride home with your mom. Tim and I will stay here." Paul gave Sheena a look that let her know that it was not up for discussion.

Tim tried to hand Adrianna to Camilla, but she stepped away. "Tim, I am staying here with you. I am not tired."

"Take Adrianna and go with Sheena. You didn't sleep much last night or on the plane. You aren't going to sit at this hospital all day. End of discussion." Tim kissed Camilla on the cheek and placed Adrianna in her arms.

"Tim, I am not…" Tim shot Camilla a look that made her shut her mouth. Sheena chuckled in the background and Paul nudged her shoulder. "Tim, you are so bossy."

Sheena grabbed the diaper bag and pulled Camilla by the arm "Let's hurry before my mom leaves. I promise you will get used to the bossiness after awhile. Paul only bosses me around when it is for my benefit. I can only imagine how it is going to be now that I am pregnant."

After the ladies left the room, Tim looked at Paul and they both chuckled. "Does Sheena ever get mad at you for telling her what to do?"

"Of course. She still does at times, but she knows I mean well."

"Man, I never just boss Camilla around for the fun of it and she rides me every single time. Sometimes I want to say 'Camilla just shut up and do what I told you to do'."

"Well, you told me that it was her strength that captivated you and now you want to fault her for that same strength."

"Then what should I do? Just let her do whatever even though it is not what's best for her, the baby, or the family?"

"Tim, why are you asking me? I have been married six months longer than you and my wife is not as feisty as yours? You are going to have to figure this one out on your own."

"You young brothers don't know anything. Pull up a chair and let me school you." They thought James had fallen asleep, but they quickly complied. He spoke through labored breaths and when Paul admonished him to save his energy he stubbornly continued.

"First of all, the man and woman must be on the same page. The word of God says we can't be unequally yoked. If you are both believers you must go to the word of God to help your wife understand your role as the head of the house. Until she understands that, there will always be a constant struggle for authority in your house. Once she understands and accepts what God has mandated it will be easier for her to adhere to what you say. God instructs us to love our wives as Christ loves the church. There are some things that Christ doesn't ask us to do, He outright commands us to do it. But even with His command, we still have a choice."

"Okay, you just lost me." Tim was more confused than he was before their conversation. "I should tell her what to do, but she doesn't have to do it?"

"No, what I am trying to say is your wife is not your slave, and if you plan on being married any length of time, you cannot force her to do anything. But, just as Christ's love is so good to us that we don't mind doing the things He commands, love your wives the same way. Love them so good that they don't mind doing what you tell them."

"So you're saying Camilla hates doing what I tell her, because, I am not loving her right."

"No. I think you are doing it right; if not, she would still be sitting here refusing to listen to you. I think you need to open the lines of communication and give it some time. When we first loved the Lord, doing what He commanded wasn't easy. It was scary and confusing. In time, she will know your love and all that it encompasses."

Paul could see the tiredness on his father-in-law's face and abruptly ended the conversation. "Mr. Walker you get some rest. We will be here for a few hours, so if you need anything you just holler."

The women had just made it home and Sheena was helping Camilla bathe Adrianna. Adrianna was the only one who slept all night and she was full of energy, splashing water all over the place, blowing spit bubbles, and getting on Camilla's nerves.

"Camilla, what is wrong? I have never seen you this frustrated with Adrianna." Sheena watched as tears filled Camilla's eyes. "Come on, let's finish this bath, so we can talk." Sheena quickly bathed and dressed Adrianna, then took her downstairs to April.

"Okay Camilla, talk to me." Sheena grabbed her hand, making her sit on the bed.

"Sheena, how do you put up with Paul being so bossy? Tim is the bossiest man I have ever been with and it drives me crazy."

Sheena chuckled, "I know exactly how you feel. When Paul and I were dating, I hated being bossed around. I remember the first time he did it. We met for coffee and when I arrived, he was already there. Paul stood and placed his hands on my shoulders. I thought he was going to kiss me, but all he said was, *Where is your sweater?* It was mid-summer, summer school was almost over. I had on a sleeveless, knee-length business dress. The only things visible were my shoulders and arms. I told him it was going to be a hot day, so I didn't bring one and he told me to go home and get one. He said it was in appropriate for a high school principal to look so sexy in front of teenage boys."

Camilla laughed, "Oh my God, Sheena. What did you say?"

"I told him my daddy lives in Texas. Then, he gave me that sexy smile that drives me crazy, kissed me on the cheek and said, *Go get a sweater. I will get us some coffee to go, and meet you at your office.* Then, he walked away."

"Sheena, please tell me you told him off."

"No, I didn't tell him off, but I didn't go get a sweater either. I went straight to work and when he walked in to my office, I could tell he was livid. Before he could say anything I told him, *I do not need you to tell me how to dress, and if you like spending time with me I suggest you tone down the bossiness.* Girl, he handed me my coffee, turned around, and walked out. My heart sank. He was the first man to ever excite me and I didn't want to lose him, but I had friends who dated demanding controlling men. I refused to be one of them."

"So how did you guys hook back up?"

"That's the funny part. Summer school had just let out for the day. I was still pretty upset that Paul just left the way he did, so I was going home. There were still quite a few students waiting around for rides. I was coming around the corner headed for the staff parking lot when I overheard a group of boys talking. One of them said, minus the curse words of course, *Did you see Mrs. Walker today? Just give me five minutes alone with her and I'll have her screaming my name."* I was so embarrassed that I stood there barely breathing until I was sure they were gone. Then, I hopped in my car and went straight to Paul's office, walked right pass his secretary, and into his office without knocking. I walked right up to him and kissed him in a way that I'd never kissed a man before. I told him what the group of boys said and how embarrassed I was. For the first time he told me he loved me saying, "I love you and would never try to control you. I just want what is best for you." I told him I loved him, too. After that, it still took me awhile to get used to it, but it did help me to stop and think before I told him off. Take today for instance. How dare he tell me that I can't stay at the hospital with my sick father, but when you think about it I am pregnant. I have been awake for over twenty-four hours and have not eaten anything. So, it was better for me to leave, eat, rest, and come back later."

"I guess you're right, but I don't know if I will ever get used to it."

"Trust me, you will, as long as you stop fighting and let him be the head. After you accept it, the way he takes care of you will be a turn on."

Camilla gasped, "What?"

"You heard me," Sheena laughed "Now stop tripping and take a nap before I call Tim." Sheena walked out of the room laughing hard. Camilla tried to throw a pillow at her, but she had slammed the door shut. Camilla drifted off to sleep and slept for hours. Her cell phone rang and she jumped up out of her sleep. She looked at the caller ID and sighed as she answered, "Hey Latrice, I am sorry I missed our lunch date, but I had a family emergency and had to rush out of town."

"Oh, is everyone okay?"

"Sheena's father is in the hospital, but it looks like he is going to pull through."

"That is good to hear. Call me when you get back, because I really need to talk to you."

"I will. You take care." Camilla didn't understand why Latrice insisted on talking to her face to face, but the whole situation was starting to worry her. She could not figure out where Latrice could've met Tim. She just hoped they hadn't slept together.

"Who were you talking to?" Tim walked in as Camilla was hanging up the phone. Camilla looked at Tim, rolled her eyes, placed her head down, and tried to go back to sleep. Tim climbed on top of her kissing her neck. "Baby, what's wrong?"

"Tim, you know I am mad at you. Get off of me."

"Naw, you aren't mad at me." Tim pinned her arms above her head slightly kissing them. She closed her eyes trying to ignore him, but he knew exactly how to touch her. He knew what she liked and used it against her. He tried to kiss her lips and she pressed her lips together refusing to let him inside. He mumbled against her lips as he licked them, "Baby, let me in. I am sorry, but you needed to rest. I couldn't let you sit at the hospital all day." Camilla's breathing sped up and her heart raced. No matter how hard she tried to resist Tim she couldn't. Camilla opened her mouth to tell him to stop, but he slid his tongue into her mouth. With a few quick flicks of the tongue she succumbed to his advances.

"Baby, please don't be mad at me." Camilla pressed her face against his neck, her chest rose and fell as she tried to catch her breath. Between each deep breathe she whispered, "Tim you don't fight fair."

"Camilla, I am not trying to fight. I needed you to calm down so you could understand that I am not trying to control you, but I do have a responsibility to take care of you."

"Look, I love you and I understand that you are the head of the house with the responsibility of our welfare, but you have to watch your tone when you are telling me what to do. You don't have to be so forceful and aggressive."

"I am only forceful because you go against everything I say. If you stop fighting me, then I will ease up. Do we have a deal?" Camilla looked up at Tim as he leaned over her with a sincere expression on his face. She searched his face for a hint of deception, but all she found was genuine love. She accepted his offer, praying for the strength to hold her peace and allow a man to make decisions for her.

21

Paul woke up early one morning. He was still at his in-laws' house and hadn't gotten a good night sleep since he got there. He had a hard time sleeping in a different bed. He rolled over to cuddle his wife, hoping that the warmth from her body would help him get back to sleep, but when he reached for her, she was gone. He sat up, looking around the dark room and trying to see where she was when he saw a light coming from the bathroom.

Knocking on the door, Paul placed his ear to it, listening for her response, but there was none. All he heard was a faint cough and moaning. He slowly opened the door and saw his wife kneeling in front of the toilet with her head buried inside the bowl. Kneeling next to her, he rubbed her back to offer some sort of comfort. He sat next to her, rubbing her back and wiping her forehead until her stomach settled. He helped her brush her teeth and carried her to bed.

Paul climbed in bed next to Sheena and pulled her close, laying her head on his chest. Sheena clung to him, her body weak from all the vomiting. He ran his fingers thru her hair, helping her relax.

"Paul?" Sheena lifted her head to look in his eyes. "Is this what I have to look forward to?"

"Baby, I don't know, but whatever you have to go through, I am going to be right by your side. Next time, wake me up. You don't have to be sick by yourself."

"I know. I just didn't want you to see me throw up."

"Well from what I hear, some of the things that go on during

177

pregnancy and child birth are worse than throwing up. You better get used to me seeing everything now so that it won't bother you later, because I don't plan on missing anything."

There was a soft knock on the door. Sheena sat up immediately fearing the worst. "Come in." Her eyes widened as April stepped into the room. "Oh my God. April, is everything all right with dad?"

"Relax Sheena, he is fine. I have an early class this morning, I wanted to talk to you, but hadn't gotten the opportunity, so I wanted to catch you before you get busy."

"Can this wait until later? Your sister is not feeling well. She had her first round of morning sickness and—"

"Paul, I am feeling much better. Can you give us a few minutes, so we can talk?"

"No, he can stay. I kind of need to talk to both of you, if that's okay?"

Paul was a little leery about what April needed to talk about. He hadn't had much interaction with her and was curious about why she needed to talk to him.

"Shut the door and have a seat." Paul with his usual take charge demeanor sat up a little straighter and wrapped his arm around Sheena's shoulders.

Sheena looked at Paul and nudged him in his ribs.

"What was that for?" Paul asked, fighting the smile pulling at the corners of his mouth. He knew exactly what it was for.

"Stop being bossy. What if she doesn't want to sit?"

"I wasn't being bossy. I was being hospitable."

"Sheena, it's okay. I didn't take it that way." April sat on the edge of the bed and took a deep breath while trying to formulate her thoughts. "Well, as you know, I have been in school for about two and half years and I still don't have a major, but I think I have finally decided what I want to do."

"That is great. So what's the problem?" Sheena had been bugging April to pick a major for quite some time, and her answer was always,

"What's the rush? I still have time."

"Well I want to study journalism, and to be the best, I want to study at one of the best schools for journalism. That's where you guys come in."

"Whatever you need, Sheena and I will try out best to get it."

"Good, because I have already applied and been accepted; I am transferring to San Diego State in the fall and…"

Sheena screamed loudly and jumped off the bed, causing April to hit the floor. Sheena rushed to help her up, "I am sorry, I'm just excited you are moving close to us."

"Well, that's what I actually wanted to talk to you about. Mom and Dad are already going to have to pay more money for out-of-state tuition. I don't want to burden them with the cost of room and board. So, I was hoping I could stay with you guys."

"April, you're my wife's sister and you are always welcome in our home, but if you want to live on campus, I will pay your room and board. You don't have to stay with us unless you really want to."

"Thanks for the offer, but I really want to stay with you guys. I want a quiet place to study besides the library. I have friends that stay in the dorms here and I hear horror stories about their roommates. I don't want to deal with that. I was also hoping Sheena and I could get a little closer and have a real sister relationship."

"I would like that. We have plenty of room, but I don't know how quiet it is going to be once I have the baby. We would love an extra set of hands to help change diapers."

April laughed. "I don't mind at all. I am glad I'll be there to get to know my little niece or nephew."

Sheena walked April to the door reassuring her that everything would be all right and that she would help break the news to their parents. April had never been away from home and Sheena knew her parents were going to be totally against the idea.

Sheena was headed back into the room when Camilla stuck her head out of the bedroom across the hall. "Is everything okay? What are you doing up so early?"

"Go back to sleep, nosy rosy."

"I have been saying the same thing for the past hour." Tim stepped behind her.

"I can't. I'm nauseous this morning. I wish I would just throw up and get it over with so my stomach will feel better."

Sheena held her stomach. "Please don't talk about being sick. I threw up for the first time this morning and it drained my entire body."

"That is why you need to come back to bed." Paul joined them in the hall and slid his hand around Sheena's waist. The baritone of his voice made Sheena's heart flutter and his hand made her quiver. Paul's breath on her neck deepened his effect. "Are you coming back to bed?"

Paul had almost sucked Sheena into his trance when Camilla burst out laughing, "Dang Sheena, are you that whipped? He had you under some kind of spell."

Sheena playfully pushed Camilla. "I don't know why you are laughing when you are whipped too."

"Not like that. You forgot we were even standing here."

"I'm sorry. Please remind me how long you knew Tim before he persuaded you to marry him. If my memory serves me correctly you weren't even a couple."

Camilla stopped laughing and folded her arms across her chest.

"That's what I thought, now come downstairs and help me make breakfast. Try not to burn anything."

Paul and Tim watched their wives walk away, looked at each other, and without a word fell out laughing. Neither one of them thought their wives were whipped and, if truth be told, they felt like they were the ones who were whipped. Both had made drastic lifestyle changes after meeting their wives. The only reason they always put their woman in a trance was because they couldn't keep their hands off of them. Every curve of their bodies, their long silky hair, and the perfection in their skin had Paul and Tim hooked from day one.

Tim was getting washed up for breakfast and Camilla's cell phone kept ringing. He checked the caller ID and decided to answer. "Hey Delisa, is everything all right?"

"Everything is fine. I was just calling to see how Uncle James is doing."

"He is actually doing great. They are releasing him from the hospital sometime today. Of course Sheena protested, but they said four days is standard hospital stay for those types of surgeries. The doctor reassured her that James was going to be fine, so she let them off the hook."

"Good, we have been so worried, but it is good to hear that the Lord has worked a miracle." Delisa had some other things that she needed to get off of her chest. "Tim, is my sister around?"

"She is downstairs helping Sheena cook. If you give me a few seconds to finish changing Adrianna, I will take the phone to her."

"That's okay. I just wanted to let you guys know that I am sorry for how I have been acting. Uncle James having a heart attack helped me see that tomorrow is not promised to any of us. It is better to love while you can, because you never know who will be gone tomorrow. So tell my sister I love her, that I am happy for her, and have her call me when she gets a chance."

"Thank you, Delisa. I am sure she will be glad to hear that. I know she has some things she wants to say to you, so I will have her give you a call. All right, talk to you later."

Camilla walked into the room as Tim was hanging up the phone, curious as to why he was talking on her phone. "Who was that?"

"That was your sister. She wanted to check on your uncle and apologize for how she has been acting." Tim finished putting on his shirt and walked to the kitchen with Camilla. "She also said she loves you and is happy for you. She wants you to call her back later." Tim sat down at the table and Camilla's phone started ringing again.

Tim passed the phone to Camilla, so she could answer. It was rare that he got a home-cooked breakfast, and he was ready to eat. He didn't know how they cooked all that food so fast, but he planned on enjoying every single bite. Tim was getting ready to crack a joke about his wife's cooking when he saw the grim expression on her face. "Baby, is everything all right?"

"Yeah, this is Latrice. I am going to talk in the other room." Camilla got up from the table, glad that Latrice finally decided to end this game and tell her what was going on. "Okay Latrice, what is bothering you?"

"Well, I'd rather tell you in person, but you are taking too long to come back, and you need to know as soon as possible before you do something crazy like marry this man. He has probably been stalking you this whole time."

"What?" Camilla was already frustrated with Latrice and was not going to tolerate her saying anything negative about Tim. "Latrice, what are you talking about? Tim is a good man."

"I hope you're right. Do you remember the night we partied before our senior year?"

"Of course I remember."

"We said we were going to have a good time, get drunk, and get the partying out of our system, so we could buckle down and knock out our senior year. You got more drunk than I'd ever seen you."

"I said I remember." Camilla's tone was short and sharp. "How could I forget? That's the night I got pregnant with Adrianna."

"Oh my God, Camilla I never even thought about that."

"What Latrice?" Camilla was on her feet, pacing around the room, trying very hard not to tell Latrice off and hang up the phone.

"Well, like I said you were really drunk and this man was coming on to you. He seemed just as drunk as you were. You guys couldn't keep your hands off of each other and I tried to take you home, but you told me you were a grown woman who could make decisions for herself. You left with him even though I told you were crazy."

"Latrice get to your point."

"My point is that man was Tim."

"What?" Camilla's mind was racing with thoughts of that night.

182

She remembered going out and dancing with a few guys who weren't Tim, but the rest of the night was a blur. She remembered waking up in a hotel with a strange man, but she was so scared she grabbed her clothes and left without looking at his face. Since the day she found out about her pregnancy, she'd regretted not staying and finding out his name.

"Hello, Camilla, you still there?"

"Yeah I'm here. Latrice this is crazy. Tim lived in a whole other state; it couldn't be him."

"I am almost 100 percent sure it is. Ask him. Maybe he was in town visiting his brother."

Camilla gasped. "Latrice, I have to go." She hung up the phone. Camilla's pacing became more frantic and her pulse raced with her mind remembering that night was the same night as Sheena's engagement party. There was a good chance that Tim was in town that weekend.

Camilla heard laughter coming from the kitchen and it brought her back to reality. She slowly inched toward the kitchen, searching her mind for the words to say. She had to get to the bottom of it and the only way was to talk to Tim. She walked through the door with tears in her eyes and her chest heaving with anxiety. Tim immediately passed Adrianna to Sheena and rushed to Camilla's side.

"Baby, what's wrong?" Tim helped Camilla to her seat and gave her a glass of juice, hoping to calm her nerves.

Camilla forced herself to calm down and slowly began searching for answers. "Tim did you go to Paul and Sheena's engagement party?"

"Why? Is that where Latrice thinks she saw me?"

"No. Were you there?" Camilla held her breath as she waited for his answer.

"Yes, I was there, but I left early…"

Camilla got up from the table pacing back and forth hysterically crying out, "Oh my God, oh my God."

Tim grabbed her by the shoulders. "Camilla, you have to calm down and talk to me. This stress cannot be good for the baby. Now take a deep breath and tell me what Latrice said." Tim sat down and pulled

Camilla onto his lap, massaging her back to help her calm down.

"Okay, the night of the engagement party," Camilla spoke slowly, trying to remain calm. "I went out with Latrice and a few other friends. I remember, because Sheena wouldn't speak to me for a week when I told her I was not coming to her party. Well, my friends and I decided we were going to party hard and get all the partying out of our system so we could focus on our senior year. But, I was the only one who got sloppy drunk. The majority of that night is a blur, all I remember is waking up the next morning in a hotel with some man I didn't know and I left so fast I didn't get his name, number, or even look at his face." Tears rolled down Camilla's face as she tried to come to terms with the whole situation. "Latrice seems to think, in fact, she said she is 100 percent sure that you are the guy I left the club with."

"What? There is no way…."

"Wait a minute, Tim." Paul stood trying to make sense of everything. "You did leave the party early, and the next morning, I had to pick you up from some hotel because you did not know where you were."

"Oh my God!" Camilla was back on her feet pacing again. "Tim, if you are the man I left the club with, you have to be the man I woke up with, and if you are the man I woke up with, you have to be Adrianna's father," Camilla cried hysterically.

"Oh my goodness." Sheena had been sitting quietly, praying that whatever Latrice had to say would not ruin Tim and Camilla's marriage, but never expected the bomb that just dropped. She watched Tim as he watched Adrianna who was in her lap oblivious to what had just taken place. "Tim, are you all right?" Sheena waited for his response, but he said nothing.

Tim smiled as he watched Adrianna drooling and blowing spit bubbles. He reached out to grab her and Adrianna stood in Sheena's lap, bouncing up and down with excitement and chanting, "Da Da Da Da." Tim scooped her up into his arms and left the room, trying to hide his emotions.

Sheena embraced Camilla, trying to calm her down before she

made herself sick, and Paul went after Tim. By the time Paul caught up to Tim, he was sitting on the couch in the living room cradling Adrianna with one hand and wiping his tears with the other.

He saw Paul coming toward him and tried to man up, but failed. "Paul, she has to be my daughter. It explains so much, like the crazy connection we have with each other."

"I know. The whole situation has me dumbfounded. Just think, men and women hook up all the time in clubs, make babies, and the father never gets a chance to know his child. God has blessed you to not only meet your daughter, but to fall in love with her mother and be a family. I know you have a lot to take in, but right now Camilla needs you. You have another child to be concerned about, and if Camilla doesn't calm down, it is going to affect the baby. So give me my niece and go take care of your wife."

Tim stopped to take a deep breath and calm his nerves before he entered the kitchen. He walked in and his heart melted when he saw Camilla lying on the floor crying hysterically. He reached over Sheena and lifted Camilla to her feet. He moved her hair out of her face, wiped her tears, and covered her lips with his. He molded her body against his, relieving her tension. Her cries tapered off as she relaxed into his embrace.

"Camilla, baby, don't be upset. We should be praising God right now for letting us find each other again and for giving us a chance to be a family. If you want, we can have a paternity test done just to be sure, but I am convinced she is my daughter."

"I am so sorry. I should have talked to you before I left and we wouldn't be in this situation."

"Shhh! We are not going to dwell on that. This just proves that we are meant to be together."

Tim carried Camilla to bed and caressed her with his hands, his words, and his heart. Once she had fallen asleep, he played with his daughter until she was ready for a nap. He rocked her to sleep then laid her next to her mother. Tim was so grateful to God for giving him an opportunity to be a father to his child. He remembered how much he wanted his father to be a real father and would never want any of his children to experience any of the pain he went through.

22

Delisa rolled over and narrowed her eyes at the sun beaming through her bedroom window. Last night was the best sleep she'd had in months. The nightmares of her daughter's death seemed to be tapering off, and she'd made it through the night without getting up. There had been some horrible nightmares. Some nights, she woke up drenched in sweat. Other nights, she woke in tears from dreaming of how life would be if Jalisa hadn't gone up those stairs.

Jaleel lay next to her still sleeping and her eyes scanned his flawlessly cut torso. The cut of each muscle was enhanced by the silky chocolate hue of his skin. Her fingers trailed from one pectoral muscle to the next. Desire rose within her, but she forced herself to resist.

Climbing out of bed, she made her way to the kitchen to begin cooking breakfast for her man. The smell of bacon and coffee filled the house and the aroma drifted to the bedroom, waking up Jaleel. He walked into the kitchen to find Delisa cooking and singing. He stopped and watched for a moment. Delisa danced and bounced around the kitchen as she sang one of her favorite church hymns. It had been so long since she looked happy. This joy was a welcome change.

Slowly, he approached her, rubbing his hands down her back hoping not to scare her, but his attempt failed. Delisa jumped and sucked in her breath when she felt his presence. They both chuckled at her reaction. Jaleel softly kissed Delisa on the back of her neck. "I am sorry baby. I didn't mean to scare you."

Delisa turned to offer him her lips, which he willingly accepted. "I was not expecting you to get up. I was trying to cook quietly so I could serve you breakfast in bed."

"I'm sorry, but you have it smelling so good in here I had to come see what was cooking. If you want, I will get back in bed and wait for you." That sexy smile that always captivated Delisa's heart, spread across Jaleel's face and Delisa's pulse raced.

Over the past few weeks, Delisa had seen Jaleel in another light. He had become her strength, her best friend, and her seducer. He loved her back in to her right frame of mind and strengthened her when she felt like giving up on life. On the days she cried, he prayed. On the days she did not want to get out of bed, he joined her and made love to her, relieving her stress. Jaleel had become the man of her dreams, her knight in shining armor, her lover, and protector. She finally had the love she'd been waiting for her whole life.

Jaleel's touch or simply his look of passion captivated her mind and put her in a trance. Delisa had seen Sheena and Camilla being put under the very same trance and often wondered how it felt to be consumed by love. Finally, she understood what they felt and how it could make them change their entire life for a man. It was a love that lifted your spirit, encouraged your heart, and gave you goose bumps.

"Jaleel." Delisa placed the spatula on the counter and stepped closer to him. "Have I ever told you how gorgeous you are? You are the finest brother I have ever seen. I don't know what has come over me lately, but I am finding it harder and harder to resist you. If you don't get out of this kitchen soon, you may not get breakfast."

Jaleel backed her up against the refrigerator, lifted her off the ground, wrapped her legs around his waist, and whispering against her lips. "I am going to have breakfast one way or another." He sucked her lips and pressed himself between her legs until she moaned. He brought her to the point where she could no longer resist him then let her go, smiled, and walked away.

"Jaleel, where are you going?" Delisa panted, wanting him to consume her right there.

"I will be waiting for my breakfast upstairs. I just wanted to give you a little preview of what is waiting for you when you get there."

Delisa rushed to finish making breakfast. She arranged it nicely on a tray and headed for the bedroom. She stopped just before reaching the bedroom. *Two can play this game.* She took off all her clothes and marched into the bedroom with the tray. She placed the tray on the dresser and turned to Jaleel. "Which breakfast do you prefer?"

Jaleel's mouth dropped and his eyes scanned her body from head to toe. Without saying a word, Jaleel lifted her to the bed. They spent the rest of the day in bed, making love and watching movies until the sun went down.

Jaleel's stomach growled; it had been several hours since they devoured the tray of breakfast and he was starving. "Baby?" He tickled his nose against Delisa's cheek. She had fallen asleep during the last movie. "Baby, wake up. Let's go out to eat."

Delisa opened one eye to look at Jaleel, moaned, pulled the covers over her head, and tried to go back to sleep. Jaleel was not having it. He tickled her ribs, which always drove her crazy. Delisa screamed and squirmed away from him. She bucked so hard trying to get away that they both fell off the bed. Jaleel fell over first and grabbed Delisa trying to keep his balance, but pulled her down with him. She landed on top of him. Both were laughing so hard they could barely breathe.

Jaleel's laughing faded to a soft chuckle as he watched his wife who was doubled over in laughter. He ran his fingers through her hair, admiring her beauty. Delisa finally noticed him staring at her. She stretched out to lay prostrate against him. They lay eye to eye and mouth to mouth, silently watching each other as they exchanged breaths wondering what the other was thinking.

"Jaleel, what's wrong?"

"Nothing's wrong. It's just good to hear you laughing again. You had me worried for a while, but God has really strengthened you."

"Yes He has, but He used you to do it. I wouldn't have made it these past couple of months without you. I know it was rough when I first came home, but you stood by me no matter how much it hurt you. I will never be able to thank you enough." Delisa placed her lips upon Jaleel's and was just about to consume them, but right on queue the phone rang.

In one quick movement, Jaleel stood with Delisa in his arms, wrapped her legs around him, and walked to answer the phone. Delisa's heart raced as she watched him answer the phone. His masculine strength turned her on and she planned to attack him as soon as he hung up, but he passed the phone to her. "It's Sheena."

Delisa grabbed the phone and Jaleel tried to remove her legs from around his waist so she could have some privacy, but she squeezed tighter and frowned signaling for him to stay. Jaleel chuckled and walked her to the bed, laid her on her back, and rested between her legs until she finished her phone call.

Delisa tried to focus on what Sheena was saying, but she hadn't heard a word because Jaleel kept nibbling on her making it impossible to focus. They were both still as naked as could be and Jaleel was using it to his advantage. Delisa's head sank into the bed and she was just about to hang up the phone when she heard Sheena say, "To make a long story short, Tim might be Adrianna's father."

Delisa sat up so fast that her chest bumped Jaleel in his nose. "Sheena, what did you say?"

"You heard right. Tim might be Adrianna's father and Camilla is hysterical."

"How is that even possible? Tim lived in a different state."

"Delisa were you listening? I told you he was in town that weekend for my engagement party."

"Oh. I'm sorry I was a little distracted." Delisa smiled at Jaleel.

"Well the main reason I called was because I need a favor." Sheena paused. She knew she was about to walk into dangerous territory and if she did not use the right words the conversation could end in disaster.

"Sheena, what is it? You know I would do anything for you."

"I am glad you said that because I want you to meet us at the airport on Thursday. We are going straight to the hospital to do a DNA test and Camilla really needs you. Now, I know things are not great between you guys right now, but she is still your sister. You being by her side would make all of this easier for her."

"Okay. I will be there. What time does your flight come in?"

Sheena was at a loss for words, not believing how quickly Delisa agreed to be there for Camilla. "Wow that was easy. Are you feeling all right?"

Delisa chuckled. "I am fine. Camilla is my sister and I want the best for her. Besides, I know how guilty she has felt about not knowing who Adrianna's father was. I was there for her then and I will be there for her now."

Sheena gave Delisa their flight itinerary and as much detail as she could about the conversation Camilla had with Latrice. Like everyone else, Delisa was amazed at the power of God and how His will would be done regardless of complications and interference. He took two strangers who consummated a union in an act of drunken lust, reconciled them unto Himself, reunited them as one, and blessed them through their act of indiscretion.

Jaleel watched intently as Delisa talked on the phone. He tried to read between the lines and figure out what was going on, but all he could figure out was something was going on with Tim and Camilla. It wasn't bad news, but it was shocking. He waited impatiently for Delisa to get off the phone and no sooner than she hung up, he started in with the questions. Delisa relayed the whole conversation while Jaleel listened attentively with eyebrows raised and mouth hanging open. When she finished all Jaleel could say was, "Jesus."

Sheena ended her conversation with Delisa and went downstairs to check on her father. She was relieved that he was doing better and was able to come home. She immediately feared the worst when she heard he

191

was sick, but God had intervened and rapidly healed her father. Sheena found her father sitting in the family room talking to Paul. Slowly, she backed out of the room before they saw her and stood in the hallway, eavesdropping.

"I laid in that hospital bed with nothing to do but think." Sheena wished she hadn't missed the beginning of the conversation. Her father's voice was somber and she wondered what had him in such a serious mood. "My wife and daughters mean the world to me. God has blessed me to provide for them, but what if this situation did not turn out so good and I did not make it. Sure, I have life insurance, but how long will that last?"

Sheena heard Camilla and Tim walking behind her and immediately signaled for them to be quiet. She wanted to hear what her father had to say, but knew Adrianna was not going to stay quiet for too long.

"The only thing that gives me comfort," James continued, voice shaken with emotion, "...is you. Knowing Sheena has you has lifted a huge weight. I have to admit, I was a little concerned about her marrying a man so much older than her, but you have proven yourself to be a good man who loves my daughter."

"Mr. Walker…" Paul started to speak, but James cut him off.

"Son, I have been distant and for that I apologize, but I hear you call my wife *Mom* and I would be honored if you would call me *Dad*. Sheena told me your father didn't really take an interest in you and your brother. She said he neglected and abused you, and that you practically raised Tim. I don't want to sound condescending, but I want you to know that I am proud of you. I am sure plenty of easier opportunities were presented, but you chose the road less traveled and made sure your brother followed your lead. You are a good man and have achieved more without parents than most men can with two parents."

Paul sat quietly trying to contain his emotions before he spoke. "I—I—um," Paul held his head down and a tear silently rolled down his cheek. He quickly wiped it away, hoping it went unnoticed. "I have wanted for so long to hear my own father say he was proud of me. I

192

graduated from law school at the top of my class and he didn't even bother to show up. After that, I stopped caring about what he thought or how he was doing. I tried to erase him from my life. I appreciate everything you said and I would be honored to call you Dad. I promise that if anything were to happen to you, I will take care of April and Mom, so don't worry about them."

Both men stood and embraced, trying to hide their emotions. Sheena was not as discreet. Tears flowed freely down her face. She sobbed and sniffled until Camilla nudged her in the shoulder, telling her to be quiet before Paul heard her. Sheena turned to give Camilla the evil eye while Adrianna spit out her pacifier and cried out "Dada Dada". They looked at each other, and without saying a word, ran into the kitchen. Tim and Camilla sat at the table and pretended like they were playing with Adrianna. Sheena started pulling food out the refrigerator, pretending like she was going to cook.

Paul stepped into the hallway and it was empty. He walked toward the kitchen and stepped on Adrianna's pacifier. Paul picked up the pacifier and stormed into the kitchen. "You guys know how I feel about eavesdropping." Paul tossed the pacifier onto the table. "This proves you two were out there listening. Sheena, were you out there too?"

"Paul, stop being a lawyer and sit down." Sheena kept pulling food out of the refrigerator trying to avoid making eye contact. Paul stood in front of her trying to make her stop, but she stepped around him.

Paul laughed, "Do you think I would be the lawyer I am today if I wasn't able to read people?" He grabbed Sheena by the elbow and pulled her back to him. He covered her lips with his and whispered against them, "Stop being so nosy, before it gets you in trouble."

Sheena placed her hand on her hip and looked directly into his eyes. "I am not nosy."

Paul laughed again. "Are you trying to intimidate me?"

Sheena smiled. "Is it working?"

"It's working all right, just not the way you want it to." Paul grabbed both of her hands and pinned them behind her back, pushing her body against his and causing her breath to catch in her chest.

Sheena heard her father coming and tried to break free from Paul's grip, but he held her hands against her back with one hand and firmly pressed her body against his. With his free hand, he held her head in place, kissing her until he felt the fight and tension leave her body. Paul let her arms go and tried to step back to see if she was upset, but she slipped her hand around his neck pulling him back into their kiss.

James squeezed passed them. "You two don't mind me. I am just getting a glass of water."

Sheena broke their kiss. "I will get it for you Dad."

Sheena tried to walk away, but Paul yanked her back against his body. "She will bring it to you in a second. You go relax." Paul waited until James left the room before he released Sheena. "You have given me a little problem and you can't just walk away leaving me exposed. You know these thin basketball shorts don't hide anything." Paul whispered, hoping Tim and Camilla would not over hear.

Sheena looked over her shoulder to see if Tim and Camilla were watching, and then playfully slid her hand up the front of his shorts. "I did not give you a problem. I am your problem." Sheena tried to walk away and again Paul snatched her back.

"I am going to be your problem if you don't stop playing."

Sheena laughed. "What do you want me to do? I can't stand here all day."

"Just give me a minute to calm down then we can go upstairs and handle this problem once and for all."

"Okay, what can we talk about to take your mind off the arising situation?"

Paul laughed. "You got jokes."

"What are you guys doing over there giggling and whispering?" Camilla played with Adrianna, hoping Paul would forget about their snooping, but it seemed like he had moved on to something else and totally forgot they were in the room.

Paul and Sheena jumped. Sheena spun around to face Camilla.

"What did you say?"

"Never mind. Are you still mad at us for listening to your conversation?"

"Nope, it's all good." Paul smiled. Camilla interrupting their conversation quickly helped him calm down, and he was free and clear to walk away. "Baby, I am going to go upstairs. I know your Dad is waiting for his water."

"Are you sure you're all right?"

"I'm good for now." Paul flashed that sexy smile that made Sheena's heart skip beats, and walked away.

"Sheena, what was that all about?" Camilla waited for Sheena to respond, but there was no answer. "Is Paul all right?" Camilla waited, but still no answer.

Sheena just stared at Paul with a silly little grin on her face as he walked away.

Camilla pushed Sheena to get her attention. "Sheena, that is pitiful." Camilla shook her head and walked away.

"Don't act like you don't know what it feels like to be so in love with a man you can't think straight."

"Yeah, I know how that feels, but from the look on your face, you need to repent for the thoughts that were running through your mind."

Tim doubled over laughing. "I am sorry little sister, but you do have it bad for my brother."

"Oh please, Tim. Don't let me get started on you. You are ten times worse than me. Now stop making fun of me, so I can get my father some water."

Sheena practically threw the glass of water at her father and ran upstairs to be with Paul. James chuckled as she ran away. He often worried if she'd find love, but now that she had, he was ecstatic. She always had her head into a book, which turned most men off, and the men who stuck around never captured her heart. His baby found love and happiness. He couldn't have been happier for her.

23

Tim sat next to his wife, waiting for their plane to take off. The past two days had been full of excitement, confusion, and lots of questions. He was happy to be going home so he could get some answers. Paul had called his client again to see if a paternity test could be rushed and once again he came through. They were to go straight to the hospital to give DNA samples when they got off the plane, but the results would take a while.

The plane made it to full altitude and the seatbelt light was turned off. Tim took a sleeping Adrianna out of her car seat and laid her on his shoulder. Adrianna squirmed and whined until she found her favorite position. With her face against Tim's neck, she drifted back to sleep.

Camilla laughed. "Tim, you are spoiling her. She could have slept in her car seat."

"I know, but she is more comfortable up here."

Camilla rubbed her hand down his arm. "You mean you are more comfortable when she is in your arms." Camilla moved the car seat that sat between them. "I have noticed that ever since you found out you might be her real father you have been real overprotective. You barely even let me touch her. I am not going to take her away from you if that's what you think."

"No, I know you would never do anything like that. I just want to make sure she knows I am her dad. She was already five months when I met her and I have to make up for lost time."

"I don't think that is necessary. She already likes you more than she likes the rest of my family. Sometimes, I think she likes you better than me. I may sound crazy, but I think she always knew you were her father. Do you love her more now that she is your real daughter?"

"It's not that I love her more, because she's had my heart since the first day I met her, the same way you have. I just used to keep my distance and let you take the lead, because I was only her stepfather, but all of that is going to change." Tim saw the look on Camilla's face and knew he'd better clarify before she jumped down his throat. "I think you are a great mother. I need to be a great father, not just mom's husband. I know that doesn't involve much since she is so young, but I will be involved in every decision that concerns her, no matter how big or small." Tim pulled Camilla in to his arms to rest on his free shoulder. She snuggled close to him, resting her face on his chest as he rubbed her back soothing her until she fell asleep.

Paul rubbed Sheena's back as she vomited into the barf bag. Her morning sickness was not mixing well with their early morning flight. He wished he listened when she asked to take a later flight. The turbulence from the plane was adding to her queasiness and he felt guilty for insisting they take their scheduled flight. The people sitting around them were starting to complain and the bathroom was occupied so there was nowhere else for them to go.

The convulsions in her stomach finally ceased. Sheena laid her head back to rest while she waited for the flight attendant to bring some 7-Up. Paul wiped her mouth and prayed for God to calm her stomach.

Not knowing what else to do, Paul went to get Camilla. He couldn't stand seeing his wife suffer. She looked weak and fragile; each convulsion seemed to strain every muscle in her body. He walked back to Camilla avoiding eye contact with the surrounding passengers. The negative comments were trying his salvation, and he was trying to maintain his composure.

Camilla was resting comfortably in Tim's arms when Paul woke them up. "Camilla, I am sorry to wake you, but I need your help. Sheena is sick and I don't know what to do."

Camilla laughed, "There is nothing you can do. Tell Sheena to relax and she will feel better in a couple of hours."

"A couple of hours? The people up there are ready to throw us off the plane. You have to go up there and help her."

"I'm sorry, but I can't go up there, because if I see her throw up then I am going to throw up. Or, did you forget I'm pregnant, too? Sorry big brother, you are on your own." Camilla patted Paul's shoulder, laid her head on Tim's chest, and closed her eyes.

"Sorry big brother, just do what I do. Keep your mouth shut, don't apologize for her being sick, and hold her hair back so it doesn't get dirty. I know it sucks seeing your wife suffer like that, but there is really nothing you can do about it. Now go away before you wake up Adrianna."

Paul got back to Sheena just in time to grab a clean bag, and pull her hair back for another round of vomiting. Paul was tired of all the staring and rude comments from the people sitting across the aisle and decided to address it. "Excuse me sir, is there a problem?"

"As a matter of fact there is, if you knew she was sick you should have stayed at home. Germs are easily spread in confined spaces and I don't want to spend my vacation with a stomach virus."

"For your information she is not sick, she is pregnant, and you shouldn't judge someone until you have all the facts." Paul watched the man's look turn from frustration and disgust to embarrassment.

Paul felt vindicated as the man sank back into his seat. He knew everyone around them heard the conversation because all the mumbling stopped. He was able to tend to his wife without the scrutiny of other passengers.

Sheena laid her head in Paul's lap, lifting it occasionally to sip her cup of 7-up. She took slow, deep breaths, forcing her mind to relax. The nausea had passed, but she was still very tense. Under normal circumstances, she would've been mortified about being sick in public, but she was just relieved to be feeling better. The slow rhythmic stroke of

Paul's hand up and down her back calmed her nerves and slowly she drifted off to sleep.

Not too long after falling asleep, Sheena felt Paul nudging her, telling her it was time to get off the plane. He had somehow sat her up and put her seat belt on without her knowing. Sheena looked around and the plane was just about empty. "Where is everybody?"

"I let everyone exit so we would not have to rush." Paul rested his head on the side of her face to whisper in her ear. "I should have listened to you and took a later flight; I'm sorry. Are you feeling better?"

"I feel much better and there is no need to apologize. Yes, I wanted to take a later flight, but we would just now be leaving San Antonio instead of arriving in San Diego. I am so glad we are home now. All is forgiven."

Paul and Sheena rushed to catch up with Tim and Camilla who were already at the baggage claim pulling their luggage off the conveyor belt. They all grabbed their bags, turned to walk outside, and to their surprise Delisa and Jaleel were standing behind them.

"Hey Camilla." Delisa hadn't seen Camilla since she found out about the wedding and the only time they had spoken was When Camilla called to tell Delisa that their Uncle James was in the hospital. "How are you feeling?"

"I am good. You know it was not necessary for you to pick us up. We left our cars here."

"I know, but..." Delisa closed the gap between them and grabbed Camilla's hand. "Sheena called and told me what went down with you and Tim. I wanted to be here for you. Is that okay?"

Camilla embraced her sister. "It is more than okay. In fact, I am glad you're here. I need to apologize. You have been there for me through the roughest times of my life. You held me and prayed for me. I know it tormented you to see me keep going back to the same behaviors that were destroying me, but you were always by my side when I fell apart. I am so sorry for shutting you out and not allowing you to share in my happiness. I don't know why I assumed you would try to ruin my happiness when you have prayed for me to be happy. Please forgive me. I need you in my life."

"All is forgiven. Now let's get to this hospital and get this test done. Tim, I am going to follow you, so don't speed."

"What? I don't know where I'm going. I am following Paul, and he has been driving like a snail ever since he found out Sheena is pregnant."

Delisa turned to Sheena with excitement. "You're pregnant?"

"Yes. I had just found out a few minutes before I got the call about my father. Sorry I did not tell you sooner. Things have been a little hectic this week."

"Don't worry about that. I am happy for you. Jaleel and I have been considering having another baby. We are going to have to hurry up, so the three babies can grow up together."

"Are you sure you're ready for that?"

"Yeah, we had been considering it before Jalisa passed, but then we separated and, naturally, things got put on hold. I am always going to miss her and she can never be replaced, but we have to move on and live our lives."

The women continued their conversation as if they were old friends who had not seen each other in years. The men waited patiently, not wanting to interrupt the much needed reconciliation. Paul and Jaleel talked about last night's basketball game. Tim played with Adrianna, making her laugh hysterically. He tossed her one too many times and she spit up on his forehead. Tim screamed for Camilla to help him. Everyone saw the mess sliding down the side of his face and Adrianna chuckling like she did it on purpose; they doubled over in laughter.

Delisa took Adrianna from Tim. "Daddy upset your stomach tossing you into the air like that." Delisa laughed as she cleaned Adrianna's mouth. "But you showed him real good. I bet he won't do that again."

Adrianna started to whine and reached for Tim.

"All right, All right, calm down. He is not leaving you." Delisa handed Adrianna back to Tim. "Who needs a test to prove he is your daddy? The way you act is all the proof I need."

200

Adrianna laid her head on her daddy's chest and stared at her auntie. Delisa tried to rub her back, but Adrianna pushed her hand away before Delisa could touch her.

"Ooh, Adrianna stop treating your auntie like that. She is the only one you have."

"No she's not." Everyone looked at Sheena with confusion. "If Tim is her father, I am her uncle's wife which makes me her aunt too."

Camilla gasped. "Oh my God, Jerry Springer is going to be calling us. Let's get out of here and get this test done."

They all headed to the hospital and, thanks to Paul's connection, they were in and out of the hospital in a matter of minutes. Camilla was a bundle of nerves the whole time, and even as she sat in the car going home she continued to bite her fingernails.

"Camilla what is wrong? You have been really quiet since we left the airport."

"I was just thinking, what if all of this is just a coincidence?" Camilla turned to get a better look at his face. "It all seems so surreal. What if you're not her father?"

"Then nothing changes. I am not going to love you any less or her any less. It's not like you told me I was Adrianna's father to trick me in to marrying you. Even if the test is negative, I am still her father."

"I know you will be a good father to her, but you don't know how many days I cried, wishing I knew who her father was. What will I tell her when she gets older, or what if her father's family has some sort of hereditary disease? I hear stories of adults who are searching for their absent fathers and it seems like it consumes their whole life. I want Adrianna to know her biological father, and with everything within me, I pray that it is you. I can't help but think what if it's not."

"If I am not her father, we will raise Adrianna to know that we love her. When the time is right we will explain that we both made some poor choices and pray she understands. Now stop stressing and biting your nails before you make them bleed." Tim rubbed Camilla's knee, trying to reassure her that everything was going to be all right.

A loud growl echoed through the car. Tim and Camilla looked at each other and laughed. They hadn't eaten all day, and Camilla's stomach was starting to rumble. She was getting into the always-hungry stage of her pregnancy, which Tim preferred over the morning sickness. Any man in his right mind would rather feed his woman than watch her be sick.

"What do you want to eat?" Tim exited the freeway and headed toward their apartment. "I can stop and get you something or cook you something."

"Wow, you mean you are actually going to let me eat fast food?" Tim had been monitoring what she ate ever since they found out she was pregnant. "If that's the case, I want five rolled tacos with guacamole and cheese."

"Camilla, you know I am not letting you eat that greasy Mexican food, what about a sub sandwich?"

"Ugh, nobody likes sandwiches but you. Please get me some tacos. I ate them when I was pregnant with Adrianna and she is fine."

"It's not going to happen. Pick something else."

Camilla smacked her lips and rolled her eyes, "Fine, if I can't have tacos then I want you to cook. I want shrimp and pasta with those little crescent rolls you always make and some steamed broccoli."

"I see how you are. I won't let you have what you want so you are going to make me slave in the kitchen."

Camilla put on her pouty face and her whiney voice. "Baby, please get me some tacos."

Tim parked in front of their apartment. Without responding he got out of the car, took Adrianna out of her car seat, and helped Camilla out of the car. Once inside, he placed Adrianna in her crib and then checked the refrigerator for the things he needed to make dinner. All the while, Camilla pouted because she could not have her way. The items needed for dinner weren't in the refrigerator and Tim sat on the couch to make a quick grocery list, trying to ignore Camilla's pouting. When he was finished, he caressed Camilla's cheek and planted soft kisses on her lips. She did not return his kiss, but kept a straight face, trying to look past him.

"So you are just going to ignore me?"

Camilla rolled her eyes and continued watching TV.

"I am going to the store. Do you want anything?"

Camilla looked at Tim rolled her eyes and turned back to the TV. Tim shook his head with confusion, kissed her again, grabbed his keys, and left.

Tim walked around the store and could not get Camilla's pouty face out of his mind. He purchased everything he needed for dinner, even getting Camilla's favorite ice cream in hopes of appeasing her anger. Tim drove past a taco shop on the way home and without second thought made a u-turn, ordered Camilla five rolled tacos, and kicked himself for allowing her sulking to get to him.

Still sitting in the same spot on the couch, Camilla heard the door knob turn and instantly prepared her face for more sulking. Tim placed all of his bags on the kitchen table and put the groceries away. He stood in the doorway with the bag of rolled tacos behind his back watching Camilla. She sat Indian style on the sofa. She had showered while he was gone and her hair was damp and draped across her shoulders. Slowly, he made his way to her and kneeling in front of her he placed the small brown bag containing the tacos in her lap. "Now will you kiss me?"

Camilla looked at the bag and knew exactly what was inside. She looked at the bag then back at Tim. "I'm sorry I was being a brat, but you were being difficult." Camilla smiled and planted small kisses all over Tim's face. With every bite of the tacos, Camilla moaned with satisfaction. Tim made himself a sandwich and watched his wife enjoy her greasy, fattening guacamole and cheese-covered tacos. She devoured every last bite, not once offering Tim any. When finished, she stretched her arms above her head, yawned, and thanked Tim with a big greasy kiss. She pulled Tim close so she could finish watching TV. Not even thirty minutes later, she was in the bathroom bent over the toilet with Tim holding her hair back. Her stomach convulsed until every last bit of taco was out. Tim wanted to gloat and say I told you so, but he hated seeing her sick and hoped she learned her lesson about eating greasy food.

"I should have listened to you." Camilla's stomach settled and Tim carried her to bed.

"Yeah, you should have. You think I am being bossy, but I only want what is best for you. Now get some rest."

"I am not sleepy. I am hungry."

"What? You just threw up. How can you even think about eating?"

Camilla sheepishly smiled. "Don't make fun of me. I threw up and now my stomach is empty."

"Okay. I will cook while you rest." Tim left the room shaking his head in amazement. He had never seen someone get sick and almost immediately think about eating again.

Tim peeled shrimp and chopped onions to sauté and almost cut his finger when Camilla slid her hands up his back. "What are you doing up? Go lay down."

"I was just thinking that it is not fair that you work and pay all the bills…"

"We are not having this conversation. Go back to bed."

"Tim, just listen. You do everything and all I do is clean. If I am going to be home all day, I could at least cook."

Tim laughed. "You have been cooking."

Camilla punched him in the arm. "Yes, and I see your face while you are trying to eat it."

Tim put the knife down, washed his hands, and gave her his undivided attention. "Okay, what is on your mind?"

"I want you to teach me how to cook. I am starting to feel like a pampered princess and I don't like it."

Tim was shocked. He thought all women wanted a man to wait on them hand and foot, but she was not like most women. Plus, the more she did not need him to do for her, the more he wanted to do. "Okay, I will teach you, but I have been meaning to ask you if you felt up to going back to work."

"I would love to go back to work, but who will hire a pregnant woman?"

"I will. I am getting swamped. I have eight major business and several personal accounts. Before you say no, I want you to know that you will not be a secretary. You will manage all the personal accounts and run the front of the office. When we get a few more clients, we can hire a receptionist." Camilla thought for a second and Tim watched her facial expression, trying to read her thoughts. "Okay, but you have to treat me like an employee, not your wife."

"What, you mean I can't call you into my office to take care of a little personal business?"

"No, you can't. We have to keep things separate. That is rule number one: no sex at work, and rule number two: no work at home. Agreed?"

"If you say so. I will try my best." Tim agreed, knowing he was not going to play fair.

24

Sheena rested her head on the desk, silently praying for her morning sickness to pass. It was only nine in the morning and she had already made three trips to bathroom and felt the fourth coming on. Her body was drained. Another trip to the bathroom might wipe her out. Paul had tried to convince her not to go to work, but she was the principal and could not let a little morning sickness keep her from doing her job. Sheena headed to the bathroom for round four and everyone looked at her like she had the plague. She knew she would have to explain what was going on before everyone started avoiding her.

Sheena's secretary stopped her as she gradually headed back to her office. "Mrs. Matthews, I see that you are not feeling well. You only have one appointment for today and I can reschedule it. You should go home."

"Thanks for being concerned, but that will not be necessary. Please ask everyone to come to my office for a real quick meeting." Sheena rushed into her office to call Paul, hoping his voice would soothe her before everyone showed up, but he didn't answer. She left him a voicemail, in the most pathetic voice she had, explaining how sick she was and how she wished she had taken his advice and stayed home.

Silently, Sheena watched as secretaries, counselors, the receptionist, attendance clerk, registrar, health clerk, and vice principal filed into her office, all keeping their distance. Some looked like they were holding their breath, trying not to contract whatever virus was in the air. Sheena laughed inwardly at how quickly it had spread around the office that she was sick. "I am pretty sure everyone has heard that I am sick. I just wanted to assure you that I am not contagious." There were a few sighs and deep breaths, but surprisingly everyone genuinely looked concerned. She had made a few enemies who felt she was too young and lacked the experience needed to be a principal. She accepted the job hoping to earn their respect. Now it looked like she had done just that. "I'm pregnant and I will try my best to do my job, but as you can see, I have an extreme case of morning sickness. So, I am asking in advance for your forgiveness and understanding if I come in late or don't come in at all. I know the end of the year is approaching…" Sheena was interrupted by a knock on her door. "Come in."

Paul walked in and the office erupted with applause. Paul was a little startled and confused. "Okay, what is going on?"

"I was just informing everyone that I'm pregnant. Will you all please excuse us?"

Paul shook a few congratulatory handshakes as everyone exited. His chest stuck out with pride as he exchanged smiles and greetings. Sheena stood behind him then shut and locked the door after the last person left. Paul grabbed her tried to kiss her, but she pulled away.

"I am sorry, but I have been throwing up all morning and I am pretty sure you don't want to kiss that. I have been so sick everyone was staring at me. It looked like they wanted to lock me in my office and call the health department. So, I decided to tell them I was pregnant. What are you doing here?"

"I just finished my meeting and was in the neighborhood. Are you feeling any better?"

"A little. How was your meeting?"

Paul smiled and pulled her to the sofa. "Why are you at work? Let me take you home?"

"I can't. There is so much that needs to be done and being pregnant does not fit into the plan right now."

"Baby, don't say that. I thought you were happy about having a baby."

"I'm sorry, but you know how busy I get toward the end of the school year, and being sick is slowing me down."

"I am not even going to pretend to know what you're dealing with, but I do know that you are an amazing woman with a tremendous amount of strength. If anyone can do this you can. Two years ago, when we first met, it was around this time and you were overwhelmed with work, but made it through. Last year, we were planning our wedding around this time and you said it was bad timing, but you did it. I know you can make it through this. Just let me know what I can do to help."

"I am glad you said that, because I was thinking about hiring someone to help around the house. I just don't have the energy to clean and cook."

Paul could not believe she was actually considering hiring a housekeeper, and what was even more unbelievable, she was going to spend his money for the first time since they married. She always insisted on taking care of her own needs and did not want him to think she was after his money. He was about to get excited until Sheena opened her mouth and ruined everything.

"I checked my finances and I can afford someone to come two days out of the week."

"Are you serious?"

"What? Am I serious about hiring someone?"

"I have tried to be patient, but now I am a little insulted. You are my wife and I am well capable of taking care of everything you need. I understand your desire to keep working, but your need to pay your own way is ridiculous."

"Paul, calm down."

"Don't tell me to calm down. I have never accused you of being a gold digger. I've never even thought of you like that. If I did, I would not have married you. I don't care what you have to say. I am paying for someone to come every day and from now on, money will be deposited into your account every week to take care of your extra expenses. You will allow me to be your husband in every way." Paul got up and stormed out of her office.

Sheena sat for a second in shock, not understanding why Paul was so upset. She wanted to follow him and give him a piece of her mind, but did not want to make a scene. The way he stormed out of the office, everyone probably already knew they had some sort of argument. So she decided to call him instead.

Paul answered the phone more upset than when he was in the office. "What?"

"What do you mean, *what*?" Sheena could not believe how rude he was being. "What is the matter with you? You know what? Forget it. If you want to be mad for no reason, go ahead." Sheena hung the phone up and tried to calm down. She needed some air and did not want the staff to see her so emotional.

Walking around the campus was not helping. Sheena was still upset and confused, so she hopped in her car and headed to Tim's office, hoping he could help her understand why Paul was upset.

To her surprise, Camilla greeted her when she came through the door. "Hey what are you doing here?" Camilla came around the desk to give her a hug and kiss.

"Tim asked me to work for him. I just started a couple of weeks ago. What are you doing here?"

"Paul and I just had the most ridiculous little argument and I wanted to ask Tim a question. Is he here?"

"No. Paul called him a few minutes ago and the way Tim rushed out of here, your little argument might not have been as small as you think. Come sit down so we can talk."

"I don't think you can help me. I think Paul has some sort of male ego problem that is why I wanted to talk to Tim."

"Well, you are going to have to settle for me until Tim gets back. What happened?"

"Everything was fine. Paul came by my office. I was sick and regretting the pregnancy. Paul was being really sweet. Then, I mentioned wanting to hire a housekeeper and that I had checked my account to see what I could afford and Paul flipped out."

"Sheena, you're an idiot." Camilla sat back shaking her head.

"How am I an idiot? Please explain it to me, because I really don't understand why he is so upset. I am very capable of taking care of myself."

"That is just it. You act like you don't need him."

"But I do need him. I just don't need his money."

"Sheena, you are an idiot."

"Camilla, I'm leaving. You aren't helping. You're just making me more upset."

"Okay, calm down. Paul is a real man, and if he is anything like his brother, he takes pride in being able to provide for his family. He has worked hard to get to where he is and wants to share it with you, but you insist on paying half the bills, paying for your meal when he takes you out, and now this. You're insulting him and he is tired of it."

"Camilla, I have never let any man besides my father pay for anything."

"I know. And Paul is not just any man. He is your husband. You are pushing him away and I know why. You are afraid to be totally dependent on him financially, because you think he is going to wake up one day, realize he shouldn't have married you, and leave you."

Sheena sank back into her chair, her eyes filled with tears. She tried to find a quick come back to refute what Camilla had said, but couldn't. Camilla was right and Sheena felt so ashamed. She insisted on paying part of the bills to maintain some sense of control. The thought of being completely dependent on Paul financially made her feel vulnerable.

"You don't have to say anything. I know I'm right. I also know that man loves you and is not going anywhere. Stop expecting your marriage to fail, and enjoy it. Your husband is very driven and determined. There may come a time where he does not have to work anymore. What are you going to do? Work at the school while he is out traveling the world?"

"You are right. I am an idiot." Sheena wrapped her arms around Camilla and squeezed tight. "You have been married for only a few months and already know more than me."

"I don't know more about marriage. I have just been with enough losers and in so many terrible relationships that I know when I see real love. You guys have it, Delisa and Jaleel have it, and now, I finally have it."

Camilla and Sheena had been talking for almost an hour before Tim came back. "Paul and I are going..." Tim walked through the door talking, expecting Camilla to be alone at the front desk, but Sheena sitting in the lobby had completely caught him off guard.

Sheena smiled. "Where are you and Paul going?"

"We are going to the gym to burn off a little steam."

"It's that bad?" Sheena frowned. "Call his cell and ask him to come in for a minute."

"I really don't think that is a good idea, but if that's what you want, I'll call."

Tim made the call and everyone waited quietly for Paul to come in. Paul walked in and Tim immediately blocked the door so he couldn't leave. Paul saw Sheena and turned to leave. Tim stepped into his face. "That is your wife. Calm down and listen to what she has to say."

Paul wanted to cave Tim's chest in, but after the altercation he had with Jaleel, he never wanted Sheena to see him so out of control. "Okay, I am listening." Paul backed down and leaned against the counter.

Sheena stood in front of him, her heart broken from his reaction to seeing her. She smoothed her hand up his chest stopping at his neck to adjust his tie. She spoke slowly, choosing her words carefully so that she wouldn't upset him any further. "I'm sorry. You are an awesome man and I have been an idiot." Sheena felt the softening of his body, looked into his eyes, and knew her caress was soothing his anger. "I am afraid to be totally dependent on you financially, because if you leave me, I will have nothing. Our life, our relationship, the way you love me all seems too good to be true. I am afraid you will find someone better."

Paul slid closer to her and planted small kisses on her neck. Tim, taking that as his queue to leave, grabbed Camilla by the hand and escorted her to his office. He left the lobby, reserving the right to rag on

211

his brother for giving in to Sheena so quickly. Tim was learning that when a man loves a woman there is nothing he wouldn't do for her, but Paul had it bad. Tim didn't understand how Sheena could think he would leave her.

Chills rolled through Sheena's body as Paul slowly slid his fingers up and down her spine. He spoke between the kisses, and his breath against her skin drew her further into the allure of his presence. "Don't you know there is no one else for me? You know I have been with other women and none of them can compare to the woman you are. I am not going anywhere." Tears slid down Sheena's face and landed on Paul's cheek. He hadn't noticed she was crying. Her tears always softened his heart causing him to cave in to her desires. "If paying your own way makes you feel more secure, I guess I will learn to accept it."

Abruptly, Sheena tore from Paul's embrace pacing the floor searching for the words to end her idiocy, but surrendering your own desire is never easy. Sheena dug in her purse as Paul watched with confusion. Pulling her debit and credit cards out of her wallet Sheena handed it to Paul. "Let's start with this. These are all of my credit cards. If I need to buy something, I will come to you. I also have a balance on a few of those cards, so I guess I will give you the bill when we get home. Last but not least, here is my debit card. Maybe we can get a joint account or I can have my check deposited into your account."

Paul grabbed the scissors from Camilla's desk and cut all Sheena's credit cards, then pulled out his wallet. "Thank you, this really means a lot to me, but I think you are a little confused about what I want. I don't want to control you by making you come to me for money." Paul took four new cards out of his wallet and handed them, along with a debit card, to Sheena. "These are your new credit cards; feel free to get whatever you want. The blue one is a debit card to my personal account. Your credit cards have pretty high balances, so you may never need it, but feel free to use it. As for your own checking account, keep it."

"No." Sheena jumped toward him shoving her debit card into his hand. "This is hard enough for me as it is. Please let me deposit my check into your account so I can contribute something. I know you don't need it, but it will make me feel like I am paying for something."

Paul took the card and watched Sheena's reaction as she looked over her new cards. He laughed when she looked up in confusion. "You want to know how I got your name on the cards so fast."

"Yes, and I also want to know how you got my name on the cards without my consent."

"First of all, I ordered the cards after we were married and have been carrying them all this time. As for how I got your name on them, it's simple. I am a very good customer and I hate to say it, but money talks."

Sheena laughed and rolled her eyes. Why did she even ask? Paul could persuade anyone to do anything. Sheena turned to walk away, but Paul grabbed her by the elbow. "I am just getting my purse so you can take me out to lunch, or do you have something to do?"

"I had another meeting, but I cancelled it. I would have ripped that man apart if I went in there with the anger I had."

"Yeah, you were pretty upset. I am sorry and it will not happen again, well, at least not over that."

They blew off the rest of the work day and went to Fashion Valley mall. Everything Sheena touched, Paul made her buy. He enjoyed every minute of it and the call from the credit card company notifying him that his card was suddenly showing a lot of activity made the day even better.

25

Tim and Camilla sat at the kitchen table reading over the results of the DNA test, proof that he was Adrianna's father. Tears silently rolled down Camilla's face. Tears of joy for the relief of guilt she felt for not knowing Adrianna's father. It took longer to get the results than what they initially expected, but now she could finally stop beating herself up for being so foolish and careless. Tim laughed to himself, realizing that even in a drunken stupor he had to have Camilla. Neither of them remembered much about that night, but Adrianna was proof that they were together.

Tim wiped Camilla's tears and lifted her head to look into her eyes. "Are you all right? Does this upset you?"

"I am more than all right. Knowing that I married my one night stand makes me feel less like a tramp. It makes me think that we must have had an awesome connection that night and I surrendered to the connection not the alcohol."

"I am glad you feel that way, and I hope you are as happy after I say what I have to say." Tim paused to find the right words. He did not want to upset or frighten her, but he had to do what was best for the family. "I am going to ask Paul to find me a lawyer. I want Adrianna's last name changed and I want to be added to the birth certificate."

"I know we can get her named changed, but is it possible to change a birth certificate?"

"That is what I plan to find out. So, you are okay with this?"

"Why wouldn't I be okay with it? You are my husband and if the test proved you weren't her father, I was going to ask you to adopt

Adrianna and have her name changed. Now we get to skip all the adoption paperwork."

"I just don't want you to think I am trying to take her from you."

"I am not worried. You are not going anywhere." Camilla smiled and seductively walked away.

Tim followed behind her. "What is that supposed to mean?"

"Baby, I can feel it in your touch and see it in your eyes, you cannot live without me."

Tim watched her hips sway as she walked away. He knew every word she said was true. He would not trade his life with her for anything. The years he spent with an abundance of women could not compare to the few months he'd had with the right woman.

"And another thing…" Camilla turned around to further tease Tim about how hooked he was and caught him staring at her with a mischievous little grin on his face. "See that's exactly what I am talking about. I make you lose focus." Camilla laughed and blew him a kiss.

Tim chased after Camilla. She ran into her room screaming and tried to shut the bedroom door, but Tim was too quick. He caught her just as she turned to shut the door. He grabbed her by the waist and she screamed so loud that she woke up Adrianna.

"You are so lucky," Tim whispered against her neck as he left a trail of kisses.

Left heaving in the doorway, Camilla watched Tim walk into Adrianna's room and whispered to herself, "I'm not lucky yet, but I will be as soon as she goes back to sleep."

Tim stepped back in to the hallway laughing. "I heard that. You just say the word and we will get a sitter for tonight."

"But it's a weeknight."

"So what? Paul and Sheena can watch her and take her to daycare in the morning or Delisa can keep her."

Camilla's eyes widened, remembering the last time Delisa watched Adrianna. "No, I don't think Delisa is ready to keep another baby, but I will call Sheena."

Tim lifted Adrianna out of the crib and frowned. "Can you take care of this stinky diaper first?"

Camilla laughed. "No, you are no longer step-daddy and I no longer feel obligated to take the stinky ones. Besides, you said yourself that you needed to make up for lost time." Camilla laughed as she went to make her phone call.

Tim placed Adrianna back in the crib to collect everything he needed. He grabbed baby powder, diaper rash ointment, baby wipes, air freshener, and three diapers just in case he messed up. He picked up Adrianna and held her as far away from him as possible, laid her on the changing table, and slowly began removing her diaper.

Once the diaper was off, Adrianna took that as her queue to get up and began squirming all over the changing table. She kicked the dirty diaper on to the floor, getting a little poop on her sock. Tim tried to gain control and avoid her messy foot, but had no such luck. Adrianna squirmed and kicked, trying to get free, and her messy foot landed right on the back of Tim's hand. The hairs on the back of his neck stood up and he screamed for Camilla to come help.

Camilla ran into the room expecting to see something horrible, but what she saw made her double over in laughter. Tim had one hand on Adrianna's chest holding her down and his dirty hand was stretched as far out as he could get it. "Tim, please don't tell me that is what I think it is on the back of your hand."

"That is exactly what it is. Now quit laughing and come help me."

The doorbell rang as Camilla was making her way toward Tim and she stopped mid-step. "I will be right back." She ran off to answer the door ignoring, Tim's plea for her to finish changing Adrianna.

The smile on Camilla's face quickly faded when she opened the door. She had been avoiding her parent's phone calls ever since Tim told everyone they were married, and now here they were standing on her doorstep. They stared each other down and, without invitation, her parents walked in and sat on the couch. Camilla stood at the door for a minute, trying to build up the courage to face her parents.

"Are you going to close the door and sit with us or are you kicking us out of your house the way you kicked us out of your life?"

Her mother's words pierced her heart and what little courage she had melted away. Camilla softly shut the door and sat on the sofa opposite her parents. Silently, they stared each other down; no one moved and no one spoke. The room was thick with tension. Camilla prayed for a way to escape and praised God when Adrianna came crawling into the living room followed by Tim.

One look at the fear on Camilla's face and Tim knew Johnny and Felicia's visit was not going to be a pleasant one. He took a seat next to Camilla and waited for them to finish playing with their granddaughter. Tim silently gave himself a pep talk to stay respectful and demand respect in return. He would respect Camilla's parents, but he was the head of the house and would not let his authority be challenged by anyone.

"So Mr. and Mrs. Walker, what brings you by?"

Felicia cut her eyes toward Tim. "Do we have to have a reason to stop by?"

"Well, you did not call first, so I just assumed it was something too important to discuss over the phone." Tim maintained eye contact even when he felt Camilla dig her nails into his arm.

Felicia jumped to her feet and was ready to storm into Tim's face to tell him off, but Johnny stopped her. "You are absolutely right. You are the head of this household and we will respect you by calling before we come by." Out of the corner of his eye, Johnny saw the look Felicia gave him and tried his best to ignore her.

"I appreciate that." Tim reached under his arm and pulled Camilla's nails out. "I know you are concerned about your daughter's well-being and are unsure of my intentions. I want to assure you that I am very capable of taking care of my wife and all of our children. You don't have to worry."

"We just think you got married too soon and that once the new love stage wears off, your relationship will not have a leg to stand on. We don't want to see our daughter hurt again."

217

"But Daddy, it is more than love. I have been in love before and it can't compare to what I feel for him."

"I hear you sweetheart, but do you really know who he is, his family history, what kind of man he is when he's upset, and the little things everyone hides when they first meet someone?"

"I know exactly what kind of man he is. He is a man that stood by me during a rough time, lost his job to be with me while I mourned, changed his entire life because he loved me, and accepted my daughter as his own. What else do I need to know? How he takes his coffee or how he eats his eggs is something I will learn as we go."

"Camilla, you sound foolish. You can't judge a man's character in few short months. You must see him at his best and worst to have a full understanding of his character." Felicia was fuming, but maintained her composure.

"Mr. and Mrs. Walker, I understand your concern." Tim was finished having a pointless conversation. "But we are married, and that is not going to change. So there is no need to keep going back and forth over why we should have waited. Yes, we handled things wrong by being secretive, and for that I am sorry, but I will not apologize for marrying the woman I love. I hope in time you will see how good we are for each other, but right now Camilla needs your support."

Camilla held her breath as she waited for her parent's response, hoping Tim's tone and attitude was not misconstrued as dismissive, but received as a reflection of his love for her.

"You're right. There is no point arguing over something we can't change. My wife and I have always supported Camilla and we will continue to do just that, but from what I can tell, she may not need us as much as she used to." Johnny was pleasantly surprised by Tim's assertiveness and felt a sense of relief for his daughter's well-being.

Camilla breathed a sigh of relief as she watched her husband and father shake hands. She could tell her mother was still upset, but if her father was comfortable with the situation, he would have no problem persuading her mother.

Shutting the door after her parents left, Camilla turned toward Tim and screamed. "I can't believe you talked to my parents like that." She plopped next to him on the sofa and laid her head in his lap. "I know my mom wanted to slap you, but I think you earned my father's respect."

"And your mother will respect me, too, once she's had a chance to think things over, but that's enough of all of that. What did Sheena say about watching Adrianna tonight?"

"She said she did not see a problem with keeping her, but had to talk to Paul. Then she would call me back."

"Okay." Tim lifted Camilla's head and adjusted her to sit in his lap. "But while we wait, I think I owe you a little payback for leaving me stuck changing that nasty diaper."

A playful little grin spread across Camilla's face as she grabbed Tim's hand preventing him from stroking her face again. "I hope you washed all that poop off your hand."

"You're trying to be funny. Now I am going to have to teach you a lesson." Tim slid his hand up Camilla's shirt and she stopped him.

"That sounds like fun, but you forgot your daughter is still here."

Resting his head on Camilla's chest Tim slid his hand back out of her shirt. "I guess you're safe for now, but you better watch your back, because I'm coming for you."

"Good, I'm looking forward to it."

It was after eight when they finally arrived at Sheena's to drop Adrianna off. Camilla sat in the car while Tim took Adrianna inside. Paul answered the door and Adrianna screamed at the top of her lungs when Tim passed her to Paul. Sheena hurried over and tried to soothe her, but nothing worked. Adrianna screamed insistently as she reached for her daddy. He reached to take her back, but Sheena stopped him, reassuring him that Adrianna would be fine once he left.

Tim reluctantly got in the car, heartbroken from seeing Adrianna cry so hard. He had forced himself to walk to the car and each step was harder than the first. He felt guilty for leaving her and instantly opened the car door to go get his baby.

Camilla heard Adrianna and couldn't believe how hard she was crying. She laid it on thick and Tim was playing right into her hand. Camilla grabbed Tim by the arm before he could get all the way out of the car. "Baby, she is going to be fine."

"I can't leave her crying like that." Tim tried to get out of the car, but Camilla pulled him back in.

"Honey, we really need this time alone. Let's give her a few minutes and if she is still crying, we will get her and go home."

Not even a full minute went by before the screaming tapered off. Tim still wasn't convinced and had to call Sheena to be sure Adrianna was alright. Sheena laughed at him, but once she explained that Adrianna was too captivated by Roscoe and his playful antics to worry about her missing parents, Tim finally pulled away from the curb.

To Camilla's surprise, Tim pulled up to a drive-thru and ordered two ultimate bacon cheeseburgers with fries and drinks. She was so excited about actually being able to eat a burger that being taken to a fast food restaurant did not bother her at all. When the cashier passed Tim the bag, Camilla wanted to snatch it and tear into it, but he placed it on the back seat and told her she had to wait.

They reached their destination and Tim gathered all of their things out of the back seat then helped Camilla out of the car. It was practically deserted because it was a week night and it was still pretty cold outside. Camilla loved the beach. She watched the cold wind blow the blanket as Tim tried to lay it down. She tried not to focus on the burgers, but the aroma was torture. Tim had made her skip the snack she was making before they left, saying he was buying her a special treat and didn't want her appetite to be spoiled. Now she was starving and he was taking too long to put the blanket down.

Once the blanket was down, Camilla grabbed her food, passed the rest to Tim, and dug in, not saying a word until the last bite was gone. When she was done, she finished it off with a nice loud burp. "Excuse me." Camilla covered her mouth in embarrassment.

Seeing her embarrassment, Tim slid behind her with a leg on each side and leaned her back against his chest. Then, he wrapped them both in the extra blankets he brought. He assured her that there was no need to be embarrassed as he gently caressed her neck and shoulders.

"Tim, do you think what we feel for each other will wear off?"

"Don't tell me you let your parents get to you."

"They did have a valid point. We barely know each other."

"I know that I have never met a woman like you, never had these feelings for a woman, and never wanted to protect a woman, even if it meant giving up my own life. I am not going to sit here and pretend like I have all the answers, because I don't, but there is one thing I know for sure. We have the potential to have a great marriage; we just have to work at it."

"But, we are both stubborn and set in our ways."

"I know, but the way we feel about each other overrides all that. I am just going to let my love for you lead me, and I hope you do the same."

Camilla turned to face him. She needed to look in his eyes to see his sincerity. "Does your heart love me enough to stick around when your head tells you to leave?"

Pulling her close enough to where their lips almost touched, Tim stared deep into her eyes as he whispered, "I wish I could find the words to express how desperately I need you. I have never loved until I found you and I refuse to lose the love we have."

They sat for moments, staring deep into each other's eyes, neither moving. The only sound was coming from the hypnotic rhythm of the waves crashing against the shore. Tim slid his hand up the back of Camilla's neck to release her hair from the bun and the windswept it up in to the breeze. Her hair flowed in gentle waves as it was caught up in the current of the wind.

No longer able to bare Tim's penetrating glare, Camilla lowered her eyes to the sand and traced the ridges of a seashell with her finger. Tim's question made her freeze.

"Do you regret marrying me?"

"Marrying you is one of the few things in my life that I don't regret. You are a great guy who could have any woman he wants, but you chose me. Then, it turns out that you are Adrianna's father. It all seems too good to be true. It feels like any minute I am going to wake up and realize it was all just a dream."

Tim pulled Camilla closer. "Well it is not a dream, and I am not going anywhere, so relax and let me love you." He wrapped his arms around her trying to protect them both from the cold.

The temperature was dropping and they clung to each other trying to stay warm, but their efforts were futile. Deciding they could no longer take the cold, they packed up their things and ran to the car.

26

Sheena stood in the restroom at work, her heart racing with fear. She had found a few drops of blood in her panties and the fear of miscarriage had her pulse racing. She was sweating profusely and her fingers began to tingle. She was on the verge of hyperventilating when her secretary walked in.

"Mrs. Matthews are you all right?"

"No. Please help me to my office."

Slowly, Marcy escorted Sheena to her office. Everyone they passed was obviously alarmed by her physical appearance, but no one dared to ask what was going on. Once behind her desk, Sheena leaned back, tried to relax, and begged Marcy to call Paul.

Marcy called Paul's office and Lillian, the receptionist, refused to transfer her call unless she told her what the emergency was. Sheena was tired of hearing them go back and forth. She snatched the phone, hung it up, and dialed Paul's direct line.

Paul felt fire roll through his veins when Sheena told him about Lillian. He told Ellen to clear his schedule for the remainder of the day and stopped to talk to Lillian before he left the office. Without compassion or explanation he angrily looked her in the eyes. "Clear out your desk. You are fired. Don't come back. I will have your final check mailed to you." With mouth hanging open and eyes filled with tears, Lillian watched Paul walk away.

Paul made it to Sheena's office, rushed in without speaking to anyone, lifted her out of her seat, and as fast as he rushed in, he rushed out, carrying her to the car. Sheena begged him twice to slow down as he drove to the hospital, but he didn't respond. He just drove faster and faster until he pulled into the hospital parking lot.

Thanks to Paul's hospital connections, Sheena was immediately taken to a private room and examined. They sat quietly as the nurse took a couple tubes of blood and the ultrasound technician took pictures of her womb. After the room was empty, Sheena looked to Paul with tears in her eyes and cried. "I don't want to lose my baby."

"Don't think like that." Paul cupped his hand against her cheek and planted small kisses on her lips. "Think positive. Everything is going to be fine." He slid his hand down to rest on her stomach and interceded for the life of their unborn child. He contained his emotions as he prayed and forced himself to be the strength his wife needed. Paul climbed into the hospital bed with Sheena and held her close. She cried into his chest as he pleaded for God to intervene.

Their prayer was interrupted when the doctor walked in and Sheena was shocked to see her obstetrician. "Dr. Shiel, what are you doing here?"

"I received a call from a very concerned husband who begged me to meet him here."

Paul stood to shake the doctor's hand. "Thanks for coming. I really appreciate you taking time out of your busy schedule to take care of my wife."

"It's not a problem, but I am concerned about her. I have tried to explain how important it is for her to take it easy and avoid stress as much as possible. First pregnancies are very delicate and at high risk for miscarriage. With that said, I hope you heed my advice."

Sheena sat up and dried her tears with her hand. "So I'm not losing the baby?"

"I reviewed your chart and spoke with the doctor who examined you. We don't think the amount of blood you described is significant enough for us to be alarmed. Your hormone levels are exactly where they should be, but I looked over your ultrasound and there is something I want to discuss with you." Everything seemed to move in slow motion as Sheena watched the doctor pull out the ultrasound pictures. She held her breath as Dr. Shiel fastened the pictures to the board. "Okay, this first picture you see one big circle with two smaller circles inside. Those two circles are amniotic sacks."

"So, is it abnormal to have two?" Sheena looked at the doctor with confusion.

Dr. Shiel laughed and went on to the next picture. "If you look closer at the two sacks you will see another tiny oval shape inside each sack." Dr. Shiel leaned back and waited for them to realize what she was saying.

"What you are saying is…" Paul shook his head in unbelief. "We are having twins."

"That is exactly what I am saying, which means, Sheena, you are going to have to take it easy. I know you are a principal and things are probably hectic right now, but find a way."

Sheena sat dumbfounded, unable to say a word. She watched as the doctor left the room. Several times she turned to Paul to speak, but her mind was so flooded with thoughts and questions she couldn't form a sentence. She dressed in silence and rode all the way home without speaking a word.

"Honey." Sheena gripped Paul's hand as he led her into the house. "Are we going to be able to do this? We had a hard time with Adrianna the other night. How much harder is it going to be with two?"

"We can do all things through Christ, and as for the other night, it will not be like that in the beginning. By the time our babies are that active we will be pros." Paul lifted Sheena and carried her up to their bedroom. "Stop worrying. You will be a great mother. We will hire a nanny and do whatever we have to, so stop stressing." Paul walked into the bathroom to fill the tub with water and when he returned Sheena was still in the same spot with the same tormented look on her face. "Baby, what is wrong?"

"You said we are going to hire a nanny. I don't want a nanny." Sheena stepped closer to Paul and slid her hands up his chest. "I think I am

225

going to quit my job."

Trying to hide his excitement, Paul worded his sentences carefully. He wanted her to quit her job when they got married, and was ecstatic she was finally considering it, but did not want her to have any regrets or blame the babies for ruining her life. "Are you sure that is what you want? You have worked hard to get where you are. Quitting is not the only solution."

"I know. I also know that we are not hurting for money, so why risk my health and the health of our babies just for career success? I don't want a nanny or daycare raising my kids. Not many women have the opportunity or the means to stay home with their children. I do."

"Well, if that is what you really want I will support you."

Sheena laughed. "Oh please, you know you feel like running around this room praising God that I finally decided to quit my job."

"You're right, but I just want you to be sure this is what you want, so take some time and think about it."

"I have. Today just helped me make my final decision. I will make the necessary phone calls in the morning." Sheena went to enjoy her bath, leaving Paul standing alone in their room, free to let his excitement show.

Sheena sank into the tub of hot water, turned on the jets, and leaned back. She closed her eyes to relax and let go of the stress she had been carrying. With a few deep breaths, she was drifting off to sleep.

The air was filled with a rich aroma. Jaleel walked through the front door and his stomach growled. He had been so busy at work he didn't have time to take a lunch break. The smell of fried chicken had his stomach begging for a taste. Without hesitation, Jaleel marched into the kitchen and his stomach's growling intensified when he saw the spread of food Delisa was placing on the table.

Seeing Jaleel walk in the room put a smile on her face. She had been planning all day to cook for him and was worried about her timing. Each day, the time he came home varied and she wanted the food to be fresh and hot when he arrived. His arrival couldn't have been more perfect.

After throwing his coat to the side and washing his hands, Jaleel sat at the table, ready to dig in. He piled his plate with chicken, cabbage, candied yams, macaroni and cheese, and cornbread. His eyes widen when he saw Delisa place a peach cobbler in the oven.

Delisa double checked the oven temperature, washed her hands, and prepared to join her husband for dinner. When she turned around, Jaleel was shoveling food in his mouth so fast that he barely finished one bite before the next one was on its way in. He had already finished two pieces of chicken and was reaching for his third.

After four pieces of chicken and two servings of everything else, Jaleel was finally done eating. Delisa laughed as she watched him lean back in his chair, sipping on a can of soda. He unbuttoned his pants and let out the loudest burp possible.

"Excuse me." Jaleel wiped his mouth and stood to stretch his body. "Baby, you threw down. You have not cooked like that in a while and it could not have come at a better time. I didn't take a lunch and my stomach was on E."

"Well that explains why you came in here and inhaled all this food without even speaking to me." Delisa laughed. "I haven't seen you eat like that since college."

"I am sorry, but when I saw all that food I could not think straight." Jaleel walked to her side and pulled her out of her seat, wrapping his arms around her. He placed light kisses up the side of her neck, leaving a trail that led to her lips. "So, how was your day?"

"It was tormenting. I couldn't get you out of my mind. I called you at work several times, and each time they said you were away from your desk. Then, I tried calling your cell phone, but you left it here. All I wanted was to hear your voice and I couldn't catch a break."

"I'm sorry, but we had a major issue with the network. Today was the most stressful day I've had since I started working there."

"Well, why don't you go upstairs, take a hot shower, and I will give you a back massage when you get out."

"Sounds good, but I am not going anywhere until I get a bowl of peach cobbler. I hope you bought some vanilla ice cream. You know I like it right out of the oven, so the ice cream can melt all over it."

"After everything you just ate, how can you even think about eating anything else?" Delisa rubbed her hand across Jaleel's stomach, "You are going to make yourself sick being so greedy."

"It is well worth it, and…" Jaleel slid his hand under the front of her shirt, "I am going to have a good time working it off tonight."

"Oh, is that a fact?" Delisa leaned in to give him better access to her body. She had been craving his affection and the warmth of his hand on her bare skin was the satisfaction she had been waiting for.

Jaleel whispered against her lips, "Most definitely." He tried to grab her legs and wrap them around his waist, but Delisa stopped him.

"No, you are not about to put me under your spell."

"What spell? I am just trying to kiss you. Is it a crime to kiss my wife?" Jaleel grabbed her arm as she tried to run away, then spun her around and lifted her unto the counter.

"Jaleel, what are you doing?"

"Stop tripping. You know exactly what I am doing." He slowly started to unbutton her shirt, but the phone rang and before he could stop her, Delisa jumped off the counter and ran to answer the phone.

"Hello?" Delisa looked back at Jaleel, laughing at the look of disbelief on his face.

"Hey baby girl, how have you been?"

"I am much better than I used to be. How are you?"

"I am real good. I need to talk to you and my son. Do you mind if I stop by?"

"It would be good to see you and I just made a peach cobbler, so we will wait until you get here. We can eat it together." Delisa cut her eyes to Jaleel as he sucked his teeth and sighed.

"That sounds good. I am in the neighborhood, so I'll see you in a few."

228

Shaking her head as she hung up the phone, Delisa could not believe Jaleel was being so selfish. "Don't get mad. This is a big peach cobbler. There will be plenty left over."

"I am not upset about that. I was trying to do some things and you just invited someone over here."

"It was not just someone. It was your father and he needs to talk to us. So, I guess what you were planning is going to have to wait." Delisa pulled the peach cobbler out of the oven and threw the pot holder at Jaleel, hitting him right in the face.

Without hesitation, Jaleel chased after Delisa. She ran out of the kitchen and up the stairs screaming. Jaleel was right on her heels. He took the stairs two at a time and caught her about halfway up. He pulled her against him. She could feel his chest heaving against her back. The sensation of his hands gliding up her side made her shiver. He slid his hand all the way up her side, following every curve and lifting her arms to wrap around his neck.

A low moan escaped her as Jaleel caressed her body and grazed his lips along the side of her neck. He chuckled and whispered between kisses. "I thought my plans had to wait."

Delisa grabbed him by the belt and led him up the stairs to the bedroom, where they ripped through their clothes, tussling with each other to gain the upper hand. Jaleel won the struggle, but was rudely interrupted by the doorbell. He growled in frustration, begging Delisa not to answer. She punched him in the chest and scolded him for not caring about what was going on with his father.

Jaleel answered the door, and Delisa went to the kitchen to prepare bowls of peach cobbler and ice cream. Opening the door, Jaleel was shocked to see that his father was not alone. "Hey Dad, come on in. Head to the kitchen, Delisa is waiting on us." Jaleel eyed the woman as she walked by. She was a fair-skinned older woman with a head full of gray hair. He did not know who she was or why she was with his father, but he was sure going to figure it out.

Delisa stood in shock as her father-in-law walked into the kitchen with a woman until Jaleel elbowed her. "I am sorry." Delisa turned and fumbled with the bowls of peach cobbler. "I didn't realize you were bringing a friend. I need to make another bowl."

They all sat in silence, eating their dessert, chewing each bite slowly. They all wanted to evade the looming conversation. Jaleel had an assumption of what his father wanted to say and was trying to brace himself for the impact.

"Son, I am not going to take up too much of your time." He placed his spoon into the bowl and wiped his mouth. "But there are some things going on in my life right now that I want you to know. Your mother put me through a lot and distorted both of our views on love. I am glad you did not hold on to it as long as I have and were able to find love with Delisa." He grabbed the woman's hand and looked her in the eye. "The Lord has blessed me to find love in my old age. I do not want to spend the rest of my days on this earth alone. I hope you understand and give us your blessing, because Janine and I are getting married next week."

Clearing his throat, Jaleel searched for the words to congratulate his father. "You have been through a lot, and all I have ever wanted was for you to be happy. I only wish you would have told me you were seeing someone and given us a chance to get to know each other before you got married. But, if she makes you happy, then you have my blessing."

Delisa sat, silently praying for her husband. He was very protective of his father and she prayed he was really okay with his father getting married. She watched as he stood and embraced Janine, welcoming her into the family. After everyone said goodbye and Jaleel walked them to the door, Delisa questioned his reaction. "Are you really okay with this?"

"What choice do I have? I just wish I knew her a little better, so I could see her true intentions."

"Maybe that is why he kept it from you. He probably wanted to get to know her before you shooed her off."

"Come on, Delisa. I am not that bad."

"No, you are worse. You spent so much time trying to protect him from women like your mother that you scared off a couple of good ones in the process. Now behave and let your father be happy. He is a grown man and can take care of himself. I saw the look in his eyes. He really loves this woman, and if you chase her off I am going to hurt you."

"He did look happy, didn't he?"

"Yes he did. Promise me you will leave her alone."

"You have my word. I will not interfere."

"Good, now help me do these dishes. I'll wash, you dry."

"I have a better idea. Why don't we throw all of these dishes into the dishwasher, go upstairs, and finish what we started?"

Delisa watched as Jaleel raced around the kitchen collecting dishes and throwing them into the dishwasher. There was no organization to his stacking. He just tossed them in as fast and as tight as he could. He didn't bother to put the soap in the little compartment. He just squeezed it into the bottom of the machine, slammed the door shut, turned it on, picked up Delisa, and raced up the stairs.

27

The weeks ticked by and Camilla and Sheena's stomachs began to protrude as their pregnancies progressed. Sheena decided to wait, but Camilla was anxious to find out the gender of her baby. When they found out she was having a boy, Tim was elated. Sheena was twice as big as Camilla and had officially been placed on bed rest. She whined and pouted, but Paul did not give in. He stood his ground, moving them into one of the downstairs bedrooms and hiring a nurse to look after Sheena while he was at work.

After a long battle with her parents, April finally moved to San Diego. Just in time to begin summer classes at SDSU. During her first week living with Sheena, they stayed up late talking and laughing. They were up so late, Paul slept in another room to give them their privacy. One morning, he had finished dressing for work and went to the kitchen for his morning caffeine fix. April was sitting at the table waiting for him.

"Hey Paul. I wanted to catch you before you left for work."

"Is everything all right?" They did not know each other that well and were still a little uncomfortable talking to each other.

"Yes, everything is fine. I just wanted to apologize for taking over your room, and thank you for giving me an opportunity to have a relationship with my sister."

"Don't mention it. You are family and I am happy that you are here."

"I want you to know that I came here to build a relationship with you also. I have always wanted a brother and you are as close as I am going to get to having one, so please don't leave the room when Sheena and I are talking. I really want you to be involved."

Paul sipped his cup of coffee, giving himself time to think of an appropriate response. "I apologize. Don't take it personal. I just didn't want to make you uncomfortable. I would really like to get to know you a little better. So, I give you my word. I will not walk out on you guys anymore." Paul raised his right hand and made a cross over his chest with the left hand.

April laughed. "Thanks, you have a good day at work. See you later."

Paul tiptoed into his room, hoping to check on Sheena without waking her. When he walked into the room, Sheena snatched the covers over her head. He thought she was playing around until he heard sniffling. Paul sat on the edge of the bed and rubbed her back. "Baby what's wrong? I know you're crying, so please don't hide from me." He slowly pulled the covers away from her face and it was drenched in tears. Her hair was disheveled and her nose was runny. "Baby, please talk to me."

"Paul, do you love me?"

"You know I do. You are the only woman I have ever loved."

"Do you think I am fat?"

"What? Sheena you are pregnant. You're supposed to gain weight." Paul was getting more and more confused as the conversation progressed.

"Are you still attracted to me?"

"Of course I am."

Sheena wailed even louder. "Then why haven't you made love to me in weeks?"

Paul kneeled on the floor in front of her to kiss away her tears. "You are the most beautiful woman I have ever seen and the fact that you are pregnant with my child is even more of a turn on."

"Not enough of a turn on for you to make love to me?"

Paul chuckled. "That is not the case at all. I am scared that I might hurt you, but it has not stopped me from desiring you.

"Every night after I rub oil on your stomach, I have to take an extra

233

long shower to calm myself down. Then I climb into bed with you and the same problem pops back up." Paul helped Sheena sit up on the edge of the bed and removed her night gown. He locked their door and called his office letting them know he was going to be late.

Tenderly, he caressed his wife, giving her the affection she craved, and although he did not make love to her, the intimacy was just as satisfying. He kissed his favorite parts of her body and with every kiss he whispered why he loved that part. Sheena leaned back, letting him soothe her fears.

When he was done, he helped her back into bed, then whispered in her ear. "Don't ever think that I don't want you. Not being able to make love to you is killing me, but it is what is best for you and the babies. So, I will just have to suffer."

Paul left for work, trying to clear his mind, but failed. Sheena's moans echoed through his mind and the scent of her body wash was still in his nostrils. He closed his eyes at the stop light, reliving every kiss and every touch. The cars honking behind him brought him to the present and the ache of his erection throbbed against his zipper for the remainder of his commute.

Lying in her bed watching TV, Sheena patiently awaited Dr. Shiel's phone call. She had called the doctor's office after Paul left, asking for clarification on her bed rest status. Every time the phone rang, Sheena anxiously jumped, hoping it was the doctor. Twice it was Paul and once it was Delisa, checking to see if she needed anything from the store.

An hour later, Dr. Shiel finally called. "Hello Mrs. Matthews. The nurse tells me you have some concerns. How can I help you?"

Sheena had given herself a pep talk to be upfront and honest. For the first time, she attacked the subject head on. "My husband will not have sex with me because he thinks he will hurt me or the babies."

"He has a right to be concerned. You are in a very delicate stage right now. Like we've discussed before, pregnancies like yours are very high risk. Sex is an added risk. That being said it doesn't mean you can't be intimate. Find other ways besides vaginal intercourse to be affectionate." Sheena's heart sank with each word, but the doctor's last statement gave her renewed hope. She hung up the phone more determined than ever to get what she needed from her husband.

Sheena grabbed her cell phone, typed the most explicit text of her life, and sent it to her husband.

Sheena worked herself up into a frenzy imagining the possibilities as she waited for Paul's response, but it never came. She rolled over to sip her glass of water and Paul busted through their bedroom door, pulling off his suit in the process. He kicked his shoes off and slid into bed with his wife. No words were exchanged. The passion in his eyes said enough.

He read her text at least ten times. He practically had it memorized. Trying to prove that he was still attracted to her had him dangling on the edge of a cliff all morning and her text finally pushed him over the edge.

Your touch is enough to ignite my body and your mouth can bring me so much pleasure. Between the two you have the power to turn me into a sexually charged inferno. I yearn for you to set me ablaze. I promise to do the same to you. He was already on fire. He'd understood her hidden directive. They could make love without intercourse. After he'd left the house that morning he'd been thinking the same thing. The moment her hands and mouth touched his skin he was incinerated. His thoughts and everything not related to the passion between them, incinerated beyond recognition.

Through the fog of his dream, Paul heard a knock on his bedroom door. "Who is it?"

"It's April, there is some man at the door demanding to see you."

"What?" Paul sat up and grabbed his pants.

"He will not give me his name. He said you will know who he is when you see him. He was freaking me out, so I left him on the porch and locked the door."

"Okay, give me a minute and when I come out, I want you to come in here with Sheena and lock the door."

By this time Sheena had woken up. "Baby, what is going on?"

"Nothing, there is just someone at the door. I need you to calm down and put some clothes on."

"Don't tell me *nothing*. Why is April coming in here and locking the door?"

Without responding, Paul picked up her robe, wrapped her up, finished putting on his clothes, and left the room. April came in, locked the door, and sat quietly as they waited for Paul to come get them.

Paul opened the door and the sight of his visitor instantly made his blood boil. "What are you doing here?"

"I need to talk to you. May I come in?"

Paul stared him down, wanting to tear him apart, but slowly stepped to the side, letting the man enter. "Sit right here. I will be right back. Would you like something to drink?"

"Sure, a glass of cold water would be nice."

Paul left the room and called Tim, offering him no explanation, just telling him to hurry and get there. Then he went in the kitchen to make a couple glasses of ice water, taking his time, hoping that Tim would show up so he would not have to deal with this issue alone. His mind was racing and he was unable to process a clear thought.

With glasses in hand, Paul stopped by the bedroom to get Sheena. Carefully, he helped her dress then brought her to the family room to meet their guest. Sheena was so excited that Paul was letting her out of the room. She didn't care why he was letting her out.

They sat quietly sipping their glasses of water. Paul was searching for a way to handle the situation, and praying for the door to ring so he would have a little back up. When the door finally rang, he jumped up to answer it.

"What's up, little brother?" They embraced as Tim and Camilla walked in.

"Come into the family room. You will never guess who just showed up at my door today."

Tim walked into the room and almost dropped Adrianna when he saw who was sitting on the couch. The hairs stood up on the back of his neck and his nostrils flared. "What are you doing here?" The disgust in Tim's tone was not concealed, and Camilla placed her hand on his back hoping to calm the rage.

"I guess I could ask you the same question. I didn't know you lived out here."

"Okay Paul, you guys are scaring me. Who is this man?" Sheena stood waiting for an answer and when Paul didn't answer, the man did.

"I'm their father."

Camilla and Sheena both gasped in disbelief. Everyone stood in silence for a minute until Camilla, with her fiery mouth, decided to give him a piece of her mind. "You bastard! You have some nerve showing up here, unannounced, after everything you put them through."

"I am sorry, but who are you?

Tim stepped next to Camilla and pulled her behind him. "She's my wife."

"What? I thought you would never get married."

"Well, people change. Now what do you want?" Tim had no respect for his father and no desire to have a relationship with him. He couldn't believe the audacity of this man, showing up unannounced after years of no contact.

"I am glad you said that, people do change, and I have. I was hoping we could have some sort of relationship."

Sheena stepped up and wrapped her arms around Paul. "Are you okay? If not make him leave."

"I am fine." Paul eyed his father. He tried to control his temper for his wife's sake, but the longer he looked at his father, the angrier he became.

"Is she your wife, Paul?"

Staring his father down, all the pain of neglect and abuse flooded back to his mind, and a whirlwind of rage was building up inside of him. "You can't do this. Show up here after not seeing us in years, after all the childhood abuse, acting like everything is all good. If you wanted to be a part of our lives you would've been there when it mattered most!" Paul was pacing back and forth. Little beads of sweat had formed on his brow. Sheena kept reaching for him to calm him, but her fragile state limited her movement.

"Please, please just hear me out before you kick me out."

"We don't have to hear you out!" Tim gruffly yelled as he rushed into his father's face. His anger was spiraling out of control and all he could think about was beating his father down.

April jumped up and ran between them. "I don't know what he has done to you, but I can tell it must have been horrible. I know I am not into the church the way you guys are, but I do know God wants us to forgive."

"She's right." Sheena grabbed Paul's hand and led him to the sofa. "Now, everyone sit down, calm down, and let's talk like adults. Mr. Matthews, I am Sheena, Paul's wife. This is April, my sister. Over there is Camilla, Tim's wife, and Adrianna, their daughter."

Trying to relax, Paul took a few deep breaths, and Sheena rubbed his back, silently praying for his strength. She had never seen him so angry. If truth be told, she wanted to slap his father and kick him out, but Paul needed healing to move forward. Confronting his father was the best way.

"I know you guys hate me and you have every right, but I am here because I want to do the right thing for once in my life. There is someone in the car I want you to meet. I asked her to wait so that I could clear the air. She's your sister. Apparently, her mother knew how much of a jerk I was and never told me about her. She is twenty years old and begged her mother to tell her who I was. She tracked me down all by herself, and when I told her that I had two sons, she demanded that I find you."

"So what do you expect us to do? Accept you back into our lives and the four of us live happily ever after? She may be able to forgive you for not being in her life, but it's not that easy for me," Tim spoke with clenched teeth and balled fist. The veins on his temple were bulging and rage was radiating from him.

"Okay, we need a break." Camilla passed Adrianna to April and pulled Tim out of the room. "Baby, you need to calm down." She reached to caress him, but his anger startled her.

Tim turned to face her and yelled. "Don't tell me…" Tim paused when he saw Camilla flinch and back away from him. Her fear of him immediately softened his demeanor. He pulled her close and apologizing for being a jerk.

Rubbing her hands up and down his chest Camilla tried to soothe him. "I know you're upset, but you have to calm down and find a way to forgive him. Staying angry at him is only giving him power over you. God is giving you an opportunity for healing and closure. Take it. No matter what happens, you still have me and possibly a relationship with your sister."

Tim took a few deep breaths then walked into the family room. "Where did he go?"

"He went to get her out of the car. Are you all right with this? I couldn't care less about him, but if we have a sister, I would like to meet her."

"I could have gone the rest of my life without seeing him and I would have been fine. His showing up like this brings back memories that I had long forgotten. I hate him more than I thought."

Paul embraced his brother, "That's all the more reason for us to see this through. I don't want my hatred for him to keep me out of heaven."

"Paul, baby, you can do this. You don't want your sister's first impression of you to be a bad one, so stay calm and remember this is about you getting closure, not about your father."

"Thank you, baby." Paul led her back to the sofa. "You need to stay seated or I am going to put you in the bed." Before she sat down, he planted his lips upon hers to alleviate his frustration.

Mr. Matthews cleared his throat when he walked into the room to grasp everyone's attention. "Everyone this is Candice. Candice, this is Paul and Tim, your brothers."

Instantly she broke into tears. "Both of them are here? I thought you didn't know where Tim was."

"I didn't." Mr. Matthews backed up to give them space to get acquainted.

With eyes filled with tears, Paul embraced his sister and introduced her to his wife. Tim followed suit. When Tim introduced Candice to Adrianna, she cried harder. "I'm an Auntie? May I hold her?" Surprisingly, Adrianna went straight to her, but did not stay long before she whined for her daddy.

Tears rolled uncontrollably down Candice's face as she spoke. "You have no idea how much this means to me. My mother is an only child and I am her only child. Now my mother is sick. I was so scared she was going to die and leave me all alone. Then, she told me about my father. I resented her at first for keeping me from him, but after I met him, he explained that she was only trying to protect me from the horrible person he used to be."

There wasn't a dry eye in the room. Even Mr. Matthews cried as Candice finished her story. "Our dad told me how horrible he was to you guys and he was so ashamed of the type of father he was that he did not want to face you. I begged and pleaded for him to find you. Then, I slapped a guilt trip on him to make him bring me. Please, for me, try to forgive him. I know it may take a while, but we are family. And even though you may not want to admit it, we all need each other."

Candice watched Paul and Tim stare each other down as she waited for their response. They stared at each other long and hard trying to read each other's thoughts. Paul had spent the majority of his childhood protecting Tim and was not about to allow their father back in to tear him apart all over again. Tim grew up with Paul as his father figure and saw his dad as the man that stopped by to beat him. He never loved his father and was not about to start now.

"Candice, we would love to get to know you better." Paul looked his dad in the eye. "But asking us to have a relationship with our father is virtually impossible."

Gently placing her hand on Paul's cheek, Candice turned him to look in his eyes. "I hear you, but at least we could try."

Paul and Tim both agreed to try, knowing that it was going to take a miracle from God to help them get over the past. They sat and talked for hours until Sheena started cramping and Paul led her to bed. They made plans to hang out while Candice was still in town and invited her to come out as often as she liked.

28

Tim walked out of the realtor's office ready to burst with excitement. He finally closed on the house he had been battling over for months. It was a long, hard battle, but he refused to compromise on price. All the stress of negotiating was now paying off. He had the keys to his house and would be able to give the house to Camilla for her birthday.

The added stress of dealing with his father was starting to wear him out. The house was just the excitement he needed. He was planning a surprise birthday party for Camilla, so Candice agreed to stay a little longer to help him with the arrangements. After their father left, she checked out of the hotel and moved in with Paul.

It was Candice's idea to throw the party inside the new house, suggesting they rent tables and chairs, then decorate it like they would an event hall. Tim was all for it and left all the decorating to Candice and April. The girls spent two whole days together shopping for decorations and at night they hit up one of the local clubs. They built a friendship over a short time and April really did not want Candice to leave. Having someone her age to hang with at family functions was a welcome change.

The day of the party arrived. April and Candice busied themselves with decorating. They wanted everything to be perfect. They took their time making sure everything was in its place. Once finished, they sat around talking while they waited for some furniture that Tim purchased to be delivered.

"Candice, I have really enjoyed hanging with you this week. I wish you could stay longer."

"I know. It was great meeting my brothers, but my mom is sick and she needs me."

"I was thinking about what you said. Her insurance really won't pay for some of her treatment?"

"That's not the problem. We don't have insurance, and if we don't come up with some money soon my mom will die."

"Have you thought about asking Paul?"

"Yes, I noticed that he is pretty well off, but I don't want him to think that I came out here to borrow money."

"Well you may not have to borrow money. Paul is some big shot medical malpractice attorney and he has a lot of connections. He may be able to hook you up. You may have to move out here, but that wouldn't be so bad. Just ask him. The worst he could say is no."

"Let me think about it."

"Okay, but Paul is a really good guy who bends over backwards for his family."

The bedroom furniture for the master bedroom and Adrianna's room was finally delivered. They made sure everything was put together and arranged properly, then rushed to shower and dress before the guests arrived.

The party was in full swing. Camilla was totally surprised when she came in the door. She had no idea Tim was throwing her a party and cried when she saw all of her friends and family who were in on the surprise. After greeting all her guests, she pulled Tim to the side to express her gratitude.

"Tim, I love you so much. You're the only man I've been with that cared enough to celebrate my birthday. They have never taken me out or even given me a card." Wrapping her arms around him, Camilla sank as far into Tim as her pregnant belly would allow and smothered his mouth with hers.

Tim licked his lips as he pulled out of their kiss. "You better save some of that for later, because this night is going to be full of surprises." Tim deviously smiled and walked away.

Camilla watched as he greeted a few brothers from the church, kissed Candice on the cheek, and grabbed Adrianna from Felicia. The swagger of his walk turned her on. Although she was happy about the party, she wished everyone was gone, so she could rightfully express her gratitude.

She was still watching Tim when her mother walked up. "What is wrong with your husband? Why did he take the baby from me?" Felicia waited for an answer, but there wasn't one. She watched Camilla daydream then elbowed her in the arm. "What is wrong with you? Don't you hear me talking to you?"

"Ouch." Camilla grabbed her arm and turned to her mother in confusion. "Why are you hitting me? I didn't hear you."

"I said, why did your husband take Adrianna from me?"

"Maybe because he is her father and he has every right to do so."

"Well, I am her grandmother. Doesn't that give me certain rights?"

"Of course it does... Right after her mother and father. I really wish you would give Tim a chance. He is a good husband and father. If you gave him a chance, I know you would love him." Camilla walked away, leaving her mother standing there with her mouth hanging open. She refused to stand around and argue at her party. She walked around, mingling with guests and looking for Tim.

Delisa saw the whole exchange of words between her mother and sister and figured she better intervene before her mother chased after Camilla and turned the party out. "Hey Mom, what's going on?"

"Can you believe your sister is being so stupid?"

"Oh Lord, what did she do now?"

"This whole Tim situation is out of control and she refuses to listen to reason."

"What? This whole Tim situation is the best decision she has ever made. She would have been crazy to let him go. For one, the brother is as fine as can be. Two, he turned out to be Adrianna's biological father. And

244

three, he makes Camilla happier than I have ever seen her. If you don't accept him, Camilla is going to shut you out. She is about to give you another grandchild. It would be a shame for you to never see him." Delisa left her mother to think, hoping she would get over the past and let Camilla be happy.

Tim turned the music down and interrupted everyone's conversation to make a special announcement. "Can I get everyone's attention please? I wanted to thank everyone for coming and helping me celebrate my wife. As you all know, Camilla captivated my heart from the first day I met her, and being with her has made my life worth living. Now, I want to give her a little something to say thank you."

Camilla watched Tim from across the room, wondering what he was up to. His little speech practically had her in tears and anything else would be too much to bear. She held her breath and held back her tears as Tim continued his announcement.

"Baby, I need to apologize because I told you a little lie. I told you that we were going to a friend's house to have a get together, but this is not a friend's house. This is your house." Tim pulled the keys out of his pocket and screams echoed through the house, none of which were from Camilla. Camilla covered her mouth with her hands and tears flowed down her face. He held the keys out and Adrianna kept trying to grab them. He put the keys in Adrianna's hand and told her to take them to her mother. He placed Adrianna on her feet and she waddled across the floor to give Camilla the keys.

Felicia cried when she saw Adrianna walking. She didn't know her granddaughter could walk. Her foolishness was causing her to miss out on her granddaughter's life. What Delisa said was now ringing loud and clear, and Felicia resigned to accept the inevitable before she lost what was really important to her.

Candice tried to enjoy the party, but all she could think of was her mother and the things April had said. She searched through the crowded room until she found Paul and Sheena.

"Can I talk to you guys outside for a minute?"

They followed Candice outside and waited patiently for her to begin talking.

"First of all, I don't want you to think I came out here to hit you up for money, but I would not be able to live with myself if something happened to my mother and I did nothing to prevent it. I was talking to April and she told me you have a lot of medical connections. I was wondering if there was anyone you could talk to that could help my mother. We don't have medical insurance and if we don't come up with some money to pay for her treatment she will die."

With hands trembling and tears rolling down her face, Candice anxiously waited for Paul's response. Paul did not feel comfortable giving money to someone he just met, but the torment Candice was suffering due to her mother's illness was obvious.

"I tell you what, when you get home, fax me all of your mother's medical records. I will show them to a few doctors I know, and we'll see what they can do. More than likely you will have to bring her out here. Are you okay with that?"

"That's fine." Candice's disposition picked up. "I have some money saved up, so plane tickets won't be a problem." She bounced around in excitement, thanking Paul and Sheena for her their help.

Tim escorted Camilla around the house, giving her a tour of her birthday present. She could not stop smiling and got more excited with each room they viewed. The last room he took her to was the master bedroom. She jumped with excitement when she saw all of the beautiful furniture Tim had purchased. Tim lay on the bed laughing as he watched Camilla running around to check out the room. Camilla looked in the drawers, under the bed, and checked out the closet.

"Do you think this closet is going to be big enough for both of us?"

"No, that is my closet your closet is in the bathroom."

Camilla ran through the bathroom and screamed when she walked into her closet. There was more than enough room for all of her things and there was a built-in shoe rack. She came out of the bathroom clapping, jumping, and spinning around with excitement.

Tim shook his head and laughed at her. "Will you come lay down with me before you make my baby dizzy?"

Smacking her lips and rolling her eyes, Camilla climbed into the bed. "You got jokes. Your baby is perfectly fine." She scooted as close to him as she could and turned toward him, resting her stomach against his. Tim lifted her shirt and caressed his baby. He placed little kisses on her stomach as he talked to his son.

They totally forgot about the party downstairs and would have stayed in there all night enjoying each other's company, but they heard Delisa and Sheena coming down the hall calling their names. Camilla adjusted her clothing and sat up. "We are in here."

"Did you guys forget there are people downstairs?" Delisa walked in and kissed Camilla on the cheek and Sheena followed right behind her.

"I saw the way she's been watching Tim all night and I don't think she cares how many people are here." Sheena and Delisa doubled over laughing, but Sheena abruptly stopped when she heard Paul's voice.

"Sheena where are you? I know you're up here. Aunt Felicia told me she saw you come up here. You know you shouldn't climb the stairs. And if she's up here, Delisa I know you are too."

Delisa placed her finger over her lips signaling for everyone to be quiet, but Tim yelled out anyway. "They're in here." Delisa jumped up and put Tim in a headlock. Jaleel and Paul walked in just in time to see Delisa drag Tim off the bed with her arm wrapped around his neck.

"All right little sister, I am going to give you until the count of five to let me go or I will not be held responsible for the pain that is inflicted."

Laughing, Delisa squeezed harder. "I am a big girl, I can take it."

Tim stood hunched over as he counted. He counted to five and Delisa still wouldn't let him go. He stood up straight, grabbed Delisa by the legs, and lifted her above his head. She screamed loud with her arms flailing at her sides.

Sheena laughed so hard she got a pain in her side and had to sit down. "You guys stop being so silly before you make me go into labor from laughing so hard."

Tim put Delisa down and she punched him in the arm as hard as she could then ran to Jaleel, almost knocking him over, which made everyone laugh even harder.

They sat upstairs talking for a while before they rejoined the party. They reflected on the ups and downs of the months past, praising God for the victory and strength. They rejoiced even more when they thought about their current status. Everyone was happily married, in good health, financially stable, and full of joy. It made them realize how blessed they were.

To be a part of a family was more than Paul and Tim could ask for. God had blessed them to even start their own. Camilla had found the man of her dreams, but more importantly, she'd renewed her relationship with the Lord. Jaleel and Delisa suffered a great loss, but had rekindled the fire in their marriage and triumphantly overcome the odds.

EPILOGUE

It was late September when Sheena's water broke. The doctors had done everything they could to stop early labor, but the babies wanted out.

Sheena endured twenty hours of labor like a champ. Paul could not stand seeing her in so much pain, but stood by her every step of the way, letting her scream, bite, and claw him as much as she needed. Thanks to Paul's client, they were treated like royalty during their stay at the hospital. Paul Jr. and Paige received the finest care. They were both healthy and able to leave the hospital with their mom. Paul was determined to be a good dad and lightened his case load to spend more time at home. Sheena's instincts took over and she took care of her son and daughter as if she had been doing it all her life.

Camilla was bummed that Sheena delivered before her and impatiently whined for two weeks until she went into labor herself. Tim Jr. came so fast, they barely made it to the hospital in time for the delivery. Felicia had gotten her act together and Tim let her be in the delivery room. With a couple of pushes, little Tim was in the world. With eyes wide open, he looked his parents in the eyes. They brought him home and Adrianna refused to let Tim hold the baby at first, but after a few days she relaxed and went into big sister mode.

Finally receiving an acceptance letter, Delisa started classes for her graduate program. It took her a minute to get into the swing of things, but she got the hang of it. Jaleel had no problem supporting her. When they found out she was pregnant he encouraged her to continue, stressing the fact that the baby was due at the end of the spring semester. She could then take the summer off and start again in the fall.

The doctors that Paul asked to look at Candice's mother turned out to be a real blessing. The death sentence the other doctors placed on her turned out to be unfounded. With medication, exercise, and the proper diet, everything was fine. They moved to San Diego so Candice could get to know her brothers better. Tim hired her as his receptionist and convinced her to go to college. She invited their dad out for the holidays, which made Paul and Tim furious, but Sheena and Camilla helped them see the bright side. Surprisingly, they were well-behaved and even had a conversation with their dad without bringing up the past.

James and Linda gave up the fight and moved to San Diego. The empty nest turned out to be more than they could tolerate. For weeks, they complained about the cost of living and high gas prices, but seeing their grandchildren made it all worthwhile. Paul evicted the couple who were renting his condo and gave it to his in-laws. They expected April to move in with them, but she had a taste of life without her parents and was not about to give it up.

This Thanksgiving, dinner was full of new faces and crying babies. Dinner was at Tim and Camilla's house, so she would not have a problem being on time and, thanks to her husband, she cooked the entire meal with very little assistance. Everyone had jokes. They were also a little leery about eating the food, but were pleasantly surprised at how good everything tasted. The day brought memories of tragedy, but the warmth of family dispelled the threat of sadness. Their season of adversity had transitioned into tranquility. They made it through the storm in one piece, marriages intact, lives free from sin, and their faith unwavering.